BISON FRONTIERS OF IMAGINATION

GLADIATOR

Philip Wylie

INTRODUCTION TO THE BISON BOOKS EDITION BY
Janny Wurts

UNIVERSITY OF NEBRASKA PRESS
LINCOLN AND LONDON

⊗

First Nebraska paperback printing: 2004

Library of Congress Cataloging-in-Publication Data
Wylie, Philip, 1902–1971.
Gladiator / Philip Wylie; introduction by Janny Wurts.
p.   cm.—(Bison frontiers of imagination)
ISBN 0-8032-9840-4 (pbk.: alk. paper)
1. Human experimentation in medicine—Fiction.   2. Alienation
(Social psychology)—Fiction.   3. Fathers and sons—Fiction.
4. Muscle strength—Fiction.   5. Loneliness—Fiction.   I. Title.
II. Series.
PS3545.Y46G58   2004
813'.52—dc22
2003022025

FOR
MICHAEL SHEPARD

Introduction

There are many reasons to read a story beyond the thrill of being entertained. Stretching the mind to explore new concepts or bending thought to understand history can lend us valuable insights. With each new generation, ideas shift focus. Thoughts that are considered important change and evolve over time.

Philip Wylie was a storyteller with strong views concerning women, and that the values of the society in which he lived influenced the way he viewed and interpreted his world. Yet there is a timeless concept that impels the tale he has created on these pages.

Most human beings spend their lives in search of themselves, first learning to orient to the surroundings that shape them, and then reaching beyond that birthright to discover their greatness that lies above and beyond the ordinary. Some lose their dreams early. Others try and fail. Others meet discouragement, pick themselves up, and never find the way out of the box. The very few discover the bigger picture, and the slim handful of those actually stay on course and develop their genius. That genius lives in all of us, but few find the will or the space to nurture the seed of the dream that roots their uniqueness.

Philip Wylie's *Gladiator* takes this age-old trial of the human condition and stands it on its head. His hero is born with exceptional strengths, and the quest he follows shows his trials and triumphs in trying to adapt himself into the context of a society that, in Wylie's assuredly cynical view, does not look upon differences kindly.

A wiser being than I once pointed out that as human beings we tend to annihilate differences. We disown them, we separate from them, we denigrate them with labels, or we consider ourselves above them. We handle differences by eliminating them, one way or another, not by learning to share them, grow beside them, integrate them, or even in, sadly, so many cases, learning to coexist with them.

To me the hero of Wylie's story demonstrates this principle with graphic poignancy. If some of the viewpoints of Wylie's time frankly put my back up, it is a lesson to me—that I am as narrow in viewpoint as that past generation, if I cannot bend my thoughts, stretch my mind, and climb down from my high horse of judgment.

I am impelled to rise to the challenge—not to eliminate the difference, not to disown the feelings, not to lightly dismiss a story in which this author put so much of his heart and his anguish.

To strive with Wylie's exceptional hero and to follow his quest for belonging became a marvel of insights. Not as an example of how human beings might treat one another, when confronted with the exceptional that lies outside of the normal parameters, or beyond the reach of consensus understanding—but as a celebration of the enduring quality of will, that men and women who are ordinary, and also those who find their way to claim genius, must possess in order to surmount their quest to reconcile differences. That authority and that drive to seek freedom from society's hidebound constrictions is one of the gifts of our human spirit.

The ultimate quest is to reconcile and appreciate differences and to honor the impact of diversity that poses our greatest world challenge today. Wylie's story dares to explore this ground by reversing the view through the telescope. The large man, the strong man, the exceptional spirit whose quest is to find himself in the context of an ordinary society is as bold an undertaking now as in the era when the book was first published.

To the last page, Philip Wylie has left us a challenge: whether we in the new millennium stand any closer to resolving the crises posed to us by his dream.

GLADIATOR

ONCE UPON a time in Colorado lived a man named Abednego Danner and his wife, Matilda. Abednego Danner was a professor of biology in a small college in the town of Indian Creek. He was a spindling wisp of a man, with a nature drawn well into itself by the assaults of the world and particularly of the grim Mrs. Danner, who understood nothing and undertook all. Nevertheless these two lived modestly in a frame house on the hem of Indian Creek and they appeared to be a settled and peaceful couple.

The chief obstacle to Mrs. Danner's placid dominion of her hearth was Professor Danner's laboratory, which occupied a room on the first floor of the house. It was the one impregnable redoubt in her domestic stronghold. Neither threat nor entreaty would drive him and what she termed his "stinking, unchristian, unhealthy dinguses" from that room. After he had lectured vaguely to his classes on the structure of the *Paramecium caudatum* and the law discovered by Mendel, he would shut the door be-

3

hind himself, and all the fury of the stalwart, black-haired woman could not drive him out until his own obscure ends were served.

It never occurred to Professor Danner that he was a great man or a genius. His alarm at such a notion would have been pathetic. He was so fascinated by the trend of his thoughts and experiments, in fact, that he scarcely realized by what degrees he had outstripped a world that wore picture hats, hobble skirts, and straps beneath its trouser legs. However, as the century turned and the fashions changed, he was carried further from them, which was just as well.

On a certain Sunday he sat beside his wife in church, singing snatches of the hymns in a doleful and untrue voice and meditating, during the long sermon, on the structure of chromosomes. She, bolt upright and overshadowing him, like a coffin in the pew, rigid lest her black silk rustle, thrilled in some corner of her mind at the picture of hell and salvation.

Mr. Danner's thoughts turned to Professor Mudge, whose barren pate showed above the congregation a few rows ahead of him. There, he said to himself, sat a stubborn and unenlightened man. And so, when the weekly tyranny of church was ended, he asked Mudge to dinner. That he accomplished by an argument with his wife, audible the length of the aisle.

They walked to the Danner residence. Mrs. Danner changed her clothes hurriedly, basted the roast, made milk sauce for the string beans, and set three places. They went into the dining-room. Danner carved, the home-made mint jelly was passed, the bread, the butter, the gravy; and Mrs. Danner dropped out of the conversation, after guying her husband on his lack of skill at his task of carving.

Mudge opened with the usual comment. "Well, Abednego, how are the blood-stream radicals progressing?"

His host chuckled. "Excellently, thanks. Some day I'll be ready to jolt you hidebound biologists into your senses."

Mudge's left eyebrow lifted. "So? Still the same thing, I take it? Still believe that chemistry controls human destiny?"

"Almost ready to demonstrate it," Danner replied.

"Along what lines?"

"Muscular strength and the nervous discharge of energy."

Mudge slapped his thigh. "Ho ho! Nervous discharge of energy. You assume the human body to be a voltaic pile, eh? That's good. I'll have to tell Gropper. He'll enjoy it."

Danner, in some embarrassment, gulped a huge mouthful of meat. "Why not?" he said. "Look at the insects—the ants. Strength a hundred times our own. An ant can carry a large spider—yet an ant is tissue and fiber, like a man. If a man could be given the same sinews—he could walk off with his own house."

"Ha ha! There's a good one. Maybe you'll do it, Abednego."

"Possibly, possibly."

"And you would make a splendid piano-mover."

"Pianos! Pooh! Consider the grasshoppers. Make a man as strong as a grasshopper—and he'll be able to leap over a church. I tell you, there is something that determines the quality of every muscle and nerve. Find it—transplant it—and you have the solution."

Mirth overtook Professor Mudge in a series of paroxysms from which he emerged rubicund and witty. "Probably your grasshopper man will look like a grasshopper—more insect than man. At least, Danner, you have imagination."

"Few people have," Danner said, and considered that he had acquitted himself.

His wife interrupted at that point. "I think this nonsense has gone far enough. It is wicked to tamper with God's creatures. It is wicked to discuss such matters—especially on the Sabbath. Abednego, I wish you would give up your work in the laboratory."

Danner's cranium was overlarge and his neck small; but he stiffened it to hold himself in a posture of dignity. "Never."

His wife gazed from the defiant pose to the locked door visible through the parlour. She stirred

6

angrily in her clothes and speared a morsel of food. "You'll be punished for it."

Later in the day Mudge and Gropper laughed heartily at the expense of the former's erstwhile host. Danner read restively. He was forbidden to work on the Sabbath. It was his only compromise. Matilda Danner turned the leaves of the Bible and meditated in a partial vacuum of day-dreams.

On Monday Danner hastened home from his classes. During the night he had had a new idea. And a new idea was a rare thing after fourteen years of groping investigation. "Alkaline radicals," he murmured as he crossed his lawn. He considered a group of ultra-microscopic bodies. He had no name for them. They were the "determinants" of which he had talked. He locked the laboratory door behind himself and bent over the microscope he had designed. "Huh!" he said. An hour later, while he stirred a solution in a beaker, he said: "Huh!" again. He repeated it when his wife called him to dinner. The room was a maze of test tubes, bottles, burners, retorts, instruments. During the meal he did not speak. Afterwards he resumed work. At twelve he prepared six tadpole eggs and put them to hatch. It would be his three hundred and sixty-first separate tadpole hatching.

Then, one day in June, Danner crossed the campus with unusual haste. Birds were singing, a gentle wind eddied over the town from the slopes of the Rocky Mountains, flowers bloomed. The professor did not heed the reburgeoning of nature. A strange thing had happened to him that morning. He had peeped into his workroom before leaving for the college and had come suddenly upon a phenomenon.

One of the tadpoles had hatched in its aquarium. He observed it eagerly, first because it embodied his new idea, and second because it swam with a rare activity. As he looked, the tadpole rushed at the side of its domicile. There was a tinkle and a splash. It had swum through the plate glass! For an instant it lay on the floor. Then, with a flick of its tail, it flew into the air and hit the ceiling of the room.

"Good Lord!" Danner said. Old years of work were at an end. New years of excitement lay ahead. He snatched the creature and it wriggled from his grasp. He caught it again. His fist was not sufficiently strong to hold it. He left it, flopping in eight-foot leaps, and went to class with considerable suppressed agitation and some reluctance. The determinant was known. He had made a living creature abnormally strong.

When he reached his house and unlocked the door of the laboratory, he found that four tadpoles, in all, had hatched. Before they expired in the unfamiliar element of air, they had demolished a quantity of apparatus.

Mrs. Danner knocked on the door. "What's been going on in there?"

"Nothing," her husband answered.

8

"Nothing! It sounded like nothing! What have you got there? A cat?"

"No—yes."

"Well—I won't have such goings on, and that's all there is to it."

Danner collected the debris. He buried the tadpoles. One was dissected first. Then he wrote for a long time in his notebook. After that he went out and, with some difficulty, secured a pregnant cat. A week later he chloroformed the tabby and inoculated her. Then he waited. He had been patient for a long time. It was difficult to be patient now.

When the kittens were born into this dark and dreary world, Mr. Danner assisted as sole obstetrician. In their first hours nothing marked them as unique. The professor selected one and drowned the remainder. He remembered the tadpoles and made a simple calculation.

When the kitten was two weeks old and its eyes opened, it was dieting on all its mother's milk and more besides. The professor considered that fact significant. Then one day it committed matricide.

Probably the playful blow of its front paw was intended in the best spirit. Certainly the old tabby, receiving it, was not prepared for such violence from its offspring. Danner gasped. The kitten had unseamed its mother in a swift and horrid manner. He put the cat out of its misery and tended the kitten with trepidation. It grew. It ate—beefsteaks and chops, bone and all.

9

When it reached three weeks, it began to jump alarmingly. The laboratory was not large enough. The professor brought it its food with the expression of a man offering a wax sausage to a hungry panther.

On a peaceful Friday evening Danner built a fire to stave off the rigours of a cold snap. He and Mrs. Danner sat beside the friendly blaze. Her sewing was in her lap, and in his was a book to which he paid scant attention. The kitten, behind its locked door, thumped and mewed.

"It's hungry," Mrs. Danner said. "If you must keep a cat, why don't you feed it?"

"I do," he answered. He refrained, for politic reasons, from mentioning what and how much he fed it. The kitten mewed again.

"Well," she repeated, "it sounds hungry."

Danner fidgeted. The laboratory was unheated and consequently chilly. From its gloomy interior the kitten peered beneath the door and saw the fire. It sensed warmth. The feline affinity for hearths drew it. One paw scratched tentatively on the door.

"It's cold," Mrs. Danner said. "Why don't you bring it here? No, I don't want it here. Take it a cover."

"It—it has a cover." Danner did not wish to go into that dark room.

The kitten scratched again and then it became earnest. There was a splitting, rending sound. The bottom panel of the door was torn away and it emerged nonchalantly, crossing the room and curling up by the fire.

For five minutes Mrs. Danner sat motionless. Her eyes at length moved from the kitten to her husband's quivering face and then to the broken door. On his part, he made no move. The kitten was a scant six inches from his foot. Mrs. Danner rose. She went to the door and studied the orifice, prying at it with her fingers as if to measure the kitten's strength by her own. Then she turned the key and peered into the gloom. That required either consummate nerve or great curiosity. After her inspection she sat down again.

Ten minutes passed. Danner cleared his throat. Then she spoke. "So. You've done it?"

"Done what?" he asked innocently.

"You've made all this rubbish you've been talking about strength—happen to that kitten."

"It wasn't rubbish."

"Evidently."

At that crisis Mr. Danner's toe trembled and the kitten, believing it a new toy, curled its paws over the shoe. There was a sound of tearing leather, and the shoe came apart. Fortunately the foot inside it was not hurt severely. Danner did not dare to budge. He heard his wife's startled inhalation.

Mrs. Danner did not resume her sewing. She breathed heavily and slow fire crept into her cheeks. The enormity of the crime overcame her. And she perceived that the hateful laboratory had invaded her portion of the house. Moreover, her sturdy religion had been desecrated. Danner read her thoughts.

"Don't be angry," he said. Beads of perspiration gathered on his brow.

"Angry!" The kitten stirred at the sound of her voice. "Angry! And why not? Here you defied God and man—and made that creature of the devil. You've overrun my house. You're a wicked, wicked man. And as for that cat, I won't have it. I won't stand for it."

"What are you going to do?"

Her voice rose to a scream. "Do! Do! Plenty— and right here and now." She ran to the kitchen and came back with a broom. She flung the front door wide. Her blazing eyes rested for a moment on the kitten. To her it had become merely an obnoxious little animal. "Scat! You little demon!" The broom came down on the cat's back with a jarring thud.

After that, chaos. A ball of fur lashed through the air. Whatnot, bird cage, bookcase, morris chair flew asunder. Then the light went out. In the darkness a comet, a hurricane, ricochetted through the room. Then there was a crash mightier than the others, followed by silence.

When Danner was able, he picked himself up and lighted the lamp. His wife lay on the floor in a dead faint. He revived her. She sat up and wept silently over the wreck of her parlour. Danner paled. A round hole—a hole that could have been made by nothing but a solid cannon shot—showed where the kitten had left the room through the wall.

Mrs. Danner's eyes were red-rimmed. Her breath came jerkily. With incredulous little gestures she picked herself up and gazed at the hole. A draught blew through it. Mr. Danner stuffed it with a rug.

"What are we going to do?" she said.

"If it comes back—we'll call it Samson."

And—as soon as Samson felt the gnawing of appetite, he returned to his rightful premises. Mrs. Danner fed him. Her face was pale and her hands trembled. Horror and fascination fought with each other in her soul as she offered the food. Her husband was in his classroom, nervously trying to fix his wits on the subject of the day.

"Kitty, kitty, poor little kitty," she said.

Samson purred and drank a quart of milk. She concealed her astonishment from herself. Mrs. Danner's universe was undergoing a transformation.

At three in the afternoon the kitten scratched away the screen door on the back porch and entered the house. Mrs. Danner fed it the supper meat.

Danner saw it when he returned. It was chasing flies in the yard. He stood in awe. The cat could spring twenty or thirty feet with ease. Then the sharp spur of dread entered him. Suppose someone saw and asked questions. He might be arrested, taken to prison. Something would happen. He tried to analyze and solve the problem. Night came. The cat was allowed to go out unmolested. In the morning the town of Indian Creek rose to find that six large dogs had been slain during the dark hours. A panther had come down from the mountains, they said. And Danner lectured with a dry tongue and errant mind.

It was Will Hoag, farmer of the fifth generation, resident of the environs of Indian Creek, church-goer, and hard-cider addict, who bent himself most mercilessly on the capture of the alleged panther. His chicken-house suffered thrice and then his sheep-fold. After four such depredations he cleaned his rifle and undertook a vigil from a spot behind the barn. An old moon rose late and illuminated his pastures with a blue glow. He drank occasionally from a jug to ward off the evil effects of the night air.

Some time after twelve his attention was distracted from the jug by stealthy sounds. He moved toward them. A hundred yards away his cows were huddled together—a heap of dun shadows. He saw a form which he mistook for a weasel creeping toward the cows. As he watched, he perceived that the small animal behaved singularly unlike a weasel. It slid across the earth on taut limbs, as if it was going to attack the cows. Will Hoag repressed a guffaw.

Then the farmer's short hair bristled. The cat sprang and landed on the neck of the nearest cow and clung there. Its paw descended. There was a horrid sound of ripping flesh, a moan, the thrashing of hoofs, a blot of dribbling blood, and the cat began to gorge on its prey.

Hoag believed that he was intoxicated, that delirium tremens had overtaken him. He stood rooted to the spot. The marauder ignored him. Slowly, unbelievingly, he raised his rifle and fired. The bullet knocked the cat from its perch. Mr. Hoag went forward and picked it up.

"God Almighty," he whispered. The bullet had not penetrated the cat's skin. And, suddenly, it wriggled in his hand. He dropped it. A flash of fur in the moonlight, and he was alone with the corpse of his Holstein.

He contemplated profanity, he considered kneeling in prayer. His joints turned to water. He called faintly for his family. He fell unconscious.

When Danner heard of that exploit—it was relayed by jeering tongues who said the farmer was drunk and a panther had killed the cow—his lips set in a line of resolve. Samson was taking too great liberties. It might attack a person, in which case he, Danner, would be guilty of murder. That day he did not attend his classes. Instead, he prepared a relentless poison in his laboratory and fed it to the kitten in a brace of meaty chops. The dying agonies of Samson, aged seven weeks, were Homeric.

After that, Danner did nothing for some days. He wondered if his formulæ and processes should be given to the world. But, being primarily a man of vast imagination, he foresaw hundreds of rash experiments. Suppose, he thought, that his discovery was tried on a lion, or an elephant! Such a creature would be invincible. The tadpoles were dead. The kitten had been buried. He sighed wearily and turned his life into its usual courses.

BEFORE THE summer was ended, however, a new twist of his life and affairs started the mechanism of the professor's imagination again. It was announced to him when he returned from summer school on a hot afternoon. He dropped his portfolio on the parlour desk, one corner of which still showed the claw-marks of the miscreant Samson, and sat down with a comfortable sigh.

"Abednego." His wife seldom addressed him by his first name.

"Yes?"

"I—I—I want to tell you something."

"Yes?"

"Haven't you noticed any difference in me lately?"

He had never noticed a difference in his wife. When they reached old age, he would still be unable to discern it. He shook his head and looked at her with some apprehension. She was troubled. "What's the matter?"

"I suppose you wouldn't—yet," she said. "But—well—I'm with child."

The professor folded his upper lip between his thumb and forefinger. "With child? Pregnant? You mean—"

"I'm going to have a baby."

Soon after their marriage the timid notion of parenthood had escaped them. They had, in fact, avoided its mechanics except on those rare evenings when tranquillity and the reproductive urge conspired to imbue him with courage and her with sinfulness. Nothing came of that infrequent union. They never expected anything.

And now they were faced with it. He murmured: "A baby."

Faint annoyance moved her. "Yes. That's what one has. What are we going to do?"

"I don't know, Matilda. But I'm glad."

She softened. "So am I, Abednego."

Then a hissing, spattering sound issued from the kitchen. "The beans!" Mrs. Danner said. The second idyl of their lives was finished.

Alone in his bed, tossing on the humid muslin sheets, Danner struggled within himself. The hour that was at hand would be short. The logical step after the tadpoles and the kitten was to vaccinate the human mammal with his serum. To produce a super-child, an invulnerable man. As a scientist he was passionately intrigued by the idea. As a husband he was dubious. As a member of society he was terrified.

That his wife would submit to the plan or to the step it necessitated was beyond belief. She would never allow a sticky tube of foreign animal matter to be poured into her veins. She would not permit the will of God to be altered or her offspring to be the subject of experiment. Another man would have laughed at the notion of persuading her. Mr. Danner never laughed at matters that involved his wife.

There was another danger. If the child was female and became a woman like his wife, then the effect of such strength would be awful indeed. He envisioned a militant reformer, an iron-bound Calvinist, remodelling the world single-handed. A Scotch Lilith, a matronly Gabriel, a she-Hercules. He shuddered.

A hundred times he denied his science. A hundred and one times it begged him to be served. Each decision to drop the idea was followed by an effort to discover means to inoculate her without her knowledge. To his wakeful ears came the reverberation of her snores. He rose and paced the floor. A scheme came to him. After that he was lost.

Mrs. Danner was surprised when her husband brought a bottle of blackberry cordial to her. It was his first gift to her in more than a year. She was fond of cordial. He was not. She took a glass after supper and then a second, which she drank "for him." He smiled nervously and urged her to drink it. His hands clenched and unclenched. When she finished the second glass, he watched her constantly.

"I feel sleepy," she said.

"You're tired." He tried to dissemble the eagerness in his voice. "Why don't you lie down?"

"Strange," she said a moment later. "I'm not usually so—so—misty."

He nodded. The opiate in the cordial was working. She lay on the couch. She slept. The professor hastened to his laboratory. An hour later he emerged with a hypodermic syringe in his hand. His wife lay limply, one hand touching the floor. Her stern, dark face was relaxed. He sat beside her. His conscience raged. He hated the duplicity his task required. His eyes lingered on the swollen abdomen. It was cryptic, enigmatic, filled with portent. He jabbed the needle. She did not stir. After that he substituted a partly empty bottle of cordial for the drugged liquor. It was, perhaps, the most practical thing he had ever done in his life.

Mrs. Danner could not explain herself on the following morning. She belaboured him. "Why didn't you wake me and make me go to bed? Sleeping in my clothes! I never did such a thing in my life."

"I couldn't wake you. I tried."

"Rubbish."

"You were sleeping so hard—you refused to move."

"Sometimes, old as you are, I'd like to thrash you."

Danner went to the college. There was nothing more to do, nothing more to require his concentration. He could wait—as he had waited before. He trembled occasionally with the hope that his child would be a boy—a sane, healthy boy. Then, in the end, his work might bear fruit. "The *Euglena viridis*," he said in flat tones, "will be the subject of to-morrow's study. I want you gentlemen to diagram the structure of the *Euglena viridis* and write five hundred words on its vital principles and processes. It is particularly interesting because it shares properties that are animal with properties that are vegetable."

September, October, November. Chilly winds from the high mountains. The day-by-day freezing over of ponds and brooks. Smoke at the tops of chimneys. Snow. Thanksgiving. And always Mrs. Danner growing with the burden of her offspring. Mr. Danner sitting silent, watching, wondering, waiting. It would soon be time.

On Christmas morning there entered into Mrs. Danner's vitals a pain that was indefinable and at the same time certain. It thrust all thought from her mind. Then it diminished and she summoned her husband. "Get the doctor. It's coming."

Danner tottered into the street and executed his errand. The doctor smiled cheerfully. "Just beginning? I'll be over this afternoon."

"But—good Lord—you can't leave her like—"

"Nonsense."

He came home and found his wife dusting. He shook his head. "Get Mrs. Nolan," she said. Then she threw herself on the bed again.

Mrs. Nolan, the nearest neighbour, wife of Professor Nolan and mother of four children, was delighted. This particular Christmas was going to be a day of some excitement. She prepared hot water and bustled with unessential occupation. Danner sat prostrate in the parlour. He had done it. He had done more—and that would be known later. Perhaps it would fail. He hoped it would fail. He wrung his hands. The concept of another person in his house had not yet occurred to him. Birth was his wife's sickness—until it was over.

The doctor arrived after Danner had made his third trip. Mrs. Nolan prepared lunch. "I love to cook in other people's kitchens," she said. He wanted to strike her. Curious, he thought. At three-thirty the industry of the doctor and Mrs. Nolan increased and the silence of the two, paradoxically, increased with it.

Then the early twilight fell. Mrs. Danner lay with her lank black hair plastered to her brow. She did not moan. Pain twisted and convulsed her. Downstairs Danner sat and sweated. A cry—his wife's. Another—unfamiliar. Scurrying feet on the bare parts of the floor. He looked up. Mrs. Nolan leaned over the stair well.

"It's a boy, Mr. Danner. A beautiful boy. And husky. You never saw such a husky baby." "It ought to be," he said. They found him later in the back yard, prancing on the snow with weird, ungainly steps. A vacant smile lighted his features. They didn't blame him,

III

CALM AND quiet held their negative sway over the
Danner ménage for an hour, and then there was a
disturbed fretting that developed into a lusty bawl.
The professor passed a fatigued hand over his brow.
He was unaccustomed to the dissonances of his offspring. Young Hugo—they had named him after a
maternal uncle—had attained the age of one week
without giving any indication of unnaturalness.
That is not quite true. He was as fleshy as most
healthy infants, but the flesh was more than normally
firm. He was inordinately active. His eyes had been
gray but, already, they gave promise of the inkiness
they afterwards exhibited. He was born with a quantity of black hair—hair so dark as to be nearly blue.
Abednego Danner, on seeing it, exercised the liberty
which all husbands take, and investigated rumours of
his wife's forbears with his most secret thoughts.
The principal rumour was that one of her lusty
Covenanter grandsires had been intrigued by a squaw

24

to the point of forgetting his Psalms and recalling only the Song of Solomon.

However that may have been, Hugo was an attractive and virile baby. Danner spent hours at the side of his crib speculating and watching for any sign of biological variation. But it was not until a week had passed that he was given evidence. By that time he was ready to concede the failure of his greatest experiment.

The baby bawled and presently stopped. And Mrs. Danner, who had put it to breast, suddenly called her husband. "Abednego! Come here! Hurry!"

The professor's heart skipped its regular timing and he scrambled to the floor above. "What's the matter?"

Mrs. Danner was sitting in a rocking-chair. Her face was as white as paper. Only in her eyes was there a spark of life. He thought she was going to faint. "What's the matter?" he said again.

He looked at Hugo and saw nothing terrifying in the ravishing hunger which the infant showed.

"Matter! Matter! You know the matter!"

Then he knew and he realized that his wife had discovered. "I don't. You look frightened. Shall I bring some water?"

Mrs. Danner spoke again. Her voice was icy, distant, terrible. "I came in to feed him just a minute ago. He was lying in his crib. I tried to—to hug him and he put his arms out. As God lives, I could not pull that baby to me! He was too strong, Abednego!

25

Too strong. Too strong. I couldn't unbend his little arms when he stiffened them. I couldn't straighten them when he bent them. And he pushed me—harder than you could push. Harder than I could push myself. I know what it means. You have done your horrible thing to my baby. He's just a baby, Abednego. And you've done your thing to him. How could you? Oh, how could you!"

Mrs. Danner rose and laid the baby gently on the chair. She stood before her husband, towering over him, raised her hand, and struck with all her force. Mr. Danner fell to one knee, and a red welt lifted on his face. She struck him again and he fell against the chair. Little Hugo was dislodged. One hand caught a rung of the chair back and he hung suspended above the floor.

"Look!" Mrs. Danner screamed.

As they looked, the baby flexed its arm and lifted itself back into the chair. It was a feat that a gymnast would have accomplished with difficulty. Danner stared, ignoring the blows, the crimson on his cheek. For once in his lifetime, he suddenly defied his wife. He pointed to the child.

"Yes, look!" His voice rang clearly. "I did it. I vaccinated you the night the cordial put you to sleep. And there's my son. He's strong. Stronger than a lion's cub. And he'll increase in strength as he grows until Samson and Hercules would be pygmies beside him. He'll be the first of a new and glorious race. A race that doesn't have to fear—because it cannot

26

know harm. No man can hurt him, no man can vanquish him. He will be mightier than any circumstances. He, son of a weak man, will be stronger than the beasts, even than the ancient dinosaurs, stronger than the tides, stronger than fate—strong as God is strong. And you—you, Matilda—mother of him, will be proud of him. He will be great and famous. You can knock me down. You can knock me down a thousand times. I have given you a son whose little finger you cannot bend with a crow-bar. Oh, all these years I've listened to you and obeyed you and —yes, I've feared you a little—and God must hate me for it. Now take your son. And my son. You cannot change him. You cannot bend him to your will. He is all I might have been. All that mankind should be." Danner's voice broke and he sobbed. He relented. "I know it's hard for you. It's against your religion—against your love, even. But try to like him. He's no different from you and me—only stronger. And strength is a glorious thing, a great thing. Then—afterwards—if you can—forgive me." He collapsed.

Blood pounded in her ears. She stared at the huddled body of her husband. He had stood like a prophet and spoken words of fire. She was shaken from her pettiness. For one moment she had loved Danner. In that same instant she had glimpsed the superhuman energy that had driven him through the long years of discouragement to triumph. She had seen his soul. She fell at his feet, and when Danner opened his eyes, he found her there, weeping. He took her in his arms, timidly, clumsily. "Don't cry, Mattie. It'll be all right. You love him, don't you?"

She stared at the babe. "Of course I love him. Wash your face, Abednego."

After that there was peace in the house, and with it the child grew. During the next months they ignored his peculiarities. When they found him hanging outside his crib, they put him back gently. When he smashed the crib, they discussed a better place for him to repose. No hysteria, no conflict. When, in the early spring, young Hugo began to recognize them and to assert his feelings, they rejoiced as all parents rejoice.

When he managed to vault the sill of the second-story window by some antic contortion of his limbs, they dismissed the episode. Mrs. Danner had been baking. She heard the child's voice and it seemed to come from the yard. Startled, incredulous, she rushed upstairs. Hugo was not in his room. His wail drifted through the window. She looked out. He was lying in the yard, fifteen feet below. She rushed to his side. He had not been hurt.

Danner made a pen of the iron heads and feet of two old beds. He wired them together. The baby was kept in the inclosure thus formed. The days warmed and lengthened. No one except the Danners knew of the prodigy harboured by their unostentatious house. But the secret was certain to leak out eventually.

Mrs. Nolan, the next-door neighbour, was first to learn it. She had called on Mrs. Danner to borrow a cup of sugar. The call, naturally, included a discussion of various domestic matters and a visit to the baby. She voiced a question that had occupied her mind for some time.

"Why do you keep the child in that iron thing? Aren't you afraid it will hurt itself?"

"Oh, no."

Mrs. Nolan viewed young Hugo. He was lying on a large pillow. Presently he rolled off its surface. "Active youngster, isn't he?"

"Very," Mrs. Danner said, nervously.

Hugo, as if he understood and desired to demonstrate, seized a corner of the pillow and flung it from him. It traversed a long arc and landed on the floor. Mrs. Nolan was startled. "Goodness! I never saw a child his age that could do that!"

"No. Let's go downstairs. I want to show you some tidies I'm making."

Mrs. Nolan paid no attention. She put the pillow back in the pen and watched while Hugo tossed it out. "There's something funny about that. It isn't normal. Have you seen a doctor?"

Mrs. Danner fidgeted. "Oh, yes. Little Hugo's healthy."

Little Hugo grasped the iron wall of his miniature prison. He pulled himself toward it. His skirt caught in the floor. He pulled harder. The pen moved toward him. A high soprano came from Mrs. Nolan.

"He's moved it! I don't think I could move it myself! I tell you, I'm going to ask the doctor to examine him. You shouldn't let a child be like that."

Mrs. Danner, filled with consternation, sought refuge in prevarication. "Nonsense," she said as calmly as she could. "All we Douglases are like that. Strong children. I had a grandfather who could lift a cider keg when he was five—two hundred pounds and more. Hugo just takes after him, that's all."

Mrs. Nolan was annoyed. Partly because she was jealous of Hugo's prowess—her own children had been feeble and dull. Partly because she was frightened—no matter how strong a person became, a baby had no right to be so powerful. Partly because she sensed that Mrs. Danner was not telling the whole truth. She suspected that the Danners had found a new way to raise children. "Well," she said, "all I have to say is that it'll damage him. It'll strain his little heart. It'll do him a lot of harm. If I had a child like that, I'd tie it up most of the time for the first few years."

"Kate," Mrs. Danner said unpleasantly, "I believe you would."

Mrs. Nolan shrugged. "Well—I'm glad none of my children are freaks, anyhow."

"I'll get your sugar."

In the afternoon the minister called. He talked of the church and the town until he felt his preamble adequate. "I was wondering why you didn't bring your child to be baptized, Mrs. Danner. And why

30

you couldn't come to church, now that it is old
enough?"

"Well," she replied carefully, "the child is rather
—irritable. And we thought we'd prefer to have it
baptized at home."

"It's irregular."

"We'd prefer it."

"Very well. I'm afraid—" he smiled—"that
you're a little—ah—unfamiliar with the upbringing
of children. Natural—in the case of the first-born.
Quite natural. But—ah—I met Mrs. Nolan today.
Quite by accident. And she said that you kept the
child—ah—in an iron pen. It seemed unnecessarily
cruel to me—"

"Did it?" Mrs. Danner's jaw set squarely.

But the minister was not to be turned aside lightly.
"I'm afraid, if it's true, that we—the church—will
have to do something about it. You can't let the
little fellow grow up surrounded by iron walls. It
will surely point him toward the prison. Little minds
are tender and—ah—impressionable."

"We've had a crib and two pens of wood," Mrs.
Danner answered tartly. "He smashed them all."

"Ah? So?" Lifted eyebrows. "Temper, eh? He
should be punished. Punishment is the only mould
for unruly children."

"You'd punish a six-months-old baby?"

"Why—certainly. I've reared seven by the rod."

"Well—" a blazing maternal instinct made her
feel vicious. "Well—you won't raise mine by a rod.

31

Or touch it—by a mile. Here's your hat, parson."
Mrs. Danner spent the next hour in prayer.

The village is known for the speed of its gossip
and the sloth of its intelligence. Those two factors
explain the conditions which preluded and surrounded the dawn of consciousness in young Hugo.
Mrs. Danner's extemporaneous fabrication of a
sturdy ancestral line kept the more supernatural ele-
ments of the baby's prowess from the public eye. It
became rapidly and generally understood that the
Danner infant was abnormal and that the treatment
to which it was submitted was not usual. At the same
time neither the gossips of Indian Creek nor the
slightly more sage professors of the college exercised
the wit necessary to realize that, however strong
young Hugo might become, it was neither right nor
just that his cradle days be augurs of that eventual
estate. On the face of it the argument seemed logical.
If Mrs. Danner's forbears had been men of peculiar
might, her child might well be able to chin itself at
three weeks and it might easily be necessary to con-
fine it in a metal pen, however inhumane the process
appeared.

Hugo was sheltered, and his early antics, peculiar
and startling as they were to his parents, escaped
public attention. The little current of talk about him
was kept alive only because there was so small an
array of topics for the local burghers. But it was not
extraordinarily malicious. Months piled up. A year
passed and then another.

Hugo was a good-natured, usually sober, and very sensitive child. Abednego Danner's fear that his process might have created muscular strength at the expense of reason diminished and vanished as Hugo learned to walk and to talk, and as he grasped the rudiments of human behaviour. His high little voice was heard in the house and about its lawns.

They began to condition him. Throughout his later life there lingered in his mind a memory of the barriers erected by his family. He was told not to throw his pillow, when words meant nothing to him. Soon after that, he was told not to throw anything. When he could walk, he was forbidden to jump. His jumps were shocking to see, even at the age of two and a half. He was carefully instructed on his behaviour out of doors. No move of his was to indicate his difference from the ordinary child.

He was taught kindness and respect for people and property. His every destructive impulse was carefully curbed. That training was possible only because he was sensitive and naturally susceptible to advice. Punishment had no physical terror for him, because he could not feel it. But disfavour, anger, vexation, or disappointment in another person reflected itself in him at once.

When he was four and a half, his mother sent him to Sunday school. He was enrolled in a class that sat near her own, so she was able to keep a careful eye on him. But Hugo did not misbehave. It was his first contact with a group of children, his first view of the larger cosmos. He sat quietly with his hands folded, as he had been told to sit. He listened to the teacher's stories of Jesus with excited interest.

On his third Sunday he heard one of the children whisper: "Here comes the strong boy."

He turned quickly, his cheeks red. "I'm not. I'm not."

"Yes, you are. Mother said so."

Hugo struggled with the two hymn books on the table. "I can't even lift these books," he lied.

The other child was impressed and tried to explain the situation later, taking the cause of Hugo's weakness against the charge of strength. But the accusation rankled in Hugo's young mind. He hated to be different—and he was beginning to realize that he was different.

From his earliest day that longing occupied him. He sought to hide his strength. He hated to think that other people were talking about him. The distinction he enjoyed was odious to him because it aroused unpleasant emotions in other people. He could not realize that those emotions sprang from personal and group jealousy, from the hatred of superiority.

His mother, ever zealous to direct her son in the path of righteousness, talked to him often about his strength and how great it would become and what great and good deeds he could do with it. Those lectures on virtuous crusades had two uses: they helped check any impulses in her son which she felt

34

would be harmful to her and they helped her to become used to the abnormality in little Hugo. In her mind, it was like telling a hunchback that his hump was a blessing disguised. Hugo was always aware of the fact that her words connoted some latent evil in his nature.

The motif grew in Mrs. Danner's thoughts until she sought a definite outlet for it. One day she led her child to a keg filled with sand. "All of us," she said to her son, "have to carry a burden through life. One of your burdens will be your strength. But that might can make right. See that little keg?"

"Mmmmm."

"That keg is temptation. Can you say it?"

"Temshun."

"Every day in your life you must bear temptation and throw it from you. Can you bear it?"

"Huh?"

"Can you pick up that keg, Hugo?"

He lifted it in his chubby arms. "Now take it to the barn and back," his mother directed. Manfully he walked with the keg to the barn and back. He felt a little silly and resentful. "Now—throw temptation as far away from you as you can."

Mrs. Danner gasped. The distance he threw the keg was frightening.

"You musn't throw it so far, Hugo," she said, forgetting her allegory for an instant.

"You said as far as I can. I can throw it farther, too, if I wanna."

"No. Just throw it a little way. When you throw it far, it doesn't look right. Now—fill it up with sand, and we'll do it over."

Hugo was perplexed. A vague wish to weep occupied him as he filled the keg. The lesson was repeated. Mrs. Danner had excellent Sunday-school instincts, even if she had no real comprehension of ethics. Some days later the burden of temptation was exhibited, in all its dramatic passages, to Mrs. Nolan and another lady. Again Hugo was resentful and again he felt absurd. When he threw the keg, it broke.

"My!" Mrs. Nolan said in a startled tone.

"How awful!" the other woman murmured. "And he's just a child."

That made Hugo suddenly angry and he jumped. The woman screamed. Mrs. Nolan ran to tell whomever she could find. Mrs. Danner whipped her son and he cried softly.

Abednego Danner left the discipline of his son to his wife. He watched the child almost furtively. When Hugo was five, Mr. Danner taught him to read. It was a laborious process and required an entire winter. But Hugo emerged with a new world open to him—a world which he attacked with interest. No one bothered him when he read. He could be found often on sunny days, when other children were playing, prone on the floor, puzzling out sentences in the books of the family library and trying to catch their significance. During his fifth year he was not allowed to play with other children. The neighbourhood insisted on that.

With the busybodyness and contrariness of their kind the same neighbours insisted that Hugo be sent to school in the following fall. When, on the opening day, he did not appear, the truant officer called for him. Hugo heard the conversation between the officer and his mother. He was frightened. He vowed to himself that his abnormality should be hidden deeply.

After that he was dropped into that microcosm of human life to which so little attention is paid by adults. School frightened and excited Hugo. For one thing, there were girls in school—and Hugo knew nothing about them except that they were different from himself. There were teachers—and they made one work, whether one wished to work or not. They represented power, as a jailer represents power. The children feared teachers. Hugo feared them.

But the lesson of Hugo's first six years was fairly well planted. He blushingly ignored the direct questions of those children whom his fame had reached. He gave no reason to anyone for suspecting him of abnormality. He became so familiar to his comrades that their curiosity gradually vanished. He would not play games with them—his mother had forbidden that. But he talked to them and was as friendly as they allowed him to be. His sensitiveness and fear of ridicule made him a voracious student. He liked books. He liked to know things and to learn them.

Thus, bound by the conditionings of his babyhood, he reached the spring of his first year in school without accident. Such tranquillity could not long endure. The day which his mother had dreaded ultimately arrived. A lanky farmer's son, older than the other children in the first grade, chose a particularly quiet and balmy recess period to plague little Hugo. The farmer's boy was, because of his size, the bully and the leader of all the other boys. He had not troubled himself to resent Hugo's exclusiveness or Hugo's reputation until that morning when he found himself without occupation. Hugo was sitting in the sun, his dark eyes staring a little sadly over the laughing, rioting children.

The boy approached him. "Hello, strong man." He was shrewd enough to make his voice so loud as to be generally audible. Hugo looked both harmless and slightly pathetic.

"I'm not, a strong man."

"Course you're not. But everybody thinks you are—except me. I'm not afraid of you."

"I don't want you to be afraid of me. I'm not afraid of you, either."

"Oh, you aren't, huh? Look." He touched Hugo's chest with his finger, and when Hugo looked down, the boy lifted his finger into Hugo's face.

"Go away and let me alone."

The tormentor laughed. "Ever see a fish this long?"

His hands indicated a small fish. Involuntarily

Hugo looked at them. The hands flew apart and slapped him smartly. Several of the children had stopped their play to watch. The first insult made them giggle. The second brought a titter from Anna Blake, and Hugo noticed that. Anna Blake was a little girl with curly golden hair and blue eyes. Secretly Hugo admired her and was drawn to her. When she laughed, he felt a dismal loneliness, a sudden desertion. The farmer's boy pressed the occasion his meanness had made.

"I'll bet you ain't even strong enough to fight little Charlie Todd. Commere, Charlie."

"I am," Hugo replied with slow dignity.

"You're a sissy. You're a-scared to play with us."

The ring around Hugo had grown. He felt a tangible ridicule in it. He knew what it was to hate. Still, his inhibitions, his control, held him in check. "Go away," he said, "or I'll hurt you."

The farmer's boy picked up a stick and put it on his shoulder. "Knock that off, then, strong man."

Hugo knew the dare and its significance. With a gentle gesture he brushed the stick away. Then the other struck. At the same time he kicked Hugo's shins. There was no sense of pain with the kick. Hugo saw it as if it had happened to another person. The school-yard tensed with expectation. But the accounts of what followed were garbled. The farmer's boy fell on his face as if by an invisible agency. Then his body was lifted in the air. The children had an awful picture of Hugo standing for a second with

39

the writhing form of his attacker above his head. Then he flung it aside, over the circle that surrounded him, and the body fell with a thud. It lay without moving. Hugo began to whimper pitifully.

That was Hugo's first fight. He had defended himself, and it made him ashamed. He thought he had killed the other boy. Sickening dread filled him. He hurried to his side and shook him, calling his name. The other boy came to. His arm was broken and his sides were purpling where Hugo had seized him. There was terror in his eyes when he saw Hugo's face above him, and he screamed shrilly for help. The teacher came. She sent Hugo to the blacksmith to be whipped.

That, in itself, was a stroke of genius. The blacksmith whipped grown boys in the high school for their misdeeds. To send a six-year-old child was crushing. But Hugo had risen above the standards set by his society. He had been superior to it for a moment, and society hated him for it. His teacher hated him because she feared him. Mothers of children, learning about the episode, collected to discuss it in high-pitched, hateful voices. Hugo was enveloped in hate. And, as the lash of the smith fell on his small frame, he felt the depths of misery. He was a strong man. There was damnation in his veins.

The minister came and prayed over him. The doctor was sent for and examined him. Frantic busybodies suggested that things be done to weaken him —what things, they did not say. And Hugo, suffering bitterly, saw that if he had beaten the farmer's boy in fair combat, he would have been a hero. It was the scale of his triumph that made it dreadful. He did not realize then that if he had been so minded, he could have turned on the blacksmith and whipped him, he could have broken the neck of the doctor, he could have run raging through the town and escaped unscathed. His might was a secret from himself. He knew it only as a curse, like a disease or a blemish.

During the ensuing four or five years Hugo's peculiar trait asserted itself but once. It was a year after his fight with the bully. He had been isolated socially. Even Anna Blake did not dare to tease him any longer. Shunned and wretched, he built a world of young dreams and confections and lived in it with whatever comfort it afforded.

One warm afternoon in a smoky Indian summer he walked home from school, spinning a top as he walked, stopping every few yards to pick it up and to let its eccentric momentum die on the palm of his hand. His pace thereby was made very slow and he calculated it to bring him to his home in time for supper and no sooner, because, despite his vigour, chores were as odious to him as to any other boy. A wagon drawn by two horses rolled toward him. It was a heavy wagon, piled high with grain-sacks, and a man sat on its rear end, his legs dangling.

As the wagon reached Hugo, it jolted over a rut. There was a grinding rip and a crash. Hugo pocketed his top and looked. The man sitting on the back had been pinned beneath the rear axle, and the load held him there. As Hugo saw his predicament, the man screamed in agony. Hugo's blood chilled. He stood transfixed. A man jumped out of a buggy. A Negro ran from a yard. Two women hurried from the spot. In an instant there were six or seven men around the broken wagon. A sound of pain issued from the mouth of the impaled man. The knot of figures bent at the sides of the cart and tried to lift. "Have to get a jack," Hugo heard them say.

Hugo wound up his string and put it beside his top. He walked mechanically into the road. He looked at the legs of the man on the ground. They were oozing blood where the backboard rested on them. The men gathered there were lifting again, without result. Hugo caught the side and bent his small shoulders. With all his might he pulled up. The wagon was jerked into the air. They pulled out the injured man. Hugo lowered the wagon slowly.

For a moment no attention was paid to him. He waited pridefully for the recognition he had earned. He dug in the dirt with the side of his shoe. A man with a mole on his nose observed him. "Funny how that kid's strength was just enough to turn the balance."

Hugo smiled. "I'm pretty strong," he admitted.

Another man saw him. "Get out of here," he said sharply. "This is no place for a kid."

"But I was the one—"

"I said beat it. And I meant beat it. Go home to your ma."

Slowly the light went from Hugo's eyes. They did not know—they could not know. He had lifted more than two tons. And the men stood now, waiting for the doctor, telling each other how strong they were when the instant of need came.

"Go on, kid. Run along. I'll smack you."

Hugo went. He forgot to spin his top. He stumbled a little as he walked.

I V

DAYS, MONTHS, years. They had forgotten that
Hugo was different. Almost, for a while, he had forgotten it himself. He was popular in school. He
fostered the unexpressed theory that his strength
had been a phenomenon of his childhood—one that
diminished as he grew older. Then, at ten, it called
to him for exercise.

Each day he rose with a feeling of insufficiency.
Each night he retired unrequited. He read. Poe, the
Bible, Scott, Thackeray, Swift, Defoe—all the books
he could find. He thrilled with every syllable of adventure. His imagination swelled. But that was not
sufficient. He yearned as a New England boy yearns
before he runs away to sea.

At ten he was a stalwart and handsome lad. His
brow was high and surmounted by his peculiarly
black hair. His eyes were wide apart, inky, unfathom-
able. He carried himself with the grace of an athlete. He studied hard and he worked hard for his
parents, taking care of a cow and chickens, of a

44

stable and a large lawn, of flowers and a vegetable garden.

Then one day he went by himself to walk in the mountains. He had not been allowed to go into the mountains alone. A *Wanderlust* that came half from himself and half from his books led his feet along a narrow, leafy trail into the forest depths. Hugo lay down and listened to the birds in the bushes, to the music of a brook, and to the sound of the wind. He wanted to be free and brave and great. By and by he stood up and walked again.

An easy exhilaration filled his veins. His pace increased. "I wonder," he thought, "how fast I can run, how far I can jump." He quickened his stride. In a moment he found that the turns in the trail were too frequent for him to see his course. He ran ahead, realizing that he was moving at an abnormal pace. Then he turned, gathered himself, and jumped carefully. He was astonished when he vaulted above the green covering of the trail. He came down heavily. He stood in his tracks, tingling.

"Nobody can do that, not even an acrobat," he whispered. Again he tried, jumping straight up. He rose fully forty feet in the air.

"Good Jesus!" he exulted. In those lonely, incredible moments Hugo found himself. There in the forest, beyond the eye of man, he learned that he was superhuman. It was a rapturous discovery. He knew at that hour that his strength was not a curse. He had inklings of his invulnerability.

He ran. He shot up the steep trail like an express train, at a rate that would have been measured in miles to the hour rather than yards to the minute. Tireless blood poured through his veins. Green streaked at his sides. In a short time he came to the end of the trail. He plunged on, careless of obstacles that would have stopped an ordinary mortal. From trunk to trunk he leaped a burned stretch. He flung himself from a high rock. He sped like a shadow across a pine-carpeted knoll. He gained the bare rocks of the first mountain, and in the open, where the horror of no eye would tether his strength, he moved in flying bounds to its summit.

Hugo stood there, panting. Below him was the world. A little world. He laughed. His dreams had been broken open. His depression was relieved. But he would never let them know—he, Hugo, the giant. Except, perhaps, his father. He lifted his arms—to thank God, to jeer at the world. Hugo was happy.

He went home wondering. He was very hungry—hungrier than he had ever been—and his parents watched him eat with hidden glances. Samson had eaten thus, as if his stomach were bottomless and his food digested instantly to make room for more. And, as he ate, Hugo tried to open a conversation that would lead to a confession to his father. But it seemed impossible.

Hugo liked his father. He saw how his mother dominated the little professor, how she seemed to have crushed and bewildered him until his mind was

unfocused from its present. He could not love his
mother because of that. He did not reason that her
religion had made her blind and selfish, but he felt
her blindness and the many cloaks that protected
her and her interests. He held her in respect and he
obeyed her. But often and wistfully he had tried to
talk to his father, to make friends with him, to make
himself felt as a person.

Abednego Danner's mind was buried in the work
he had done. His son was a foreign person for
whom he felt a perplexed sympathy. It is significant
that he had never talked to Hugo about Hugo's
prowess. The ten-year-old boy had not wished to
discuss it. Now, however, realizing its extent, he
felt he must go to his father. After dinner he said:
"Dad, let's you and me take a walk."

Mrs. Danner's protective impulses functioned
automatically. "Not to-night. I won't have it."

"But, mother—"

Danner guessed the reason for that walk. He
said to his wife with rare firmness: "If the boy wants
to walk with me, we're going."

After supper they went out. Mrs. Danner felt
that she had been shut out of her own son's world.
And she realized that he was growing up.

Danner and his son strolled along the leafy street.
They talked about his work in school. His father
seemed to Hugo more human that he had ever been.
He even ventured the first step toward other conversation. "Well, son, what is it?"

47

Hugo caught his breath. "Well—I kind of thought I ought to tell you. You see—this afternoon —well—you know I've always been a sort of strong kid—"

Danner trembled. "I know—"

"And you haven't said much about it to me. Except to be gentle—"

"That's so. You must remember it."

"Well—I don't have to be gentle with myself, do I? When I'm alone—like in the woods, that is?"

The older one pondered. "You mean—you like to—ah—let yourself out—when you're alone?"

"That's what I mean." The usual constraint between them had receded. Hugo was grateful for his father's help. "You see, dad, I—well—I went walkin' today—and I—I kind of tried myself out."

Danner answered in breathless eagerness: "And?"

"Well—I'm not just a strong kid, dad. I don't know what's the matter with me. It seems I'm not like other kids at all. I guess it's been gettin' worse all these years since I was a baby."

"Worse?"

"I mean—I been gettin' stronger. An' now it seems like I'm about—well—I don't like to boast— but it seems like I'm about the strongest man in the world. When I try it, it seems like there isn't any stopping me. I can go on—far as I like. Runnin'. Jumpin'." His confession had commenced in detail. Hugo warmed to it. "I can do things, dad. It kind of scares me. I can jump higher'n a house. I can run

48

faster'n a train. I can pull up big trees an' push 'em over."

"I see." Danner's spine tingled. He worshipped his son then. "Suppose you show me."

Hugo looked up and down the street. There was no one in sight. The evening was still duskily lighted by afterglow. "Look out then. I'm gonna jump."

Mr. Danner saw his son crouch. But he jumped so quickly that he vanished. Four seconds elapsed. He landed where he had stood. "See, dad?"

"Do it again."

On the second trial the professor's eyes followed the soaring form. And he realized the magnitude of the thing he had wrought.

"Did you see me?"

Danner nodded. "I saw you, son."

"Kind of funny, isn't it?"

"Let's talk some more." There was a pause. "Do you realize, son, that no one else on earth can do what you just did?"

"Yeah. I guess not."

Danner hesitated. "It's a glorious thing. And dangerous."

"Yeah."

The professor tried to simplify the biology of his discovery. He perceived that it was going to involve him in the mysteries of sex. He knew that to unfold them to a child was considered immoral. But Danner was far, far beyond his epoch. He put his hand on Hugo's shoulder. And Hugo set off the process.

"Dad, how come I'm—like this?"

"I'll tell you. It's a long story and a lot for a boy your age to know. First, what do you know about—well—about how you were born?"

Hugo reddened. "I—I guess I know quite a bit. The kids in school are always talkin' about it. And I've read some. We're born like—well—like the kittens were born last year."

"That's right." Danner knitted his brow. He began to explain the details of conception as it occurs in man—the biology of ova and spermatazoa, the differences between the anatomy of the sexes, and the reasons for those differences. He drew, first, a botanical analogy. Hugo listened intently. "I knew most of that. I've seen—girls."

"What?"

"Some of them—after school—let you."

Danner was surprised, and at the same time he was amused. He had forgotten the details of his young investigation. They are blotted out of the minds of most adults—to the great advantage of dignity. He did not show his amusement or his surprise.

"Girls like that," he answered, "aren't very nice. They haven't much modesty. It's rather indecent, because sex is a personal thing and something you ought to keep for the one you're very fond of. You'll understand that better when you're older. But what I was going to tell you is this. When you were little more than a mass of plasm inside your mother, I put a medicine in her blood that I had discovered. I did it with a hypodermic needle. That medicine changed you. It altered the structure of your bones and muscles and nerves and your blood. It made you into a different tissue from the weak fibre of ordinary people. Then—when you were born—you were strong. Did you ever watch an ant carry many times its weight? Or see a grasshopper jump fifty times its length? The insects have better muscles and nerves than we have. And I improved your body till it was relatively that strong. Can you understand that?"

"Sure. I'm like a man made out of iron instead of meat."

"That's it, Hugo. And, as you grow up, you've got to remember that. You're not an ordinary human being. When people find that out, they'll—they'll—"

"They'll hate me?"

"Because they fear you. So you see, you've got to be good and kind and considerate—to justify all that strength. Some day you'll find a use for it—a big, noble use—and then you can make it work and be proud of it. Until that day, you have to be humble like all the rest of us. You mustn't show off or do cheap tricks. Then you'd just be a clown. Wait your time, son, and you'll be glad of it. And—another thing—train your temper. You must never lose it. You can see what would happen if you did? Understand?"

"I guess I do. It's hard work—doin' all that."

"The stronger, the greater, you are, the harder life is for you. And you're the strongest of them all, Hugo."

The heart of the ten-year-old boy burned and vibrated. "And what about God?" he asked.

Danner looked into the darkened sky. "I don't know much about Him," he sighed.

Such was the soundest counsel that Hugo was given during his youth. Because it came to him accompanied by unadulterated truths that he was able to recognize, it exerted a profound effect on him. It is surprising that his father was the one to give it. Nevertheless, Professor Danner was the only person in all of Indian Creek who had sufficient imagination to perceive his son's problems and to reckon with them in any practical sense.

Hugo was eighteen before he gave any other indication of his strength save in that fantastic and Gargantuan play which he permitted himself. Even his play was intruded upon by the small-minded and curious world before he had found the completeness of its pleasure. Then Hugo fell into his coma.

Hugo went back to the deep forest to think things over and to become acquainted with his powers. At first, under full pressure of his sinews, he was clumsy and inaccurate. He learned deftness by trial and error. One day he found a huge pit in the tangled wilderness. It had been an open mine long years before. Sitting on its brink, staring into its pool of verdure, dreaming, he conceived a manner of entertainment suitable for his powers.

He jumped over its craggy edge and walked to its centre. There he selected a high place, and with his hands he cleared away the growth that covered it. Next he laid the foundations of a fort, over which he was to watch the fastnesses for imaginary enemies. The foundations were made of boulders. Some he carried and some he rolled from the floor of the man-made canyon. By the end of the afternoon he had laid out a square wall of rock some three feet in height. On the next day he added to it until the four walls reached as high as he could stretch. He left space for one door and he made a single window. He roofed the walls with the trunks of trees and he erected a turret over the door.

For days the creation was his delight. After school he sped to it. Until dark he strained and struggled with bare rocks. When it was finished, it was an edifice that would have withstood artillery fire creditably. Then Hugo experimented with catapults, but he found no engine that could hurl the rocks he used for ammunition as far as his arms. He cached his treasures in his fortress—an old axe, the scabbard of a sword, tops and marbles, two cans of beans for emergency rations—and he made a flag of blue and white cloth for himself.

Then he played in it. He pretended that Indians were stalking him. An imaginary head would appear at the rim of the pit. Hugo would see it through a

chink. Swish! Crash! A puff of dust would show
where rock met rock—with the attacker's head between. At times he would be stormed on all sides.
To get the effect he would leap the canyon and hurl
boulders on his own fort. Then he would return
and defend it.

It was after such a strenuous sally and while he
was waiting in high excitement for the enemy to re-
appear that Professors Whitaker and Smith from
the college stumbled on his stronghold. They were
walking together through the forest, bent on scaling
the mountain to make certain observations of an ancient cirque that was formed by the seventh great
glacier. As they walked, they debated matters of
strata curvature. Suddenly Whitaker gripped Smith's
arm. "Look!"

They stared through the trees and over the lip
of Hugo's mine. Their eyes bulged as they observed
the size and weight of the fortress.

"Moonshiners," Smith whispered.

"Rubbish. Moonshiners don't build like that. It's
a second Stonehenge. An Indian relic."

"But there's a sign of fresh work around it."

Whitaker observed the newly turned earth and
the freshly bared rock. "Perhaps—perhaps, professor, we've fallen upon something big. A lost race
of Indian engineers. A branch of the Incas—or—"

"Maybe they'll be hostile."

The men edged forward. And at the moment they
reached the edge of the pit, Hugo emerged from

his fort. He saw the men with sudden fear. He tried to hide.

"Hey!" they said. He did not move, but he heard them scrambling slowly toward the spot where he lay.

"Dressed in civilized clothes," the first professor said in a loud voice as his eye located Hugo in the underbrush. "Hey!"

Hugo showed himself. "What?"

"Who are you?"

"Hugo Danner."

"Oh—old Danner's boy, eh?'

Hugo did not like the tone in which they referred to his father. He made no reply.

"Can you tell us anything about these ruins?"

"What ruins?"

They pointed to his fort. Hugo was hurt. "Those aren't ruins. I built that fort. It's to fight Indians in."

The pair ignored his answer and started toward the fort. Hugo did not protest. They surveyed its weighty walls and its relatively new roof.

"Looks recent," Smith said.

"This child has evidently renovated it. But it must have stood here for thousands of years."

"It didn't. I made it—mostly last week."

They noticed him again. Whitaker simpered. "Don't lie, young man."

Hugo was sad. "I'm not lying. I made it. You see—I'm strong." It was as if he had pronounced his own damnation.

"Tut, tut." Smith interrupted his survey. "Did you find it?"

"I built it."

"I said"—the professor spoke with increasing annoyance—"I said not to tell me stories any longer. It's important, young man, that we know just how you found this dolmen and in what condition."

"It isn't a dolly—whatever you said—it's a fort and I built it and I'm not lying."

The professor, in the interests of science, made a grave mistake. He seized Hugo by the arms and shook him. "Now, see here, young man, I'll have no more of your impertinent lip. Tell me just what you've done to harm this noble monument to another race, or, I swear, I'll slap you properly." The professor had no children. He tried, at the same time, another tack, which insulted Hugo further. "If you do, I'll give you a penny—to keep."

Hugo wrenched himself free with an ease that startled Smith. His face was dark, almost black. He spoke slowly, as if he was trying to piece words into sense. "You—both of you—you go away from here and leave me or I'll break your two rotten old necks."

Whitaker moved toward him, and Smith interceded. "We better leave him—and come back later." He was still frightened by the strength in Hugo's arms. "The child is mad. He may have hydrophobia. He might bite." The men moved away hastily. Hugo watched them climb the wall. When they reached the top, he called gently. They wheeled.

And Hugo, sobbing, tears streaming from his face, leaped into his fort. Rocks vomited themselves from it—huge rocks that no man could budge. Walls toppled and crashed. The men began to move. Hugo looked up. He chose a stone that weighed more than a hundred pounds.

"Hey!" he said. "I'm not a liar!" The rock arched through the air and Professors Whitaker and Smith escaped death by a scant margin. Hugo lay in the wreck of the first thing his hands had built, and wept.

After a little while he sprang to his feet and chased the retreating professors. When he suddenly appeared in front of them, they were stricken dumb. "Don't tell any one about that or about me," he said. "If you do—I'll break down your house just like I broke mine. Don't even tell my family. They know it, anyhow."

He leaped. Toward them—over them. The forest hid him. Whitaker wiped clammy perspiration from his brow. "What was it, Smith?"

"A demon. We can't mention it," he repeated, thinking of the warning. "We can't speak of it anyway. They'll never believe us."

V

EXTREMELY DARK of hair, of eyes and skin, moderately tall, and shaped with that compact, breathtaking symmetry that the male figure sometimes assumes, a brilliantly devised, aggressive head topping his broad shoulders, graceful, a man vehemently alive, a man with the promise of a young God. Hugo at eighteen. His emotions ran through his eyes like hot steel in a dark mould. People avoided those eyes; they contained a statement from which ordinary souls shrank.

His skin glowed and sweated into a shiny red-brown. His voice was deep and alluring. During twelve long and fierce years he had fought to know and control himself. Indian Creek had forgotten the terrible child.

Hugo's life at that time revolved less about himself than it had during his first years. That was both natural and fortunate. If his classmates in school and the older people of the town had not discounted his early physical precocity, even his splendid vitality might not have been sufficient to prevent him from becoming moody and melancholy.

But when with the passage of time he tossed no more bullies, carried no more barrels of temptation, built no more fortresses, and grew so handsome that the matrons of Indian Creek as well as the adolescent girls in high school followed him with wayward glances, when the men found him a gay and comprehending companion for any sport or adventure, when his teachers observed that his intelligence was often embarrassingly acute, when he played on three teams and was elected an officer in his classes each year, then that half of Hugo which was purely mundane and human dominated him and made him happy.

His adolescence, his emotions, were no different from those of any young man of his age and character. If his ultimate ambitions followed another trajectory, he postponed the evidence of it. Hugo was in love with Anna Blake, the girl who had attracted him when he was six. The residents of Indian Creek knew it. Her family received his calls with the winking tolerance which the middle class grants to young passion. And she was warm and tender and flirtatious and shy according to the policies that she had learned from custom.

The active part of Hugo did not doubt that he would marry her after he had graduated from the college in Indian Creek, that they would settle somewhere near by, and that they would raise a number of children. His subconscious thoughts made reservations that he, in moments when he was intimate with himself, would admit frankly. It made him a little ashamed of himself to see that on one night he would sit with Anna and kiss her ardently until his body ached, and on another he would deliberately plan to desert her. His idealism at that time was very great and untried and it did not occur to him that all men are so deliberately calculating in the love they disguise as absolute.

Anna had grown into a very attractive woman. Her figure was rounded and tall. Her hair was darker than the waxy curls of her childhood, and a vital gleam had come into it. Her eyes were still as blue and her voice, shorn of its faltering youngness, was sweet and clear. She was undoubtedly the prettiest girl in high school and the logical sweetheart for Hugo Danner. A flower ready to be plucked, at eighteen.

When Hugo reached his senior year, that readiness became almost an impatience. Girls married at an early age in Indian Creek. She looked down the corridor of time during which he would be in college, she felt the pressure of his still slumbering passion, and she sensed his superiority over most of the town boys. Only a very narrow critic would call her resultant tactics dishonourable. They were too intensely human and too clearly born of social and biological necessity.

She had let him kiss her when they were sixteen.

And afterwards, before she went to sleep, she sighed
rapturously at the memory of his warm, firm lips,
his strong, rough arms. Hugo had gone home
through the dizzily spinning dusk, through the wind-
strummed trees and the fragrant fields, his breath
deep in his chest, his eyes hot and somewhat understanding.

Gradually Anna increased that license. She knew
and she did not know what she was doing. She
played a long game in which she said: "If our love
is consummated too soon, the social loss will be
balanced by a speedier marriage, because Hugo is
honourable; but that will never happen." Two years
after that first kiss, when they were floating on the
narrow river in a canoe, Hugo unfastened her blouse
and exposed the creamy beauty of her bosom to the
soft moonlight and she did not protest. That night
he nearly possessed her, and after that night he
learned through her unspoken, voluptuous suggestion all the technique of love-making this side of
consummation.

When, finally, he called one night at her house
and found that she was alone and that her parents
and her brother would not return until the next day,
they looked at each other with a shining agreement.
He turned the lights out and they sat on the couch
in the darkness, listening to the passing of people
on the sidewalk outside. He undressed her. He
whispered halting, passionate phrases. He asked her
if she was afraid and let himself be laughed away

from his own conscience. Then he took her and loved her.

Afterwards, going home again in the gloom of late night, he looked up at the stars and they stood still. He realized that a certain path of life had been followed to its conclusion. He felt initiated into the adult world. And it had been so simple, so natural, so sweet. . . . He threw a great stone into the river and laughed and walked on, after a while.

Through the summer that followed, Hugo and Anna ran the course of their affair. They loved each other violently and incessantly and with no other evil consequence than to invite the open "humphs" of village gossips and to involve him in several serious talks with her father. Their courtship was given the benefit of conventional doubt, however, and their innocence was hotly if covertly protested by the Blakes. Mrs. Danner coldly ignored every fragment of insinuation. She hoped that Hugo and Anna would announce their engagement and she hinted that hope. Hugo himself was excited and absorbed. Occasionally he thought he was sterile, with an inclination to be pleased rather than concerned if it was true.

He added tenderness to his characteristics. And he loved Anna too much. Toward the end of that summer she lost weight and became irritable. They quarrelled once and then again. The criteria for his physical conduct being vague in his mind, Hugo could not gauge it correctly. And he did not realize

62

that the very ardour of his relation with her was abnormal. Her family decided to send her away, believing the opposite of the truth responsible for her nervousness and weakness. A week before she left, Hugo himself tired of his excesses.

One evening, dressing for a last passionate rendezvous, he looked in his mirror as he tied his scarf and saw that he was frowning. Studying the frown, he perceived with a shock what made it. He did not want to see Anna, to take her out, to kiss and rumple and clasp her, to return thinking of her, feeling her, sweet and smelling like her. It annoyed him. It bored him. He went through it uneasily and quarrelled again. Two days later she departed.

He acted his loss well and she did not show her relief until she sat on the train, tired, shattered, and uninterested in Hugo and in life. Then she cried. But Hugo was through. They exchanged insincere letters. He looked forward to college in the fall. Then he received a letter from Anna saying that she was going to marry a man she had met and known for three weeks. It was a broken, gasping, apologetic letter. Every one was outraged at Anna and astounded that Hugo bore the shock so courageously.

The upshot of that summer was to fill his mind with fetid memories, which abated slowly, to make him disgusted with himself and tired of Indian Creek. He decided to go to a different college, one far away from the scene of his painful youth and his disillusioned maturity. He chose Webster University because of the greatness of its name. If Abednego Danner was hurt at his son's defection from his own college, he said nothing. And Mrs. Danner, grown more silent and reserved, yielded to her son's unexpected decision.

Hugo packed his bags one September afternoon, with a feeling of dreaminess. He bade farewell to his family. He boarded the train. His mind was opaque. The spark burning in it was one of dawning adventure buried in a mass of detail. He had never been far from his native soil. Now he was going to see cities and people who were almost foreign, in the sophisticated East. But all he could dwell on was a swift cinema of a defeated little boy, a strong man who could never be strong, a surfeited love, a truant and dimly comprehensible blonde girl, a muddy street and a red station, a clapboard house, a sonorous church with hushed puppets in the pews, fudge parties, boats on the little river, cold winter, and ice over the mountains, and a fortress where once upon a time he had felt mightier than the universe.

VI

THE SHORT branch line to which Hugo changed
brought him to the fringe of the campus. The cars
were full of boys, so many of them that he was
embarrassed. They all appeared to know each other,
and no one spoke to him. His dreams on the train
were culminated. He had decided to become a great
athlete. With his mind's eye, he played the football
he would play—and the baseball. Ninety-yard runs,
homers hit over the fence into oblivion. Seeing the
boys and feeling their lack of notice of him redoubled
the force of that decision. Then he stepped on to
the station platform and stood facing the campus.
He could not escape a rush of reverence and of
awe; it was so wide, so green and beautiful. Far
away towered the giant arches of the stadium. Near
by were the sharp Gothic points of the chapel and
the graduate college. Between them a score or more
of buildings rambled in and out through the trees.

"Hey!"

Hugo turned a little self-consciously. A youth in

65

a white shirt and white trousers was beckoning to him. "Freshman, aren't you?"

"Yes. My name's Danner. Hugo Danner."

"I'm Lefty Foresman. Chuck!" A second student separated himself from the bustle of baggage and young men. "Here's a freshman."

Hugo waited with some embarrassment. He wondered why they wanted a freshman. Lefty introduced Chuck and then said: "Are you strong, freshman?"

For an instant he was stunned. Had they heard, guessed? Then he realized it was impossible. They wanted him to work. They were going to haze him. "Sure," he said.

"Then get this trunk and I'll show you where to take it."

Hugo was handed a baggage check. He found the official and located the trunk. Tentatively he tested its weight, as if he were a normally husky youth about to undertake its transportation. He felt pleased that his strength was going to be tried so accidentally and in such short order. Lefty and Chuck heaved the trunk on his back. "Can you carry it?" they asked.

"Sure."

"Don't be too sure. It's a long way."

Peering from beneath the trunk under which he bent with a fair assumption of human weakness, Hugo had his first close glimpse of Webster. They passed under a huge arch and down a street lined with elms. Students were everywhere, carrying books

66

and furniture, moving in wheelbarrows and moving by means of the backs of other freshmen. The two who led him were talking and he listened as he plodded.

"Saw Marcia just before I left the lake—took her out one night—and got all over the place with her—and then came down—she's coming to the first prom with me—and Marj to the second—got to get some beer in—we'll buzz out and see if old Snorenson has made any wine this summer. Hello, Eddie— glad to see you back—I've elected the dean's physics, though, God knows, I'll never get a first in them and I need it for a key. That damn Frosh we picked up sure must have been a porter—hey, freshmen! Want a rest?"

"No, thanks."

"Went down to the field this afternoon—looks all right to me. The team, that is. Billings is going to quarter it now—and me after that—hope to Christ I make it—they're going to have Scapper and Dwan back at Yale and we've got a lot of work to do. Frosh! You don't need to drag that all the way in one yank. Put it down, will you?"

"I'm not tired. I don't need a rest."

"Well, you know best—but you ought to be tired. I would. Where do you come from?"

"Colorado."

"Huh! People go to Colorado. Never heard of any one coming from there before. Whereabouts?"

"Indian Creek."

"Oh." There was a pause. "You aren't an Indian, are you?" It was asked bluntly.

"Scotch Presbyterian for twenty generations."

"Well, when you get through here, you'll be full of Scotch and emptied of the Presbyterianism. Put the trunk down."

Their talk of women, of classes, of football, excited Hugo. He was not quite as amazed to find that Lefty Foresman was one of the candidates for the football team as he might have been later when he knew how many students attended the university and how few, relatively, were athletes. He decided at once that he liked Lefty. The sophistication of his talk was unfamiliar to Hugo; much of it he could not understand and only guessed. He wanted Lefty to notice him. When he was told to put the trunk down, he did not obey. Instead, with precision and ease, he swung it up on his shoulder, held it with one hand and said in an unflustered tone: "I'm not tired, honestly. Where do we go from here?"

"Great howling Jesus!" Lefty said, "what have we here? Hey! Put that trunk down." There was excitement in his voice. "Say, guy, do that again."

Hugo did it. Lefty squeezed his biceps and grew pale. Those muscles in action lost their feel of flesh and became like stone. Lefty said: "Say, boy, can you play football?"

"Sure," Hugo said.

"Well, you leave that trunk with Chuck, here, and come with me."

Hugo did as he had been ordered and they walked side by side to the gymnasium. Hugo had once seen a small gymnasium, ill equipped and badly lighted, and it had appealed mightily to him. Now he stood in a prodigious vaulted room with a shimmering floor, a circular balcony, a varied array of apparatus. His hands clenched. Lefty quit him for a moment and came back with a man who wore knickers. "Mr. Woodman, this is—what the hell's your name?"

"Danner. Hugo Danner."

"Mr. Woodman is football coach."

Hugo took the man's hand. Lefty excused himself. Mr. Woodman said: "Young Foresman said you played football."

"Just on a high-school team in Colorado."

"Said you were husky. Go in my office and ask Fitzsimmons to give you a gym suit. Come out when you're ready."

Hugo undressed and put on the suit. Fitzsimmons, the trainer, looked at him with warm admiration. "You're sure built, son."

"Yeah. That's luck, isn't it?"

Then Hugo was taken to another office. Woodman asked him a number of questions about his weight, his health, his past medical history. He listened to Hugo's heart and then led him to a scale. Hugo had lied about his weight.

"I thought you said one hundred and sixty, Mr. Danner?"

The scales showed two hundred and eleven, but

it was impossible for a man of his size and build to weigh that much. Hugo had lied deliberately, hoping that he could avoid the embarrassment of being weighed. "I did, Mr. Woodman. You see—my weight is a sort of freak. I don't show it—no one would believe it—and yet there it is." He did not go into the details of his construction from a plasm new to biology.

"Huh!" Mr. Woodman said. Together they walked out on the floor of the gymnasium. Woodman called to one of the figures on the track who was making slow, plodding circuits. "Hey, Nellie! Take this bird up and pace him for a lap. Make it fast."

A little smile came at the corners of Hugo's mouth. Several of the men in the gymnasium stopped work to watch the trial of what was evidently a new candidate. "Ready?" Woodman said, and the runners crouched side by side. "Set? Go!"

Nelson, one of the best sprinters Webster had had for years, dashed forward. He had covered thirty feet when he heard a voice almost in his ear. "Faster, old man."

Nelson increased. "Faster, boy, I'm passing you." The words were spoken quietly, calmly. A rage filled Nelson. He let every ounce of his strength into his limbs and skimmed the canvas. Half a lap. Hugo ran at his side and Nelson could not lead him. The remaining half was not a race. Hugo finished thirty feet in the lead.

Woodman, standing on the floor, wiped his forehead and bawled: "That the best you can do, Nellie?"

"Yes, sir."

"What in hell have you been doing to yourself?"

Nelson drew a sobbing breath. "I—haven't—done —a thing. Time—that man. He's—faster than the intercollegiate mark."

Woodman, still dubious, made Hugo run against time. And Hugo, eager to make an impression and unguided by a human runner, broke the world's record for the distance around the track by a second and three-fifths. The watch in Woodman's hands trembled.

"Hey!" he said, uncertain of his voice, "come down here, will you?"

Hugo descended the spiral iron staircase. He was breathing with ease. Woodman stared at him. "Lessee you jump."

Hugo was familiar with the distances for jumping made in track meets. He was careful not to overdo his effort. His running jump was twenty-eight feet, and his standing jump was eleven feet and some inches. Woodman's face ran water. His eyes gleamed. "Danner," he said, "where did you get that way?"

"What way?"

"I mean—what have you done all your life?"

"Nothing. Gone to school."

"Two hundred and eleven pounds," Woodman

muttered, "run like an Olympic champ—jump like a kangaroo—how's your kicking?"

"All right, I guess."

"Passing?"

"All right, I guess."

"Come on outside. Hey, Fitz! Bring a ball."

An hour later Fitzsimmons found Woodman sitting in his office. Beside him was a bottle of whisky which he kept to revive wounded gladiators. "Fitz," said Woodman, looking at the trainer with dazed eyes, "did you see what I saw?"

"Yes, I did, Woodie."

"Tell me about it."

Fitzsimmons scratched his greying head. "Well, Woodie, I seen a young man—"

"Saw, Fitz."

"I saw a young man come into the gym an' undress. He looked like an oiled steam engine. I saw him go and knock hell out of three track records without even losing his breath. Then I seen him go out on the field an' kick a football from one end to the other an' pass it back. That's what *I* seen."

Woodman nodded his head. "So did I. But I don't believe it, do you?"

"I do. That's the man you—an' all the other coaches—have been wantin' to see. The perfect athlete. Better in everything than the best man at any one thing. Just a freak, Woodie—but, God Almighty, how New Haven an' Colgate are goin' to feel it these next years!"

"Mebbe he's dumb, Fitz."

"Mebbe. Mebbe not."

"Find out."

Fitz wasted no time. He telephoned to the registrar's office. "Mr. H. Danner," said the voice of a secretary, "passed his examinations with the highest honours and was admitted among the first ten."

"He passed his entrance exams among the first ten," Fitzsimmons repeated.

"God!" said Woodman, "it's the millennium!" And he took a drink.

Late in the afternoon of that day Hugo found his room in Thompson Dormitory. He unpacked his carpet-bag and his straw suit-case. He checked in his mind the things that he had done. It seemed a great deal for one day—a complete alteration of his life. He had seen the dean and arranged his classes: trigonometry, English, French, Latin, biology, physics, economics, hygiene. With a pencil and a ruler he made a schedule, which he pinned on the second-hand desk he had bought.

Then he checked his furniture: a desk, two chairs, a bed, bed-clothes, a rug, sheets and blankets, towels. He hung his clothes in the closet. For a while he looked at them attentively. They were not like the clothes of the other students. He could not quite perceive the difference, but he felt it, and it made him uncomfortable. The room to which he had been assigned was pleasant. It looked over the rolling campus on two sides, and both windows were framed in the leaves of nodding ivy.

It was growing dark. From a dormitory near by came the music of a banjo. Presently the player sang and other voices joined with him. A warm and golden sun touched the high clouds with lingering fire. Voices cried out, young and vigorous. Hugo sighed. He was going to be happy at Webster. His greatness was going to be born here.

At that time Woodman called informally on Chuck and Lefty. They were in a heated argument over the decorative arrangement of various liquor bottles when he knocked. "Come in!" they shouted in unison.

"Hello!"

"Oh, Woodie. Come in. Sit down. Want a drink —you're not in training?"

"No, thanks. Had one. And it would be a damn sight better if you birds didn't keep the stuff around."

"It's Chuck's." Lefty grinned.

"All right. I came to see about that bird you brought to me—Danner."

"Was he any good?"

Woodman hesitated. "Fellows, if I told you how good he was, you wouldn't believe me. He's so good —I'm scared of him."

"Whaddaya mean?"

"Just that. He gave Nellie thirty feet in a lap on the track."

"Great God!"

"He jumped twenty-eight and eleven feet—running and standing. He kicked half a dozen punts for eighty and ninety yards and he passed the same distance."

Lefty sat down on the window seat. His voice was hoarse. "That—can't be done, Woodie."

"I know it. But he did it. But that isn't what makes me frightened. How much do you think he weighs?"

"One fifty-five—or thereabouts."

Woodie shook his head. "No, Lefty, he weighs two hundred and eleven."

"Two eleven! He can't, Woodie. There's something wrong with your scales."

"Not a thing."

The two students stared at each other and then at the coach. They were able to grasp the facts intellectually, but they could not penetrate the reactions of their emotions. At last Lefty said: "But that isn't—well—it isn't human, Woodie."

"That's why I'm scared. Something has happened to this bird. He has a disease of some kind—that has toughened him. Like Pott's disease, that turns you to stone. But you wouldn't think it. There's not a trace of anything on the surface. I'm having a blood test made soon. Wait till to-morrow when you see him in action. It'll terrify you. Because you'll have the same damned weird feeling I have—that he isn't doing one tenth of what he can do—that he's really just playing with us all. By God, if I was a bit superstitious, I'd throw up my job and get as much distance between me and that bird as I could. I'm telling you simply to prepare you. There's something mighty funny about him, and the sooner we find out, the better."

Mr. Woodman left the dormitory. Lefty and Chuck stared at each other for the space of a minute, and then, with one accord, they went together to the registrar's office. There they found Hugo's address on the campus, and in a few minutes they were at his door.

"Come in," Hugo said. He smiled when he saw Lefty and Chuck. "Want some more trunks moved?"

"Maybe—later." They sat down, eying Hugo speculatively. Lefty acted as spokesman. "Listen here, guy, we've just seen Woodie and he says you're phenomenal—so much so that it isn't right."

Hugo reddened. He had feared that his exhibition was exaggerated by his eagerness to impress the coach. He said nothing and Lefty continued: "You're going to be here for four years and you're going to love this place. You're going to be willing to die for it. All the rest of your life the fact that you went to old Webster is going to make a difference. But there's one thing that Webster insists on —and that's fair play. And honesty—and courage. You've come from a little town in the West and you're a stranger here. Understand, this is all in a spirit of friendship. So far—we like you. We want you to be one of us. To belong. You have a lot to learn and a long way to go. I'm being frank because I want to like you. For instance, Chuck here is a millionaire. My old man is no dead stick in the Blue Book. Things like that will be different from what you've known before. But the important thing is to be a square shooter. Don't be angry. Do you understand?"

Hugo walked to the window and looked out into the thickened gloom. He had caught the worry, the repression, in Lefty's voice. The youth, his merry blue eyes suddenly grave, his poised self abnormally disturbed, had suggested a criticism of some sort. What was it? Hugo was hurt and a little frightened. Would his college life be a repetition of Indian Creek? Would the athletes and the others in college of his own age fear and detest him—because he was superior? Was that what they meant? He did not know. He was loath to offend Lefty and Chuck. But there seemed no alternative to the risk. No one had talked to him in that way for a long time. He sat on his bed. "Fellows," he said tersely, "I don't think I know what you're driving at. Will you tell me?"

The roommates fidgeted. They did not know exactly, either. They had come to fathom the abnormality in Hugo. Chuck lit a cigarette. Lefty smiled with an assumed ease. "Why—nothing, Danner. You see—well—I'm quarterback of the football team. And you'll probably be on it this year—we haven't adopted the new idea of keeping freshmen

off the varsity. Just wanted to tell you those—well
—those principles."

Hugo knew he had not been answered. He felt,
too, that he would never in his life give away his
secret. The defences surrounding it had been too
immutably fixed. His joy at knowing that he had
been accepted so soon as a logical candidate for the
football team was tempered by this questioning. "I
have principles, fellows."

"Good." Lefty rose. "Guess we'll be going. By
the way, Woodie said you smashed a couple of track
records to-day. Where'd you learn?"

"Nowhere."

"How come, then?"

"Just—natural."

Lefty summoned his will. "Sure it isn't—well—
unhealthy. Woodie says there are a couple of diseases that make you—well—get tough—like stone."

Hugo realized the purpose of the visit. "Then—
be sure I haven't any diseases. My father had an
M.D." He smiled awkwardly. "Ever since I was a
kid, I've been stronger than most people. And I
probably have a little edge still. Just an accident,
that's all. Is that what you were wondering about?"

Lefty smiled with instant relief. "Yes, it is. And
I'm glad you take it that way. Listen—why don't
you come over to the Inn and take dinner with
Chuck and me? Let commons go for to-night. What
say?"

At eleven Hugo wound his alarm clock and set it

for seven. He yawned and smiled. All during supper he had listened to the glories of Webster and the advantages of belonging to the Psi Delta fraternity, to descriptions of parties and to episodes with girls. Lefty and Chuck had embraced him in their circle. They had made suggestions about what he should wear and whom he should know; they had posted him on the behaviour best suited for each of his professors. They liked him and he liked them, immensely. They were the finest fellows in the world. Webster was a magnificent university. And he was going to be one of its most glorious sons.

He undressed and went to bed. In a moment he slept, drawing in deep, swift breaths. His face was smiling and his arm was extended, whether to ward off shadows or to embrace a new treasure could not be told. In the bright sunshine of morning his alarm jangled and he woke to begin his career as an undergraduate.

VII

FROM THE day of his arrival Webster University felt the presence of Hugo Danner. Classes, football practice, hazing, fraternity scouting began on that morning with a feverish and good-natured hurly-burly that, for a time, completely bewildered him. Hugo participated in everything. He went to the classroom with pleasure. It was never difficult for him to learn and never easier than in those first few weeks. The professors he had known (and he reluctantly included his own father) were dry-as-dust individuals who had none of the humanities. And at least some of the professors at Webster were brilliant, urbane, capable of all understanding. Their lectures were like tonic to Hugo.

The number of his friends grew with amazing rapidity. It seemed that he could not cross the campus without being hailed by a member of the football team and presented to another student. The Psi Deltas saw to it that he met the entire personnel of their chapter at Webster. Other fraternities looked

80

at him with covetous eyes, but Lefty Foresman, who was chairman of the membership committee, let it be known that the Psi Deltas had marked Hugo for their own. And no one refused their bid.

On the second Monday after college opened, Hugo went to the class elections and found to his astonishment that he received twenty-eight votes for president. A boy from a large preparatory school was elected, but twenty-eight votes spoke well for the reputation he had gained in that short time. On that day, too, he learned the class customs. Freshmen had to wear black caps, black shoes and socks and ties. They were not allowed to walk on the grass or to ride bicycles. The ancient cannon in the center of the class square was defended annually by the sophomores, and its theft was always attempted by the freshmen. No entering class had stolen it in eight years. Those things amused Hugo. They gave him an intimate feeling of belonging to his school. He wrote to his parents about them.

Dean Aiken, the newly elected president of the freshman class, approached Hugo on the matter of the cannon. "We want a gang of good husky boys to pull it up some night and take it away. Are you with us?"

"Sure."

Left to his own considerations, Hugo recalled his promise and walked across the campus with the object of studying the cannon. It was a medium-sized piece of Revolutionary War vintage. It stood di-

GLADIATOR

rectly in the rear of Webster Hall, and while Hugo
regarded it, he noticed that two sophomores remained in the vicinity. He knew that guard, changed
every two hours, would be on duty day and night
until Christmas was safely passed. Well, the cannon
was secure. It couldn't be rolled away. The theft of
it would require first a free-for-all with the sophomores and after a definite victory a mob assault of
the gun. Hugo walked closer to it.

"Off the grass, freshman!"

He wheeled obediently. One of the guards approached him. "Get off the grass and stay off and
don't look at that cannon with longing. It isn't
healthy for young freshmen."

Hugo grinned. "All right, fella. But you better
keep a double guard on that thing while I want it."

Two nights later, during a heavy rain that had
begun after the fall of dark, Hugo clad himself in a
slicker and moved vaguely into the night. Presently
he reached the cannon yard, and in the shelter of an
arch he saw the sophomore guards. They smoked
cigarettes, and one of them sang softly. Day and
night a pair of conscripted sentries kept watchful
eyes on the gun. A shout from either of them would
bring the whole class tumbling from its slumber in
a very few moments. Hugo moved out of their
vision. The campus was empty.

He rounded Webster Hall, the mud sucking softly
under his feet and the rain dampening his face. From
beneath his coat he took a flare and lighted the fuse.

He heard the two sophomores running toward it in the thick murk. When they were very close, he stepped on to the stone flagging, looked up into the cloudy sky, gathered himself, and leaped over the three stories of Webster Hall. He landed with a loud thud ten feet from the cannon. When the sophomores returned, after extinguishing the flare, their cherished symbol of authority had vanished.

There was din on the campus. First the loud cries of two voices. Then the screech of raised windows, the babble of more voices, and the rush of feet that came with new gusts of rain. Flash-lights pierced the gloom. Where the cannon had been, a hundred and then two hundred figures gathered, swirled, organized search-parties, built a fire. Dawn came, and the cannon was still missing. The clouds lifted. In the wan light some one pointed up. There, on the roof of Webster Hall, with the numerals of the freshman class painted on its muzzle, was the old weapon. Arms stretched. An angry, incredulous hum waxed to a steady pitch and waned as the sophomores dispersed.

In the morning, theory ran rife. The freshmen were tight-lipped, pretending knowledge where they had none, exulting secretly. Dean Aiken was kidnapped at noon and given a third degree, which extorted no information. The theft of the cannon and its elevation to the roof of the hall entered the annals of Webster legend. And Hugo, watching the laborious task of its removal from the roof, seemed merely as pleased and as mystified as the other freshmen.

So the autumn commenced. The first football game was played and Hugo made a touchdown. He made another in the second game. They took him to New York in November for the dinner that was to celebrate the entrance of a new chapter to Psi Delta.

His fraternity had hired a private car. As soon as the college towers vanished, the entertainment committee took over the party. Glasses were filled with whisky and passed by a Negro porter. Hugo took his with a feeling of nervousness and of excited anticipation. The coach had given him permission to break training—advised it, in fact. And Hugo had never tasted liquor. He watched the others, holding his glass gingerly. They swallowed their drinks, took more. The effect did not seem to be great. He smelled the whisky, and the smell revolted him.

"Drink up, Danner!"

"Never use the stuff. I'm afraid it'll throw me."

"Not you. Come on! Bottoms up!"

It ran into his throat, hot and steaming. He swallowed a thousand needles and knew the warmth of it in his stomach. They gave another glass to him and then a third. Some of the brothers were playing cards. Hugo watched them. He perceived that his feet were loose on their ankles and that his shoulders lurched. It would not do to lose control of himself, he thought. For another man, it might be

84

safe. Not for him. He repeated the thought inanely.
Some one took his arm.

"Nice work in the game last week. Pretty."

"Thanks."

"Woodie says you're the best man on the team.
Glad you went Psi Delt. Best house on the campus.
Great school, Webster. You'll love it."

"Sure," Hugo said.

The railroad coach was twisting and writhing peculiarly. Hugo suddenly wanted to be in the air.
He hastened to the platform of the car and stood
on it, squinting his eyes at the countryside. When
they reached the Grand Central Terminal he was
cured of his faintness. They rode to the theatre in
an omnibus and saw the matinée of a musical show.
Hugo had never realized that so many pretty girls
could be gathered together in one place. Their scant,
glittering costumes flashed in his face. He wanted
them. Between the acts the fraternity repaired in a
body to the lavatory and drank whisky from bottles.

Hugo began to feel that he was living at last. He
was among men, sophisticated men, and learning to
be like them. Nothing like the *camaraderie,* the
show, the liquor, in Indian Creek. He was wearing
the suit that Lefty Foresman had chosen for him.
He felt well dressed, cool, capable. He was intensely
well disposed toward his companions. When the
show was over, he stood in the bright lights, momentarily depressed by the disappearance of the

long file of girls. Then he shouldered among his companions and went out of the theatre riotously.

Two long tables were drawn up at the Raven, a restaurant famous for its roast meats, its beer, and its lack of scruples about the behaviour of its guests. The Psi Deltas took their places at the tables. The dining-room they occupied was private. Hugo saw as if in a dream the long rows of silverware, the dishes of celery and olives, and the ranks of shining glasses. They sat. Waiters wound their way among them. There was a song. The toastmaster, a New York executive who had graduated from Webster twenty years before, understood the temper of his charge. He was witty, ribald, genial.

He made a speech, but not too long a speech. He called on the president of a bank, who rose totteringly and undid the toastmaster's good offices by making too long a speech. Its reiterated "dear old Websters" were finally lost in the ring and tinkle of glassware and cutlery.

At the end of the long meal Hugo realized that his being had undergone change. Objects approached and receded before his vision. The voice of the man sitting beside him came to his ears as if through water. His mind continually turned upon itself in a sort of infatuated examination. His attention could not be held even on his own words. He decided that he was feverish. Then some one said: "Well, Danner, how do you like being drunk?"

"Drunk?"

"Sure. You aren't going to tell me you're sober, are you?"

When the speaker had gone, Hugo realized that it was Chuck. There had been no feeling of recognition. "I'm drunk!" he said.

"Some one give Danner a drink. He has illusions."

"Drunk! Why, this man isn't drunk. It's monstrous. He has a weakened spine, that's all."

"I'm drunk," Hugo repeated. He knew then what it was to be drunk. The toastmaster was rising again. Hugo saw it dimly.

"Fellows!" A fork banged on a glass. "Fellows!" There was a slow increase in silence. "Fellows! It's eleven o'clock now. And I have a surprise for you."

"Surprise! Hey, guys, shut up for the surprise!"

"Fellows! What I was going to say is this: the girls from the show we saw this afternoon are coming over here—all thirty of 'em. We're going up to my house for a real party. And the lid'll be off. Anything goes—only anybody that fights gets thrown out straight off without an argument. Are you on?"

The announcement was greeted by a stunned quiet which grew into a bellow of approval. Plates and glasses were thrown on the floor. Lefty leaped on to the table and performed a dance. The proprietor came in, looked, and left hastily, and then the girls arrived.

They came through the door, after a moment of reluctant hesitation, like a flood of brightly colored water. They sat down in the laps of the boys, on

87

chairs, on the edge of the disarrayed tables. They were served with innumerable drinks as rapidly as the liquor could be brought. They were working, that night, for the ten dollars promised to each one. But they were working with college boys, which was a rest from the stream of affluent and paunchy males who made their usual escort. Their gaiety was better than assumed.

Hugo had never seen such a party or dreamed of one. His vision was cleared instantly of its cobwebs. He saw three boys seize one girl and turn her heels over head. A piano was moved in. She jumped up and started dancing on the table. Then there was a voice at his side.

"Hello, good-looking. I could use that drink if you can spare it."

Hugo looked at the girl. She had brown hair that had been curled. Her lips and cheeks were heavily rouged and the corners of her mouth turned down in a sort of petulance or fatigue. But she was pretty. And her body, showing whitely above her evening dress, was creamy and warm. He gave the drink to her. She sat in his lap.

"Gosh," he whispered. She laughed.

"I saw her first," some one said, pulling at the girl's arm.

"Go 'way," Hugo shouted. He pushed the other from them. "What's your name?"

"Bessie. What's yours?"

"Hugo."

The girl accepted two glasses from a waiter. They drained them, looking at each other over the rims. "Got any money, Hugo?"

Hugo had. He carried on his person the total of his cash assets. Some fifty dollars. "Sure. I have fifty dollars," he answered.

He felt her red lips against his ear. "Let's you and me duck this party and have a little one of our own. I've got an apartment not far from here."

He could hear the pounding of his heart. "Let's."

They moved unostentatiously from the room. Outside, in the hall, she took his hand. They ran to the front door.

There was the echo of bedlam in his whirling mind when they walked through the almost deserted street. She called to a taxi and they were driven for several blocks. At a cheap dance hall they took a table and drank more liquor. When his head was turned, she narrowed her eyes and calculated the effect of the alcohol against the dwindling of his purse. They danced.

"Gee, you're a swell dancer."

"So are you, Bessie."

"Still wanna go home with Bessie?"

"Mmmm."

"Let's go."

Another taxi ride. The lights seethed past him. A dark house and three flights of rickety stairs. The gritty sound of a key in a lock. A little room with a table, a bed, two chairs, a gas-light turned low, a disheveled profusion of female garments.

"Here we are. Sit down."

Hugo looked at her tensely. He laughed then, with a harsh sound. She flew into his arms, returning his searching caresses with startling frankness. Presently they moved across the room. He could hear the noises on the street at long, hot intervals.

Hugo opened his eyes and the light smote them with pain. He raised his head wonderingly. His stomach crawled with a foul nausea. He saw the dirty room. Bessie was not in it. He staggered to the wash-bowl and was sick. He noticed then that her clothes were missing. The fact impressed him as one that should have significance. He rubbed his head and eyes. Then he thought accurately. He crossed the room and felt in his trousers pockets. The money was gone.

At first it did not seem like a catastrophe. He could telegraph to his father for more money. Then he realized that he was in New York, without a ticket back to the campus, separated from his friends, and not knowing the address of the toastmaster. He could not find his fraternity brothers and he could not get back to school without more money. Moreover, he was sick.

He dressed with miserable slowness and went down to the street. Served him right. He had been a fool. He shrugged. A sharp wind blew out of a bright sky.

Maybe, he thought, he should walk back to Webster. It was only eighty miles and that distance could be negotiated in less than two hours by him. But that was unwise. People would see his progress. He sat down in Madison Square Park and looked at the Flatiron Building with a leisurely eye. A fire engine surged up the street. A man came to collect the trash in a green can. A tramp lay down and was ousted by a policeman.

By and by he realized that he was hungry. A little man with darting eyes took a seat beside him. He regarded Hugo at short intervals. At length he said. "You got a dime for a cup of coffee?" His words were blurred by accent.

"No. I came here from school last night and my money was stolen."

"Ah," there was a tinge of discouragement in the other's voice. "And hungry, perhaps?"

"A little."

"Me—I am also hungry. I have not eaten since two days."

That impressed Hugo as a shameful and intolerable circumstance. "Let's go over there"—he indicated a small restaurant—"and eat. Then I'll promise to send the money by mail. At least, we'll be fed that way."

"We will be thrown to the street on our faces."

"Not I. Nobody throws me on my face. And I'll look out for you."

They crossed the thoroughfare and entered the restaurant. The little man ordered a quantity of food, and Hugo, looking guiltily at the waiter, duplicated the order. They became distantly acquainted during the filched repast. The little man's name was Izzie. He sold second-hand rugs. But he was out of work. Eventually they finished. The waiter brought the check. He was a large man, whose jowls and hips and shoulders were heavily weighted with muscle.

Hugo stood up. "Listen. fellow," he began placidly, "my friend and I haven't a cent between us. I'm Hugo Danner, from Webster University, and I'll mail you the price of this feed to-morrow. I'll write down my name and—"

He got no further. The waiter spoke in a thick voice. "So! One of them guys, eh? Tryin' to get away with it when I'm here, huh? Well, I tell you how you're gonna pay. You're gonna pay this check with a bloody mush, see?" His fist doubled and drew back. Hugo did not shift his position. The fist came forward, but an arm like stone blocked it. Hugo's free hand barely flicked to the waiter's jaw. He rolled under the table. "Come on," he said, but Izzie had already vanished through the door.

Hugo walked hurriedly up the street and turned a corner. A hand tugged at his coat. He turned and was confronted by Izzie. "I seen you through the window. Jeest, guy, you kin box. Say, I know where you kin clean up—if you got the nerve."

"Clean up? Where?"

"Come on. We better get out of here anyhow."

They made their way toward the river. The city changed character on the other side of the elevated railroad, and presently they were walking through a dirty, evil-smelling, congested neighborhood.

"Where are we going, Izzie?"

"Wait a minute, Mr. Danner."

"What's the idea?"

"You wait."

Another series of dirty blocks. Then they came to a bulky building that spread a canopy over the sidewalk. "Here," Izzy said, and pointed.

His finger indicated a sign, which Hugo read twice. It said: "Battling Ole Swenson will meet all comers in this gymnasium at three this afternoon and eight tonight. Fifty dollars will be given to any man, black or white, who can stay three rounds with him, and one hundred dollars cash money to the man who knocks out Battling Ole Swenson, the Terror of the Docks."

"See," Izzie said, rubbing his hands excitedly, "mebbe you could do it."

A light dawned on Hugo. He smiled. "I can," he replied. "What time is it?"

"Two o'clock."

"Well, let's go."

They entered the lobby of the "gymnasium." "Mr.

93

Epstein," Izzie called, "I gotta fighter for the Swede."

Mr. Epstein was a pale fat man who ignored the handicap of the dank cigar in his mouth and roared when he spoke. He glanced at Hugo and then addressed Izzie. "Where is he?"

"There."

Epstein looked at Hugo and then was shaken by laughter. "There, you says, and there I looks and what do I see but a pink young angel face that Ole would swallow without chewing."

Hugo said: "I don't think so. I'm willing to try."

Epstein scowled. "Run away from here, kid, before you get hurt. Ole would laugh at you. This isn't easy money. It takes a man to get a look at it."

Izzie stamped impatiently. "I tell you, Mr. Epstein, I seen this boy fight. He's the goods. He can beat your Ole. I bet he can." His voice caught and he glanced nervously at Hugo. "I bet ten dollars he can."

"How much?" Epstein bellowed.

"Well—say twenty dollars."

"How much?"

"Fifty dollars. It's all I got, Epstein."

"All right—go in and sign up and leave your wad. Kid," he turned to Hugo, "you may think you're husky, but Ole is a killer. He's six nine in his socks and he weighs two hundred and eighty. He'll mash you."

"I don't think so," Hugo repeated.

94

"Well, you'll be meat. We'll put you second on the list. And the lights'll go out fast enough for yuh."

Hugo followed Izzie and reached him in time to see a fifty-dollar bill peeled from a roll which was extracted with great intricacy from Izzie's clothes. "I thought you hadn't eaten for two days!"

"It's God's truth," Izzie answered uneasily. "I was savin' this dough—an' it's lucky, too, isn't it?"

Hugo did not know whether to laugh or to be angry. He said: "And you'd have let me take a poke in the jaw from that waiter. You're a hell of a guy, Izzie."

Izzie moved his eyes rapidly. "I ain't so bad. I'm bettin' on you, ain't I? An' I got you a chancet at the Swede, didn't I?"

"How'd you know that waiter couldn't kill me?"

"Well—he didn't. Anyhow, what's a poke in the jaw to a square meal, eh?"

"When the other fellow gets the poke and you get the meal. All right, Izzie. I wish I thought Ole was going to lick me."

Hugo wrote his name under a printed statement to the effect that the fight managers were not responsible for the results of the combat. The man who led him to a dressing-room was filled with sympathy and advice. He told Hugo that one glance at Ole would discourage his reckless avarice. But Hugo paid no attention. The room was dirty. It smelled of sweat and rubber sneakers. He sat there for half an hour, reading a newspaper. Outside, somewhere, he could hear the mumble of a gathering crowd, punctuated by the voices of candy and peanut-hawkers. At last they brought some clothes to him. A pair of trunks that flapped over his loins, ill-fitting canvas shoes, a musty bath robe. When the door of his room opened, the noise of the crowd was louder. Finally it was hushed. He heard the announcer. It was like the voice of a minister coming through the stained windows of a church. It rose and fell. Then the distant note of the gong. After that the crowd called steadily, sometimes in loud rage and sometimes almost in a whisper.

Finally they brought Ole's first victim into Hugo's cell. He was a man with the physique of a bull. His face was cut and his eyes were darkening. One of the men heaving his stretcher looked at Hugo.

"Better beat it, kid, while you can still do it on your own feet. You ain't even got the reach for Ole. He's a grizzly, bo. He'll just about kill you."

Hugo tightened his belt and swung the electric light back and forth with a slow-moving fist. Another man expertly strapped his fists with adhesive tape.

"When do I go out?" Hugo asked.

"You mean, when do you get knocked out?" the second laughed.

"Fight?"

"Well, if you're determined to get croaked, you do it now."

In the arena it was dazzling. A bank of noisy people rose on all sides of him. Hugo walked down the aisle and clambered into the ring. Ole was one of the largest men he had ever seen in his life. There was no doubt of his six feet nine inches and his two hundred and eighty pounds. Hugo imagined that the man was not a scientific fighter. A bruiser. Well, he knew nothing of fighting, either.

A man in his shirt sleeves stood up in the ring and bellowed, "The next contestant for the reward of fifty dollars to stay three rounds with battling Ole and one hundred dollars to knock him out is Mr. H. Smith." They cheered. It was a nasty sound, filled with the lust for blood. Hugo realized that he was excited. His knees wabbled when he rose and his hand trembled as he took the monstrous paw of the Swede and saw his unpleasant smile. Hugo's heart was pounding. For one instant he felt weak and human before Battling Ole. He whispered to himself: "Quit it, you fool; you know better; you can't even be hurt." It did not make him any more quiet.

Then they were sitting face to face. A bell rang. The hall became silent as the mountainous Swede lumbered from his corner. He towered over Hugo, who stood up and went out to meet him like David approaching Goliath. To the crowd the spectacle was laughable. There was jeering before they met. "Where's your mamma?" "Got your bottle, baby?" "Put the poor little bastard back in his carriage." "What's this—a fight or a freak show?" Laughter.

It was like cold water to Hugo. His face set. He looked at Ole. The Swede's fist moved back like the piston of a great engine into which steam has been let slowly. Then it came forward. Hugo, trained to see and act in keeping with his gigantic strength, dodged easily. "Atta boy!" "One for Johnny-dear!" The fist went back and came again and again, as if that piston, gathering speed, had broken loose and was flailing through the screaming air. Hugo dodged like a beam of light, and the murderous weapon never touched him. The spectators began to applaud his speed. He could beat the Swede's fist every time. "Run him, kiddo!" "It's only three rounds."

The bell. Ole was panting. As he sat in his corner, his coal-scuttle gloves dangling, he cursed in his native tongue. Too little to hit. Bell. The second round was the same. Hugo never attempted to touch the Swede. Only to avoid him. And the man worked like a Trojan. Sweat seethed over his big, blank face. His small eyes sharpened to points. He brought his whole carcass flinging through the air after his fist. But every blow ended in a sickening wrench that missed the target. The crowd grew more excited. During the interval between the second and third rounds there was betting on the outcome. Three to one that Ole would connect and murder the boy. Four to one. One to five that Hugo would win fifty dollars before he died beneath the trip-hammer.

The third round opened. The crowd suddenly tired of the sport. A shrill female voice reached Hugo's cold, concentrated mind: "Keep on running, yellow baby!"

So. They wanted a killing. They called him yellow. The Swede was on him, elephantine, sweating, sucking great, rumbling breaths of air, swinging his fists. Hugo studied the motion. That fist to that side, up, down, now!

Like hail they began to land upon the Swede. Bewilderingly, everywhere. No hope of guarding. Every blow smashed, stung, ached. No chance to swing back. Cover up. His arms went over his face. He felt rivets drive into his kidneys. He reached out and clinched. They rocked in each other's arms. Dazed by that bitter onslaught of lightning blows, Ole thought only to lock Hugo in his arms and crush him. When they clinched, the crowd, grown instantly hysterical, sank back in despair. It was over. Ole could break the little man's back. They saw his arms spring into knots. Jesus! Hugo's fist shot between their chests and Ole was thrown violently backward. Impossible. He lunged back, crimson to kill, one hand guarding his jaw. "Easy, now, for the love of God, easy," Hugo said to himself. There. On the hand at the chin. Hugo's gloves went out. Lift him! It connected. The Swede left the floor and crumpled slowly, with a series of bumping sounds. And how the hyenas yelled!

They crowded into his dressing-room afterwards. Epstein came to his side before he had dressed. "Come out and have a mug of suds, kid. That was the sweetest fight I ever hope to live to see. I can sign you up for a fortune right now. I can make you champ in two years."

"No, thanks," Hugo said.

The man persisted. He talked earnestly. He handed Hugo a hundred-dollar bill. Hugo finished his dressing. Izzie wormed his way in. "Fifty dollars I won yet! Didn't I tole you, Mr. Epstein!"

"Come here, Izzie!"

The little man ran to shake Hugo's hand, but it was extended for another reason. "I want that fifty you won," he said unsmilingly. "When a bird tracks along for a free feed and lets another guy fight for him and has a roll big enough to stop up a rainspout, he owes money. That lunch will set you back just exactly what you won on me."

There was laughter in the room. Izzie whimpered. "Ain't you got a hundred all ready that I got for you? Ain't it enough that you got it? Ain't I got a wife wit' kids yet?"

"No, it ain't, yet." Hugo snapped the fingers of his extended hand. The other hand doubled significantly. Izzie gave him the money. He was almost in tears. The others guffawed.

"Wait up, bo. Give us your address if you ever change your mind. You can pick up a nice livin' in this game."

"No, thanks. All I needed was railroad fare. Thank you, gentlemen—and—good-by."

No one undertook to hinder Hugo's departure.

VIII

GREATNESS SEEMED to elude Hugo, success such
as he had earned was inadequate, and his friendships
as well as his popularity were tinged with a sort of
question that he never understood. By the end of
winter he was well established in Webster as a great
athlete. Psi Delta sang his praises and was envied his
deeds. Lefty and Chuck treated him as a brother.
And, Hugo perceived, none of that treatment and
none of that society was quite real. He wondered if
his personality was so meagre that it was not equal
to his strength. He wondered if his strength was
really the asset he had dreamed it would be, and if,
perhaps, other people were not different from him in
every way, so that any close human contact was impossible to him.

It was a rather tragic question to absorb a man
so filled with life and ambition as he. Yet every
month had raised it more insistently. He saw other
men sharing their inmost souls and he could never
do that. He saw those around him breaking their

hearts and their lungs for the university, and, although it was never necessary for him to do that, he doubted that he could if he would. Webster was only a school. A sentiment rather than an ideal, a place rather than a goal of dreams. He thought that he was cynical. He thought that he was inhuman. It worried him.

His love was a similar experience. He fell in love twice during that first year in college. Once at a prom with a girl who was related to Lefty—a rich, socially secure girl who had studied abroad and who almost patronized her cousin.

Hugo had seen her dancing, and her long, slender legs and arms had issued an almost tangible challenge to him. She had looked over Lefty's shoulder and smiled vaguely. They had met. Hugo danced with her. "I love to come to a prom," she said; "it makes me feel young again."

"How old are you?"

She ignored the obvious temptation to be coy and he appreciated that. "Twenty-one."

It seemed reasonably old to Hugo. The three years' difference in their ages had given her a pinnacle of maturity.

"And that makes you old," he reflected.

She nodded. Her name was Iris. Afterwards Hugo thought that it should have been Isis. Half goddess, half animal. He had never met with the vanguard of emancipated American womanhood before then. "You're the great Hugo Danner, aren't you? I've

seen your picture in the sporting sections." She read
sporting sections. He had never thought of a woman
in that light. "But you're really much handsomer.
You have more sex and masculinity and you seem
more intelligent."

Then, between the dances, Lefty had come. "She?
Oh, she's a sort of cousin. Flies in all the high alti-
tudes in town. Blue Book and all that. Better look
out, Hugo. She plays rough."

"She doesn't look rough."

Both youths watched her. Long, dark hair, wil-
lowy body, high, pale forehead, thin nose, red mouth,
smiling like a lewd agnostic and dancing close to her
partner, enjoying even that. "Well, look out, Hugo.
If she wants to play, don't let her play with your
heart. Anything else is quite in the books."

"Oh."

She came to the stag line, ignoring a sequence of
invitations, and asked him to dance. They went out
on the velvet campus. "I could love you—for a little
while," she said. "It's too bad you have to play football tomorrow."

"Is that an excuse?"

She smiled remotely. "You're being disloyal." Her
fan moved delicately. "But I shan't chide you. In
fact, I'll stay over for the game—and I'll enjoy the
anticipation—more, perhaps. But you'll have to win
it—to win me. I'm not a soothing type."

"It will be easy—to win," Hugo said and she
peered through the darkness with admiration, be-

cause he had made his ellipsis of the object very plain.

"It is always easy for you to win, isn't it?" she countered with an easy mockery, and Hugo shivered. The game was won. Hugo had made his touchdown. He unfolded a note she had written on the back of a score card. "At my hotel at ten, then."

"Then." Someone lifted his eyes to praise him. His senses swam in careful anticipation. They were cheering outside the dressing-room. A different sound from the cheers at the fight-arena. Young, hilarious, happy.

At ten he bent over the desk and was told to go to her room. The clerk shrugged. She opened the door. One light was burning. There was perfume in the air. She wore only a translucent kimono of pale-coloured silk. She taught him a great many things that night. And Iris learned something, too, so that she never came back to Hugo, and kept the longing for him as a sort of memory which she made hallowed in a shorn soul. It was, for her, a single asceticism in a rather selfish life.

Hugo loved her for two weeks after that, and then his emotions wearied and he was able to see what she had done and why she did not answer his letters. His subdued fierceness was a vehement fire to women. His fiercer appetite was the cause of his early growth in a knowledge of them. When most of his companions were finding their way into the mysteries of sex both unhandily and with much turmoil, he learned well and abnormally. It became a part of his secret self. Another barrier to the level of the society that surrounded him. When he changed the name of Iris to Isis in his thoughts, he moved away from the Psi Deltas, who would have been incapable of the notion. In person he stayed among them, but in spirit he felt another difference, which he struggled to reconcile.

In March the thaws came, and under the warming sun Hugo made a deliberate attempt to fall in love with Janice, who was the daughter of his French professor. She was a happy, innocent little girl, with gold hair, and brown eyes that lived oddly beneath it. She worshipped Hugo. He petted her, talked through long evenings to her, tried to be faithful to her in his most unfettered dreams, and once considered proposing to her. When he found himself unable to do that, he was compelled to resist an impulse to seduce her. Ashamed, believing himself unfit for a nice girl, he untangled that romance as painlessly as he could, separating himself from Janice little by little and denying every accusation of waning interest.

Then for a month he believed that he could never be satisfied by any woman, that he was superior to women. He read the lives of great lovers and adulterers and he wished that he could see Bessie, who had taken his money long before in New York City. She appealed to him then more than all the others—probably, he thought, because he was drunk and had not viewed her in sharp perspective. For hours he meditated on women, while he longed constantly to possess a woman.

But the habitual routine of his life did not suffer. He attended his classes and lectures, played on the basketball team, tried tentatively to write for the campus newspaper, learned to perform indifferently on the mandolin, and made himself into the semblance of an ideal college man. His criticism of college then was at its lowest ebb. He spent Christmas in New York at Lefty Foresman's parents' elaborate home, slightly intoxicated through the two weeks, hastening to the opera, to balls and parties, ill at ease when presented to people whose names struck his ears familiarly, seeing for the first time the exaggeration of scale on which the very rich live and wondering constantly why he never met Iris, wishing for and fearing that meeting while he wondered.

When his first year at college was near to its end, and that still and respectful silence that marks the passing of a senior class had fallen over the campus, Hugo realized with a shock that he would soon be on his way back to Indian Creek. Then, suddenly, he saw what an amazing and splendid thing that year at college had been. He realized how it had filled his life to the brim with activities of which he had not dreamed, how it had shaped him so that he would be almost a stranger in his own home, how it had aged and educated him in the business of living. When the time of parting with his new friends drew near, he understood that they were valuable to him, in spite of his questioning. And they made it clear that he would be missed by them. At last he shared a feeling with his classmates, a fond sadness, an illimitable poignancy that was young and unadulterated by motive. He was perversely happy when he became aware of it. He felt somewhat justified for being himself and living his life.

A day or two before college closed, he received a letter from his father. It was the third he had received during the year. It said:

Dear Son—

Your mother and I have decided to break the news to you before you leave for home, because there may be better opportunities for you in the East than here at Indian Creek. When you went away to Webster University, I agreed to take care of all your expenses. It was the least I could do, I felt, for my only son. The two thousand dollars your mother and I had saved seemed ample for your four years. But the bills we have received, as well as your own demands, have been staggering. In March, when a scant six hundred dollars of the original fund remained, I invested the money in a mine stock which, the salesman said, would easily net the six thousand dollars you appeared to need. I now find to my chagrin that the stock is worthless. I am unable to get back my purchase money.

It will be impossible during the coming year for me to let you have more than five hundred dollars. Perhaps, with what you earn this summer and with the exercise of economy, you can get along. I trust so. But, anxious as we are to see you again, we felt that, in the light of such information, you might prefer to remain in the East to earn what you can.

We are both despondent over the situation and we wish that we could do more than tender our regrets. But we hope that you will be able to find some solution to this situation. Thus, with our very warmest affection and our fondest hope, we wish you good fortune.

Your loving father,
ABEDNEGO DANNER.

Hugo read the letter down to the last period after the rather tremulous signature. His emotions were confused. Touched by the earnest and pathetically futile efforts of his father and by the attempt of that lonely little man to express what was, perhaps, a great affection, Hugo was nevertheless aghast at a prospect that he had not considered. He was going to be thrown into the world on his own resources. And, resting his frame in his worn chair—a frame capable of smashing into banks and taking the needed money without fear of punishment—Hugo began to wonder dismally if he was able even to support himself. No trade, no occupation, suggested itself. He had already experienced some of the merciless coldness of the world. The boys would all leave soon. And then he would be alone, unprovided for, helpless.

Hugo was frightened. He read the letter again, his wistful thoughts of his parents diminishing before the reality of his predicament. He counted his money. Eighty dollars in the bank and twelve in his pockets. He was glad he had started an account after his experience with Bessie. He was glad that he had husbanded more than enough to pay his fare to Indian Creek. Ninety-two dollars. He could live on that for a long time. Perhaps for the summer. And he would be able to get some sort of job. He was strong, anyway. That comforted him. He looked out of his window and tried to enumerate the things that he could do. All sorts of farm work. He could drive a team in the city. He could work on the docks. He considered nothing but manual labor. It would offer more. Gradually his fear that he would starve if left to his own devices ebbed from him, and it was replaced by grief that he could not return to Webster. Fourteen hundred dollars—that was the cost of his freshman year. He made a list of the things he could do without, of the work he could do to help himself through college. Perhaps he could return. The fear slowly diminished. He would be a working student in the year to come. He hated the idea. His fraternity had taken no members from that class of humble young men who rose at dawn and scrubbed floors and waited on tables to win the priceless gem of education. Lefty and Chuck would be chilly toward such a step. They would even offer him money to avoid it. It was a sad circumstance, at best.

When that period of tribulation passed, Hugo became a man. But he suffered keenly from his unwonted fears for some time. The calm and suave youth who had made love to Iris was buried beneath his frightened and imaginative adolescence. It wore out the last of his childishness. Immediately afterwards he learned about money and how it is earned. He sat there in the dormitory, almost trembling with uncertainty and used mighty efforts to do the things he felt he must do. He wrote a letter to his father which began: "Dear Dad—Why in Sam Hill didn't you tell me you were being reamed so badly by your nit-witted son and I'd have shovelled out and dug up some money for myself long ago?" On rereading that letter he realized that its tone was false. He wrote another in which he apologized with simple sincerity for the condition he had unknowingly created, and in which he expressed every confidence that he could take care of himself in the future.

He bore that braver front through the last days of school. He shook Lefty's hand warmly and looked fairly into his eyes. "Well, so long, old sock. Be good."

"Be good, Hugo. And don't weaken. We'll need all your beef next year. Decided what you're going to do yet?"

"No. Have you?"

Lefty shrugged. "I suppose I've got to go abroad with the family as usual. They wrote a dirty letter about the allowance I'd not have next year if I didn't. Why don't you come with us? Iris'll be there."

Hugo grinned. "No, sir! Iris once is very nice, but no man's equal to Iris twice." His grin became a chuckle. "And that's a poem which you can say to Iris if you see her—and tell her I hope it makes her mad."

Lefty's blue eyes sparkled with appreciation. Danner was a wonderful boy. Full of wit and not dumb like most of his kind. Getting smooth, too. Be a great man. Too bad to leave him—even for the summer. "Well—so long, old man."

Hugo watched Lefty lift his bags into a cab and roll away in the warm June dust. Then Chuck:

"Well—by-by, Hugo. See you next September."

"Yeah. Take care of yourself."

"No chance of your going abroad, is there? Because we sure could paint the old Avenue de l'Opéra red if you did."

"Not this year, Chuck."

"Well—don't take any wooden money."

"Don't do anything you wouldn't eat."

Hugo felt a lump in his throat. He could not say any more farewells. The campus was almost deserted. No meals would be served after the next day. He stared at the vacant dormitories and listened to the waning sound of departures. A train puffed and fumed at the station. It was filled with boys. Going away. He went to his room and packed. He'd leave, too. When his suit-cases were filled, he looked round the room with damp eyes. He thought that he was going to cry, mastered himself, and then did cry. Some time later he remembered Iris and stopped crying. He walked to the station, recalling his first journey in the other direction, his pinch-backed green suit, the trunk he had carried. Grand old place, Webster. Suddenly gone dead all over. There would be a train for New York in half an hour. He took it. Some of the students talked to him on the trip to the city. Then they left him, alone, in the great vacuum of the terminal. The glittering corridors were filled with people. He wondered if he could find Bessie's house.

At a restaurant he ate supper. When he emerged, it was dark. He asked his way, found a hotel, registered in a one-dollar room, went out on the street again. He walked to the Raven. Then he took a cab. He remembered Bessie's house. An old woman answered the door. "Bessie? Bessie? No girl by that name I remember."

Hugo described her. "Oh, that tart! She ran out on me—owin' a week's rent."

"When was that?"

"Some time last fall."

"Oh." Hugo meditated. The woman spoke again. "I did hear from one of my other girls that she'd gone to work at Coney, but I ain't had time to look her up. Owes me four dollars, she does. But Bessie, as you calls her—her name's Sue—wasn't never much good. Still—" the woman scrutinized Hugo and giggled—"Bessie ain't the only girl in the world. I got a cute little piece up here named Palmerlee says only the other night she's lonely. Glad to interdooce you."

Hugo thought of his small capital. "No, thanks."

He walked away. A warm moon was dimly sensible above the lights of the street. He decided to go to Coney Island and look for the lost Bessie. It would cost him only a dime, and she owed him money. He smiled a little savagely and thought that he would collect its equivalent. Then he boarded the subway, cursing himself for a fool and cursing his appetite for the fool's master. Why did he chase that particular little harlot on an evening when his mind should be bent toward more serious purposes? Certainly not because he had any intention of getting back his money. Because he wished to surprise her? Because he was angry that she had cheated him? Or because she was the only woman in New York whom he knew? He decided it was the last reason. Finally the train reached Coney Island, and Hugo descended into the fantastic hurly-burly on the street below. He realized the ridiculousness of his quest as he saw the miles of thronging people in the loud streets.

"See the fat woman, see Esmerelda, the beautiful fat woman, she weighs six hundred pounds, she's had a dozen lovers, she's the fattest woman in the world, a sensation, dressed in the robes of Cleopatra, robes that took a bolt of cloth; but she's so fat they conceal nothing, ladies and gentlemen, see the beautiful fat woman. . . ." A roller coaster circled through the skies with a noise that was audible above the crowd's staccato voice and dashed itself at the earth below. A merry-go-round whirled goldenly and a band struck up a strident march. Hugo smelled stale beer and frying food. He heard the clang of a bell as a weight was driven up to it by the shoulders of a young gentleman in a pink shirt.

"The strongest man in the world, ladies and gentlemen, come in and see Thorndyke, the great professor of physical culture from Munich, Germany. He can bend a spike in his bare hands, an elephant can pass over his body without harming him, he can lift a weight of one ton. . . ." Hugo laughed. Two girls saw him and brushed close. "Buy us a drink, sport."

The strongest man in the world. Hugo wondered what sort of strong man he would make. Perhaps he could go into competition with Dr. Thorndyke. He saw himself pictured in gaudy reds and yellows, holding up an enormous weight. He remembered that he was looking for Bessie. Then he saw another girl. She was sitting at a table, alone. That fact was significant. He sat beside her.

"Hello, tough," she said.

"Hello."

"Wanna buy me a beer?"

Hugo bought a beer and looked at the girl. Her

hair was black and straight. Her mouth was straight. It was painted scarlet. Her eyes were hard and dark. But her body, as if to atone for her face, was made in a series of soft curves that fitted exquisitely into her black silk dress. He tortured himself looking at her. She permitted it sullenly. "You can buy me a sandwich, if you want. I ain't eaten to-day."

He bought a sandwich, wondering if she was telling the truth. She ate ravenously. He bought another and then a second glass of beer. After that she rose. "You can come with me if you wanna."

Odd. No conversation, no vivacity, only a dull submission that was not in keeping with her appearance.

"Have you had enough to eat?" he asked.

"It'll do," she responded.

They turned into a side street and moved away from the shimmering lights and the morass of people. Presently they entered a dingy frame house and went upstairs. There was no one in the hall, no furniture, only a flickering gas-light. She unlocked a door. "Come in."

He looked at her again. She took off her hat and arranged her dark hair so that it looped almost over one eye. Hugo wondered at her silence. "I didn't mean to rush," he said.

"Well, I did. Gotta make some more. It'll be"— she hesitated—"two bucks."

The girl sat down and wept. "Aw, hell," she said finally, looking at him with a shameless defiance,

"I guess I'm gonna make a rotten tart. I was in a show, an' I got busted out for not bein' nice to the manager. I says to myself: 'Well, what am I gonna do?' An' I starts to get hungry this morning. So I says to myself: 'Well, there ain't but one thing to do, Charlotte, but to get you a room,' I says, an' here I am, so help me God."

She removed her dress with a sweeping motion. Hugo looked at her, filled with pity, filled with remorse at his sudden surrender to her passionate good looks, intensely discomfited.

"Listen. I have a roll in my pocket. I'm damn glad I came here first. I haven't got a job, but I'll get one in the morning. And I'll get you a decent room and stake you till you get work. God knows, I picked you up for what I thought you were, Charlotte, and God knows too that I haven't any noble nature. But I'm not going to let you go on the street simply because you're broke. Not when you hate it so much."

Charlotte shut her eyes tight and pressed out the last tears, which ran into her rouge and streaked it with mascara. "That's sure white of you."

"I don't know. Maybe it's selfish. I had an awful yen for you when I sat down at that table. But let's not worry about it now. Let's go out and get a decent dinner."

"You mean—you mean you want me to go out and eat—now?"

"Sure. Why not?"

"But you ain't—?"

"Forget it. Come on."

Charlotte sniffled and buried her black tresses in her black dress. She pulled it over the curves of her hips. She inspected herself in a spotted mirror and sniffled again. Then she laughed. A throaty, gurgling laugh. Her hands moved swiftly, and soon she turned. "How am I?"

"Wonderful."

"Let's go!"

She tucked her hand under his arm when they reached the street. Hugo walked silently. He wondered why he was doing it and to what it would lead. It seemed good, wholly good, to have a girl at his side again, especially a girl over whom he had so strong a claim. They stopped before a glass-fronted restaurant that advertised its sea food and its steaks. She sat down with an apologetic smile. "I'm afraid I'm goin' to eat you out of house and home."

"Go ahead. I had a big supper, but I'll string along with some pie and cheese and beer."

Charlotte studied the menu. "Mind if I have a little steak?"

Hugo shook his head slowly. "Waiter! A big T-bone, and some lyonnaise potatoes, and some string beans and corn and a salad and ice cream. Bring some pie and cheese for me—and a beer."

"Gosh!" Charlotte said.

Hugo watched her eat the food. He knew such pity as he had seldom felt. Poor little kid! All alone,

scared, going on the street because she would starve
otherwise. It made him feel strong and capable. Before the meal was finished, she was talking furiously.
Her pathetic life was unravelled. "I come from
Brooklyn . . . old man took to drink, an' ma beat
it with a gent from Astoria . . . never knew what
happened to her. . . . I kept house for the old man
till he tried to get funny with me. . . . Burlesque
. . . on the road . . . the leading man. . . . He flew
the coop when I told him, and then when it came, it
was dead. . . ." Another job . . . the manager
. . . Coney and her dismissal. "I just couldn't let
'em have it when I didn't like 'em, mister. Guess
I'm not tough like the other girls. My mother was
French and she brought me up kind of decent.
Well . . ." The little outward turning of her hands,
the shrug of her shoulders.

"Don't worry, Charlotte. I won't let them eat you.
To-morrow I'll set you up to a decent room and
we'll go out and find some jobs here."

"You don't have to do that, mister. I'll make out.
All I needed was a square and another day."

Charlotte sighed and smoked a cigarette with her
coffee. Then they went out on the street and mixed
with the throng. The voices of a score of barkers
wheedled them. Hugo began to feel gay. He took
Charlotte to see the strong man and watched his
feats with a critical eye. He took her on the roller
coaster and became taut and laughing when she
screamed and held him. Then, laughing louder than

before, they went through Steeplechase. She fell in
the rolling barrel and he carried her out. They
crossed over moving staircases and lost themselves in
a maze, and slid down polished chutes into fountains
of light and excited screaming. Always, afterwards,
her hand found his arm, her great dark eyes looked
into his and laughed. Always they turned toward
the other men and girls with a proud and haughty
expression that pointed to Hugo as her man, her
conquest. Later they danced. They drank more beer.

"Golly," she whispered, as she snuggled against
him, "you sure strut a mean fox trot."

"So do you, Charlotte."

"I been doin' it a lot, I guess."

The brazen crash of a finale. The table. A babble
of voices, voices of people snatching pleasure from
Coney Island's gaudy barrel of cheap amusements.
Hugo liked it then. He liked the smell and touch of
the multitude and the incessant hysteria of its presence. After midnight the music became more aggra-
vating—muted, insinuating. Several of the dancers
were drunk. One of them tried to cut in. Hugo shook
his head.

"Gee!" Charlotte said, "I was sure hopin' you
wouldn't let him."

"Why—I never thought of it."

"Most fellows would. He's a tough."

It was an introduction to an unfamiliar world.
The "tough" came to their table and asked for a
dance in thick accents. Charlotte paled and accepted.

Hugo refused. "Say, bo, I'm askin' for a dance. I got concessions here. You can't refuse me, see? I guess you got me wrong."

"Beat it," Hugo said, "before I take a poke at you."

The intruder's answer was a swinging fist, which missed Hugo by a wide margin. Hugo stood and dropped him with a single clean blow. The manager came up, expostulated, ordered the tough's inert form from the floor, started the music.

"You shouldn't ought to have done it, mister. He'll get his gang."

"The hell with his gang."

Charlotte sighed. "That's the first time anybody ever stuck up for me. Jeest, mister, I've been wishin' an' wishin' for the day when somebody would bruise his knuckles for me."

Hugo laughed. "Hey, waiter! Two beers."

When she yawned, he took her out to the boulevard and walked at her side toward the shabby house. They reached the steps, and Charlotte began to cry.

"What's the matter?"

"I was goin' to thank you, but I don't know how. It was too nice of you. An' now I suppose I'll never see you again."

"Don't be silly. I'll show up at eight in the morning and we'll have breakfast together."

Charlotte looked into his face wistfully. "Say,

kid, be a good guy and take me to your hotel, will you? I'm scared I'll lose you."

He held her hands. "You won't lose me. And I haven't got a hotel—yet."

"Then—come up an' stay with me. Honest, I'm all right. I can prove it to you. It'll be doin' me a favor."

"I ought not to, Charlotte."

She threw her arms around him and kissed him. He felt her breath on his lips and the warmth of her body. "You gotta, kid. You're all I ever had. Please, please."

Hugo walked up the stairs thoughtfully. In her small room he watched her disrobe. So willingly now—so eagerly. She turned back the covers of the bed. "It ain't much of a dump, baby, but I'll make you like it."

Much later, in the abyss of darkness, he heard her voice, sleepy and still husky. "Say, mister, what's your name?"

In the morning they went down to the boulevard together. The gay débris of the night before lay in the street, and men were sweeping it away. But their spirits were high. They had breakfast together in a quiet enchantment. Once she kissed him.

"Would you like to keep house—for me?" he asked.

"Do you mean it?" She seemed to doubt every instant that good fortune had descended permanently upon her. She was like a dreamer who anticipated a sombre awakening even while he clung to the bliss of his dream.

"Sure, I mean it. I'll get a job and we'll find an apartment and you can spend your spare time swimming and lying on the beach." He knew a twinge of unexpected jealousy. "That is, if you'll promise not to look at all the men who are going to look at you." He was ashamed of that statement.

Charlotte, however, was not sufficiently civilized to be displeased. "Do you think I'd two-time the first gent that ever worried about what I did in my spare moments? Why, if you brought home a few bucks to most of the birds I know, they wouldn't even ask how you earned it—they'd be so busy lookin' for another girl an' a shot of gin."

"Well—let's go."

Hugo went to one of the largest side shows. After some questioning he found the manager. "I'm H. Smith," he said, "and I want to apply for a job."

"Doin' what?"

"This is my wife." The manager stared and nodded. Charlotte took his arm and rubbed it against herself, thinking, perhaps, that it was a wifely gesture. Hugo smiled inwardly and then looked at the sprawled form of the manager. There, to that seamy-faced and dour man who was almost unlike a human being, he was going to offer the first sale of his majestic strength. A side-show manager, sitting behind a dirty desk in a dirty building.

"A strong-man act," Hugo said.

Charlotte tittered. She thought that the bravado of her new friend was over-stepping the limits of good sense. The manager sat up. "I'd like to have a good strong man, yes. The show needs one. But you're not the bird. You haven't got the beef. Go over and watch that damned German work."

Hugo bent over and fastened one hand on the back of the chair on which the manager sat. Without evidence of effort he lifted the chair and its occupant high over his head.

"For Christ's sake, let me down," the manager said.

Hugo swung him through the air in a wide arc. "I say, mister, that I'm three times stronger than that German. And I want your job. If I don't look strong enough, I'll wear some padded tights. And I'll give you a show that'll be worth the admission. But I want a slice of the entrance price—and maybe a separate tent, see? My name is Hogarth"—he winked at Charlotte—"and you'll never be sorry you took me on."

The manager, panting and astonished, was returned to the floor. His anger struggled with his pleasure at Hugo's showmanship. "Well, what else can you do? Weight-lifting is pretty stale."

Hugo thought quickly. "I can bend a railroad rail —not a spike. I can lift a full-grown horse with one —one shoulder. I can chin myself on my little finger. I can set a bear trap with my teeth—"

"That's a good number."

"I can push up just twice as much weight as any one else in the game and you can print a challenge on my tent. I can pull a boa constrictor straight—"

"We'll give you a chance. Come around here at three this afternoon with your stuff and we'll try your act. Does this lady work in it? That'll help."

"Yes," Charlotte said.

Hugo nodded. "She's my assistant."

They left the building, and when she was sure they were out of earshot, Charlotte said: "What do you do, strong boy, fake 'em?"

"No. I do them."

"Aw—you don't need to kid me."

"I'm not. You saw me lift him, didn't you? Well —that was nothing."

"Jeest! That I should live to see the day I got a bird like you."

Until three o'clock Hugo and Charlotte occupied their time with feverish activity. They found a small apartment not far from the sea-shore. It was clean and bright and it had windows on two sides. Its furniture was nearly new, and Charlotte, with tears in her eyes, sat in all the chairs, lay on the bed, took the egg-beater from the drawer in the kitchen table and spun it in an empty bowl. They went out together and bought a quantity and a variety of food. They ate an early luncheon and Hugo set out to gather the properties for his demonstration. At three o'clock, before a dozen men, he gave an exhibition of strength the like of which had never been seen in any museum of human abnormalities.

When he went back to his apartment, Charlotte, in a gingham dress which she had bought with part of the money he had given her, was preparing dinner. He took her on his lap. "Did you get the job?"

"Sure I did. Fifty a week and ten per cent of the gate receipts."

"Gee! That's a lot of money!"

Hugo nodded and kissed her. He was very happy. Happier, in a certain way, than he had ever been or ever would be again. His livelihood was assured. He was going to live with a woman, to have one always near to love and to share his life. It was that concept of companionship, above all other things, which made him glad.

Two days later, as Hugo worked to prepare the vehicles of his exhibition, he heard an altercation outside the tent that had been erected for him. A voice said: "Whatcha tryin' to do there, anyhow?"

"Why, I was making this strong man as I saw him. A man with the expression of strength in his face."

"But you gotta bat' robe on him. What we want is muscles. Muscles, bo. Bigger an' better than any picture of any strong man ever made. Put one here —an' one there—"

"But that isn't correct anatomy."

"To hell wit' that stuff. Put one there, I says."

"But he'll be out of drawing, awkward, absurd."

"Say, listen, do you want ten bucks for painting this sign or shall I give it to some one else?"

"Very well. I'll do as you say. Only—it isn't right."

Hugo walked out of the tent. A young man was bending over a huge sheet made of many lengths of oilcloth sewn together. He was a small person, with pale eyes and a white skin. Beside him stood the manager, eying critically the strokes applied to the cloth. In a semi-finished state was the young man's picture of the imaginary Hogarth.

"That's pretty good," Hugo said.

The young man smiled apologetically. "It isn't quite right. You can see for yourself you have no muscles there—and there. I suppose you're Hogarth?"

"Yes."

"Well—I tried to explain the anatomy of it, but Mr. Smoots says anatomy doesn't matter. So here we go." He made a broad orange streak.

Hugo smiled. "Smoots is not an anatomical critic of any renown. I say, Smoots, let him paint it as he sees best. God knows the other posters are atrocious enough."

The youth looked up from his work. "Good God, don't tell me you're really Hogarth!"

"Sure. Why not?"

"Well—well—I—I guess it was your English."

"That's funny. And I don't blame you." Hugo realized that the young sign-painter was a person of some culture. He was about Hugo's age, although he seemed younger on first glance. "As a matter of fact, I'm a college man." Smoots had moved away. "But, for the love of God, don't tell any one around here."

The painter stopped. "Is that so! And you're doing this—to make money?"

"Yes."

"Well, I'll be doggoned. Me, too. I study at the School of Design in the winter, and in the summer I come out here to do signs and lightning portraits and whatever else I can to make the money for it. Sometimes," he added, "I pick up more than a thousand bucks in a season. This is my fourth year at it."

There was in the young artist's eye a hint of amusement, a suggestion that they were in league. Hugo liked him. He sat down on a box. "Live here?"

"Yes. Three blocks away."

"Me, too. Why not come up and have supper with —my wife and me?"

"Are you married?" The artist commenced work again.

Hugo hesitated. "Yeah."

"Sure I'll come up. My name's Valentine Mitchel. I can't shake hands just now. It's been a long time since I've talked to any one who doesn't say 'deez' and 'doze.'"

When, later in the day, they walked toward Hugo's home, he was at a loss to explain Charlotte. The young painter would not understand why he, a college man, chose so ignorant a mate. On the other hand, he owed it to Charlotte to keep their secret and he was not obliged to make any explanation.

Valentine Mitchel was, however, a young man of some sensitivity. If he winced at Charlotte's "Pleased to meetcher," he did not show it. Later, after an excellent and hilarious meal, he must have guessed the situation. He went home reluctantly and Hugo was delighted with him. He had been urbane and filled with anecdotes of Greenwich Village and art-school life, of Paris, whither his struggling footsteps had taken him for a hallowed year. And with his acceptance of Hugo came an equally warm pleasure in Charlotte's company.

"He's a good little kid," Charlotte said.

"Yes. I'm glad I picked him up."

The gala opening of Hogarth's Studio of Strength took place a few nights afterwards. It proved even more successful than Smoots had hoped. The flamboyant advertising posters attracted crowds to see the man who could set a bear trap with his teeth, who could pull an angry boa constrictor into a straight line. Before ranks of gaping faces that were supplanted by new ranks every hour, Hugo performed. Charlotte, resplendent in a black dress that left her knees bare, and a red sash that all but obliterated the dress, helped Hugo with his ponderous props, setting off his strength by contrast, and sold the pamphlets Hugo had written at Smoots's suggestion—pamphlets that purported to give away the secret of Hogarth's phenomenal muscle power. Valentine Mitchel watched the entire performance.

When it was over, he said to Hugo: "Now you better beat it back and get a hot bath. You're probably all in."

"Yes," Charlotte said. "Come. I myself will bathe you."

Hugo grinned. "Hell, no. Now we're all going on a bender to celebrate. We'll eat at Villapigue's and we'll take a moonlight sail."

They went together, marvelling at his vitality, gay, young, and living in a world that they managed to forget did not exist. The night was warm. The days that followed were warmer. The crowds came and the brassy music hooted and coughed over them night and day.

There are, in the lives of almost every man and woman, certain brief episodes that, enduring for a long or a short time, leave in the memory a sense of completeness. To those moments humanity returns for refuge, for courage, and for solace. It was of such material that Hugo's next two months were composed. The items of it were nearly all sensuous: the sound of the sea when he sat in the sand late at night with Charlotte; the whoop and bellow of the merry-go-round that spun and glittered across the street from his tent; the inarticulate breathing and the white-knuckled clenchings of the crowd as it lifted its face to his efforts, for each of which he assumed a slow, painful motion that exaggerated its difficulty; the smell of the sea, intermingled with a thousand man-made odors; the faint, pervasive scent of Charlotte that clung to him, his clothes, his house; the pageant of the people, always in a huge parade, going nowhere, celebrating nothing but the functions of living, loud, garish, cheap, splendid; breakfasts at his table with his woman's voluptuousness abated in the bright sunlight to little more than a reminiscence and a promise; the taste of beer and pop-corn and frankfurters and lobster and steak; the affable, talkative company of Valentine Mitchel.

Only once that he could recall afterwards did he allow his intellect to act in any critical direction, and that was in a conversation with the young artist. They were sitting together in the sand, and Charlotte, browned by weeks of bathing, lay near by. "Here I am," Mitchel said with an unusual thoughtfulness, "with a talent that should be recognized, wanting to be an illustrator, able to be one, and yet forced to dawdle with this horrible business to make my living."

Hugo nodded. "You'll come through—some winter—and you won't ever return to Coney Island."

"I know it. Unless I do it for sentimental reasons some day—in a limousine."

"It's myself," Hugo said then, "and not you who is doomed to—well, to this sort of thing. You have a talent that is at least understandable and—" he was going to say mediocre. He checked himself—

"applicable in the world of human affairs. My talent —if it is a talent—has no place, no application, no audience."

Mitchel stared at Hugo, wondering first what that talent might be and then recognizing that Hugo meant his strength. "Nonsense. Any male in his right senses would give all his wits to be as strong as you are."

It was a polite, friendly thing to say. Hugo could not refrain from comparing himself to Valentine Mitchel. An artist—a clever artist and one who would some day be important to the world. Because people could understand what he drew, because it represented a level of thought and expression. He was, like Hugo, in the doldrums of progress. But Mitchel would emerge, succeed, be happy—or at least satisfied with himself—while Hugo was bound to silence, was compelled never to allow himself full expression. Humanity would never accept and understand him. They were not similar people, but their case was, at that instant, ironically parallel. "It isn't only being strong," he answered meditatively, "but it's knowing what to do with your strength."

"Why—there are a thousand things to do."

"Such as?"

Mitchel raised himself on his elbows and turned his water-coloured eyes on the populous beach. "Well —well—let's see. You could, of course, be a strong man and amuse people—which you're doing. You could—oh, there are lots of things you could do."

Hugo smiled. "I've been thinking about them—for years. And I can't discover any that are worth the effort."

"Bosh!"

Charlotte moved close to him. "There's one thing you can do, honey, and that's enough for me."

"I wonder," Hugo said with a seriousness the other two did not perceive.

The increased heat of August suggested by its very intensity a shortness of duration, an end of summer. Hugo began to wonder what he would do with Charlotte when he went back to Webster. He worried about her a good deal and she, guessing the subject of his frequent fits of silence, made a resolve in her tough and worldly mind. She had learned more about certain facets of Hugo than he knew himself. She realized that he was superior to her and that, in almost any other place than Coney Island, she would be a liability to him. The thought that he would have to desert her made Hugo very miserable. He knew that he would miss Charlotte and he knew that the blow to her might spell disaster. After all, he thought, he had not improved her morals or raised her vision. He did not realize that he had made both almost sublime by the mere act of being considerate. "White," Charlotte called it.

Nevertheless she was not without an intense sense of self-protection, despite her condition on the night he had found her. She knew that womankind lived at the expense of mankind. She saw the emotional respect in which Valentine Mitchel unwittingly held Hugo. He had scarcely spoken ten serious words to her. She realized that the artist saw her as a property of his friend. That, in a way, made her valuable. It was a subtle advantage, which she pressed with all the skill it required. One night when Hugo was at work and the chill of autumn had breathed on the hot shore, she told Valentine that he was a very nice boy and that she liked him very much. He went away distraught, which was what she had intended, and he carried with him a new and as yet inarticulate idea, which was what she had foreseen.

He believed that he loved her. He told himself that Hugo was going to desert her, that she would be forsaken and alone. At that point, she recited to him the story of her life and the tale of her rescue by Hugo and said at the end that she would be very lonely when Hugo was gone. Because Hugo had loved her, Mitchel thought she contained depths and values which did not appear. That she contained such depths neither man really knew then. Both of them learned it much later. Mitchel found himself in that very artistic dilemma of being in love with his friend's mistress. It terrified his romantic soul and it involved him inextricably.

When she felt that the situation had ripened to the point of action, she waited for the precise moment. It came swiftly and in a better guise than she had hoped. On a night in early September, when the crowds had thinned a little, Hugo was just buckling himself into the harness that lifted the horse. The spectators were waiting for the dénouement with bickering patience. Charlotte was standing on the platform, watching him with expressionless eyes. She knew that soon she would not see Hugo any more. She knew that he was tired of his small show, that he was chafing to be gone; and she knew that his loyalty to her would never let him go unless it was made inevitable by her. The horse was ready. She watched the muscles start out beneath Hugo's tawny skin. She saw his lips set, his head thrust back. She worshipped him like that. Unemotionally, she saw the horse lifted up from the floor. She heard the applause. There was a bustle at the gate.

Half a dozen people entered in single file. Three young men. Three girls. They were intoxicated. They laughed and spoke in loud voices. She saw by their clothes and their manner that they were rich. Slumming in Coney Island. She smiled at the young men as she had always smiled at such young men, friendlily, impersonally. Hugo did not see their entrance. They came very near.

"My God, it's Hugo Danner!"

Hugo heard Lefty's voice and recognized it. The horse was dropped to the floor. He turned. An expression of startled amazement crossed his features. Chuck, Lefty, Iris, and three people whom he did not know were staring at him. He saw the stupefied recognition on the faces of his friends. One despairing glance he cast at Charlotte and then he went on with his act.

They waited for him until it was over. They clasped him to their bosoms. They acknowledged Charlotte with critical glances. "Come on and join the party," they said.

After that, their silence was worse than any questions. They talked freely and merrily enough, but behind their words was a deep reserve. Lefty broke it when he had an opportunity to take Hugo aside. "What in hell is eating you? Aren't you coming back to Webster?"

"Sure. That is—I think so. I had to do this to make some money. Just about the time school closed, my family went broke."

"But, good God, man, why didn't you tell us? My father is an alumnus and he'd put up five thousand a year, if necessary, to see you kept on the football team."

Hugo laughed. "You don't think I'd take it, Lefty?"

"Why not?" A pause. "No, I suppose you'd be just the God-damned kind of a fool that wouldn't. Who's the girl?"

Hugo did not falter. "She's a tart I've been living with. I never knew a better one—girl, that is."

"Have you gone crazy?"

"On the contrary, I've got wise."

"Well, for Christ's sake, don't say anything about it on the campus."

Hugo bit his lip. "Don't worry. My business is—my own."

They joined the others, drinking at the table. Charlotte was telling a joke. It was not a nice joke. He had not thought of her jokes before—because Iris and Chuck and Lefty had not been listening to them. Now, he was embarrassed. Iris asked him to dance with her. They went out on the floor.

"Lovely little thing, that Charlotte," she said acidly.

"Isn't she!" Hugo answered with such enthusiasm that she did not speak during the rest of the dance.

Finally the ordeal ended. Lefty and his guests embarked in an automobile for the city.

"You know such people," Charlotte half-whispered. Hugo's cheeks still flamed, but his heart bled for her.

"I guess they aren't much," he replied.

She answered hotly: "Don't you be like that! They're nice people. They're fine people. That Iris even asked me to her house. Gave me a card to see her." Charlotte could guess what Iris wanted. So could Hugo. But Charlotte pretended to be innocent.

He kissed Charlotte good-night and walked in the streets until morning. Hugo could see no solution. Charlotte was so trusting, so good to him. He could not imagine how she would receive any suggestion that she go to New York and get a job, while he return to college, that he see her during

136

vacations, that he send money to her. But he knew that a hot fire dwelt within her and that her fury would rise, her grief, and that he would be made very miserable and ashamed. She chided him at breakfast for his walk in the dark. She laughed and kissed him and pushed him bodily to his work. He looked back as he walked down to the curb. She was leaning out of the window. She waved her hand. He rounded the corner with wretched, leaden steps. The morning, concerned with the petty business of receipts, refurbishings, cleaning, went slowly. When he returned for lunch it was with the decision to tell her the truth about his life and its requirements and to let her decide.

She did not come to the door to kiss him. (She had imagined that lonely return.) She did not answer his brave and cheerful hail. (She had let the sound of it ring upon her ear a thousand times.) She was gone. (She knew he would sit down and cry.) Then, stumbling, he found the two notes. But he already understood.

The message from Valentine Mitchel was reckless, impetuous. "Dear Hugo—Charlotte and I have fallen in love with each other and I've run away with her. I almost wish you'd come after us and kill me. I hate myself for betraying you. But I love her, so I cannot help it. I've learned to see in her what you first saw in her. Good-bye, good luck."

Hugo put it down. Charlotte would be good to him. In a way, he didn't deserve her. And when he was famous, some day, perhaps she would leave him, too. He hesitated to read her note. "Good-bye, darling, I do not love you any more. C."

It was ludicrous, transparent, pitiful, and heroic. Hugo saw all those qualities. "Good-bye, darling, I do not love you any more." She had written it under Valentine's eyes. But she was shrewd enough to placate her new lover while she told her sad little story to her old. She would want him to feel bad. Well, God knew, he did. Hugo looked at the room. He sobbed. He bolted into the street, tears streaming down his cheeks; he drew his savings from the bank—seven hundred and eighty-four dollars and sixty-four cents; he rushed to the haunted house, flung his clothes into a bag; he sat drearily on a subway for an hour. He paced the smooth floor of a station. He swung aboard a train. He came to Webster, his head high, feeling a great pride in Charlotte and in his love for her, walking in glad strides over the familiar soil.

IX

HUGO SAT alone and marvelled at the exquisite torment of his *Weltschmertz*. Far away, across the campus, he heard singing. Against the square segment of sky visible from the bay window of his room he could see the light of the great fire they had built to celebrate victory—his victory. The light leaped into the darkness above like a great golden ghost in some fantastic ascension, and beneath it, he knew, a thousand students were dancing. They were druid priests at a rite to the god of football. His fingers struggled through his black hair. The day was fresh in his mind—the bellowing stands, the taut, almost frightened faces of the eleven men who faced him, the smack and flight of the brown oval, the lumbering sound of men running, the sucking of the breath of men and their sharp, painful fall to earth.

In his mind was a sharp picture of himself and the eyes that watched him as he broke away time and again, with infantile ease, to carry that precious ball. He let them make a touchdown that he could

have averted. He made one himself. Then another.
The bell on Webster Hall was booming its pæan of
victory. He stiffened under the steady monody. He
remembered again. Lefty barking signals with a
strange agony in his voice. Lefty pounding on his
shoulder. "Go in there, Hugo, and give it to them.
I can't." Lefty pleading. And the captain, Jerry
Painter, cursing in open jealousy of Hugo, vying
hopelessly with Hugo Danner, the man who was a
god.

It was not fair. Not right. The old and early
glory was ebbing from it. When he put down the
ball, safely across the goal for the winning touchdown, he saw three of the men on the opposing team
lie down and weep. There he stood, pretending to
pant, feigning physical distress, making himself a
hero at the expense of innocent victims. Jackstraws
for a giant. There was no triumph in that. He could
not go on.

Afterwards they had made him speak, and the
breathless words that had once come so easily moved
heavily through his mind. Yet he had carried his
advantage beyond the point of turning back. He
could not say that the opponents of Webster might
as well attempt to hold back a Juggernaut, to throw
down a siege-gun, to outrace light, as to lay their
hands on him to check his intent. Webster had been
good to him. He loved Webster and it deserved his
best. His best! He peered again into the celebrating
night and wondered what that awful best would be.

He desired passionately to be able to give that—
to cover the earth, making men glad and bringing a
revolution into their lives, to work himself into a
fury and to fatigue his incredible sinews, to end with
the feeling of a race well run, a task nobly executed.
And, for a year, that ambition had seemed in some
small way to be approaching fruition. Now it was
turned to ashes. It was not with the muscles of men
that his goal was to be attained. They could not
oppose him.

As he sat gloomy and distressed, he wondered for
what reason there burned in him that wish to do
great deeds. Humanity itself was too selfish and
too ignorant to care. It could boil in its tiny preju-
dices for centuries to come and never know that
there could be a difference. Moreover, who was he
to grind his soul and beat his thoughts for the benefit of people who would never know and never care?
What honour, when he was dead, to lie beneath a
slab on which was punily graven some note of mighty
accomplishment? Why could he not content himself
with the food he ate, the sunshine, with wind in
trees, and cold water, and a woman? It was that
sad and silly command within to transcend his vegetable self that made him human. He tried to think
about it bitterly: fool man, grown suddenly more
conscious than the other beasts—how quickly he
had become vain because of it and how that vanity
led him forever onward! Or was it vanity—when
his aching soul proclaimed that he would gladly

achieve and die without other recognition or acclaim than that which rose within himself? Martyrs were made of such stuff. And was not that, perhaps, an even more exaggerated vanity? It was so pitiful to be a man and nothing more. Hugo bowed his head and let his body tremble with strange agony. Perhaps, he thought, even the agony was a selfish pleasure to him. Then he should be ashamed. He felt shame and then thought that the feeling rose from a wish for it and foundered angrily in the confusion of his introspection. He knew only and knew but dimly that he would lift himself up again and go on, searching for some universal foe to match against his strength. So pitiful to be a man! So Christ must have felt in Gethsemane.

"Hey, Hugo!"

"Yeah?"

"What the hell did you come over here for?"

"To be alone."

"Is that a hint?" Lefty entered the room. "They want you over at the bonfire. We've been looking all over for you."

"All right. I'll go. But, honest to God, I've had enough of this business for today."

Lefty slapped Hugo's shoulders. "The great must pay for their celebrity. Come on, you sap."

"All right."

"What's the matter? Anything the matter?"

"No. Nothing's the matter. Only—it's sort of sad to be—" Hugo checked himself.

"Sad? Good God, man, you're going stale."

"Maybe that's it." Hugo had a sudden fancy. "Do you suppose I could be let out of next week's game?"

"What for? My God—"

Hugo pursued the idea. "It's the last game. I can sit on the lines. You fellows all play good ball. You can probably win. If you can't—then I'll play. If you only knew, Lefty, how tired I get sometimes—"

"Tired! Why don't you say something about it? You can lay off practice for three or four days."

"Not that. Tired in the head, not the body. Tired of crashing through and always getting away with it. Oh, I'm not conceited. But I know they can't stop me. You know it. It's a gift of mine—and a curse. How about it? Let's start next week without me."

The night ended at last. A new day came. The bell on Webster Hall stopped booming. Woodie, the coach, came to see Hugo between classes. "Lefty says you want us to start without you next week. What's the big idea?"

"I don't know. I thought the other birds would like a shot at Yale without me. They can do it."

Mr. Woodman eyed his player. "That's pretty generous of you, Hugo. Is there any other reason?"

"Not—that I can explain."

"I see." The coach offered Hugo a cigarette after he had helped himself. "Take it. It'll do you good."

"Thanks."

"Listen, Hugo. I want to ask you a question. But,

first, I want you to promise you'll give me a plain answer."

"I'll try."

"That won't do."

"Well—I can't promise."

Woodman sighed. "I'll ask it anyway. You can answer or not—just as you wish." He was silent. He inhaled his cigarette and blew the smoke through his nostrils. His eyes rested on Hugo with an expression of intense interest, beneath which was a softer light of something not unlike sympathy. "I'll have to tell you something, first, Hugo. When you went away last summer, I took a trip to Colorado."

Hugo started, and Woodman continued: "To Indian Creek. I met your father and your mother. I told them that I knew you. I did my best to gain their confidence. You see, Hugo, I've watched you with a more skilful eye than most people. I've seen you do things, a few little things, that weren't— well—that weren't—"

Hugo's throat was dry. "Natural?"

"That's the best word, I guess. You were never like my other boys, in any case. So I thought I'd find out what I could. I must admit that my efforts with your father were a failure. Aside from the fact that he is an able biology teacher and that he had a number of queer theories years ago, I learned nothing. But I did find out what those theories were. Do you want me to stop?"

A peculiar, almost hopeful expression was on Hugo's face. "No," he answered.

"Well, they had to do with the biochemistry of cellular structure, didn't they? And with the production of energy in cells? And then—I talked to lots of people. I heard about Samson."

"Samson!" Hugo echoed, as if the dead had spoken.

"Samson—the cat."

Hugo was as pale as chalk. His eyes burned darkly. He felt that his universe was slipping from beneath him. "You know, then," he said.

"I don't know, Hugo. I merely guessed. I was going to ask. Now I shall not. Perhaps I do know. But I had another question, son—"

"Yes?" Hugo looked at Woodman and felt then the reason for his success as a coach, as a leader and master of youth. He understood it.

"Well, I wondered if you thought it was worth while to talk to your father and discover—"

"What he did?" Hugo suggested hoarsely.

Woodman put his hand on Hugo's knee. "What he did, son. You ought to know by this time what it means. I've been watching you. I don't want your head to swell, but you're a great boy, Hugo. Not only in beef. You have a brain and an imagination and a sense of moral responsibility. You'll come out better than the rest—you would even without your —your particular talent. And I thought you might think that the rest of humanity would profit—"

Hugo jumped to his feet. "No. A thousand times no. For the love of Christ—no! You don't know or understand, you can't conceive, Woodie, what it means to have it. You don't have the faintest idea of its amount—what it tempts you with—what they did to me and I did to myself to beat it—if I have beaten it." He laughed. "Listen, Woodie. Anything I want is mine. Anything I desire I can take. No one can hinder. And sometimes I sweat all night for fear some day I shall lose my temper. There's a desire in me to break and destroy and wreck that— oh, hell—"

Woodman waited. Then he spoke quietly. "You're sure, Hugo, that the desire to be the only one— like that—has nothing to do with it?"

Hugo's sole response was to look into Woodman's eyes, a look so pregnant with meaning, so tortured, so humble, that the coach swore softly. Then he held out his hand. "Well, Hugo, that's all. You've been damn swell about it. The way I hoped you would be. And I think my answer is plain. One thing. As long as I live, I promise on my oath I'll never give you away or support any rumour that hurts your secret."

Even Hugo was stirred to a consciousness of the strength of the other man's grip.

Saturday. A shrill whistle. The thump of leather against leather. The roar of the stadium.

Hugo leaned forward. He watched his fellows from the bench. They rushed across the field. Lefty caught the ball. Eddie Carter interfered with the first man, Bimbo Gaines with the second. The third slammed Lefty against the earth. Three downs. Eight yards. A kick. New Haven brought the ball to its twenty-one-yard line. The men in helmets formed again. A coughing voice. Pandemonium. Again in line. The voice. The riot of figures suddenly still. Again. A kick. Lefty with the ball, and Bimbo Gaines leading him, his big body a shield. Down. A break and a run for twenty-eight yards. Must have been Chuck. Good old Chuck. He'd be playing the game of his life. Graduation next spring. Four, seven, eleven, thirty-two, fifty-five. Hugo anticipated the spreading of the players. He looked where the ball would be thrown. He watched Minton, the end, spring forward, saw him falter, saw the opposing quarter-back run in, saw Lefty thrown, saw the ball received by the enemy and moved up, saw the opposing back spilled nastily. His heart beat faster.

No score at the end of the first half. The third quarter witnessed the crossing of Webster's goal. Struggling grimly, gamely, against a team that was their superior without Hugo, against a team heartened by the knowledge that Hugo was not facing it, Webster's players were being beaten. The goal was not kicked. It made the score six to nothing against Webster. Hugo saw the captain rip off his headgear and throw it angrily on the ground. He understood all that was going on in the minds of his team in

147

a clear, although remote, way. They went out to show that they could play the game without Hugo Danner. And they were not showing what they had hoped to show. A few minutes later their opponents made a second touchdown.

Thirteen to nothing. Mr. Woodman moved beside Hugo. "They can't do it—and I don't altogether blame them. They've depended on you too much. It's too bad. We all have."

Hugo nodded. "Shall I go in?"

The coach watched the next play. "I guess you better."

When Hugo entered the line, Jerry Painter and Lefty spoke to him in strained tones. "You've got to take it over, Hugo—all the way."

"All right."

The men lined up. A tense silence had fallen on the Yale line. They knew what was going to happen. The signals were called, the ball shot back to Lefty, Hugo began to run, the men in front rushed together, and Lefty stuffed the ball into Hugo's arms. "Go on," he shouted. The touchdown was made in one play. Hugo saw a narrow hole and scooted into it. A man met his outstretched arm on the other side. Another. Hugo dodged twice. The crescendo roar of the Webster section came to him dimly. He avoided the safety man and ran to the goal. In the pandemonium afterwards, Jerry kicked the goal.

A new kick-off. Hugo felt a hand on his shoulder. "You've gotta break this up." Hugo broke it up. He held Yale almost single-handed. They kicked back. Hugo returned the kick to the middle of the field. He did not dare to do more.

Then he stood in his leather helmet, bent, alert, waiting to run again. They called the captain's signal. He made four yards. Then Lefty's. He made a first down. Then Jerry's. Two yards. Six yards. Five yards. Another first down. The stands were insane. Hugo was glad they were not using him—glad until he saw Jerry Painter's face. It was pale with rage. Blood trickled across it from a small cut. Three tries failed. Hugo spoke to him. "I'll take it over, Jerry, if you say so."

Jerry doubled his fist and would have struck him if Hugo had not stepped back. "God damn you, Danner, you come out here in the last few minutes all fresh and make us look like a lot of fools. I tell you, my team and I will take that ball across and not you with your bastard tricks."

"But, good God, man—"

"You heard me."

"This is your last down."

There was time for nothing more. Lefty called Jerry's signal, and Jerry failed. The other team took the ball, rushed it twice, and kicked back into the Webster territory. Again the tired, dogged players began a march forward. The ball was not given to Hugo. He did his best, using his body as a ram to open holes in the line, tripping tacklers with his body, fighting within the limits of an appearance of human

149

strength to get his teammates through to victory. And Jerry, still pale and profane, drove the men like slaves. It was useless. If Hugo had dared more, they might have succeeded. But they lost the ball again. It was only in the last few seconds that an exhausted and victorious team relinquished the ball to Webster.

Jerry ordered his own number again. Hugo, cold and somewhat furious at the vanity and injustice of the performance, gritted his teeth. "How about letting me try, Jerry? I can make it. It's for Webster —not for you."

"You go to hell."

Lefty said: "You're out of your head, Jerry."

"I said I'd take it."

For one instant Hugo looked into his eyes. And in that instant the captain saw a dark and flickering fury that filled him with fear. The whistle blew. And then Hugo, to his astonishment, heard his signal. Lefty was disobeying the captain. He felt the ball in his arms. He ran smoothly. Suddenly he saw a dark shadow in the air. The captain hit him on the jaw with all his strength. After that, Hugo did not think lucidly. He was momentarily berserk. He ran into the line raging and upset it like a row of tenpins. He raced into the open. A single man, thirty yards away, stood between him and the goal. The man drew near in an instant. Hugo doubled his arm to slug him. He felt the arm straighten, relented too late, and heard, above the chaos that was loose, a sudden, dreadful snap. The man's head flew back and he dropped. Hugo ran across the goal. The gun stopped the game. But, before the avalanche fell upon him, Hugo saw his victim lying motionless on the field. What followed was nightmare. The singing and the cheering. The parade. The smashing of the goal posts. The gradual descent of silence. A pause. A shudder. He realized that he had been let down from the shoulders of the students. He saw Woodman, waving his hands, his face a graven mask. The men met in the midst of that turbulence.

"You killed him, Hugo."

The earth spun and rocked slowly. He was paying his first price for losing his temper. "Killed him?"

"His neck was broken—in three places."

Some of the others heard. They walked away. Presently Hugo was standing alone on the cinders outside the stadium. Lefty came up. "I just heard about it. Tough luck. But don't let it break you."

Hugo did not answer. He knew that he was guilty of a sort of murder. In his own eyes it was murder. He had given away for one red moment to the leaping, lusting urge to smash the world. And killed a man. They would never accuse him. They would never talk about it. Only Woodman, perhaps, would guess the thing behind the murder—the demon inside Hugo that was tame, except then, when his captain in jealous and inferior rage had struck him.

It was night. Out of deference to the body of the boy lying in the Webster chapel there was no celebration. Every ounce of glory and joy had been drained from the victory. The students left Hugo to a solitude that was more awful than a thousand scornful tongues. They thought he would feel as they would feel about such an accident. They gave him respect when he needed counsel. As he sat by himself, he thought that he should tell them the truth, all of them, confess a crime and accept the punishment. Hours passed. At midnight Woodman called.

"There isn't much to say, Hugo. I'm sorry, you're sorry, we're all sorry. But it occurred to me that you might do something foolish—tell these people all about it, for example."

"I was going to."

"Don't. They'd never understand. You'd be involved in a legal war that would undoubtedly end in your acquittal. But it would drag in all your friends —and your mother and father—particularly him. The papers would go wild. You might, on the other hand, be executed as a menace. You can't tell."

"It might be a good thing," Hugo answered bitterly.

"Don't let me hear you say that, you fool! I tell you, Hugo, if you go into that business, I'll get up on the stand and say I knew it all the time and I let a man play on my team when I was pretty sure that sooner or later he'd kill someone. Then I'll go to jail surely."

"You're a pretty fine man, Mr. Woodman."

"Hell!"

"What shall I do?" Hugo's voice trembled. He suffered as he had not dreamed it was possible to suffer.

"That's up to you. I'd say, live it down."

"Live it down! Do you know what that means—in a college?"

"Yes, I think I do, Hugo."

"You can live down almost anything, except that one thing—murder. It's too ugly, Woodie."

"Maybe. Maybe. You've got to decide, son. If you decide against trying—and, mind you, you might be justified—I've got a brother-in-law who has a ranch in Alberta. A couple of hundred miles from any place. You'd be welcome there."

Hugo did not reply. He took the coach's hand and wrung it. Then for an hour the two men sat side by side in the darkness. At last Woodman rose and left. He said only: "Remember that offer. It's cold and bleak and the work is hard. Good-night, Hugo."

"Good-night, Woodie. Thanks for coming up."

When the campus was still with the quiet of sleep, Hugo crossed it as swiftly as a spectre. All night he strode remorselessly over country roads. His face was set. His eyes burned. He ignored the trembling of his joints. When the sky faded, he went back. He packed his clothes in two suit-cases. With them swinging at his side, he stole out of the Psi Delta house, crossed the campus, stopped. For a long instant he stared at Webster Hall. The first light of morning was just touching it. The débris collected for a fire that was never lighted was strewn around the cannon. He saw the initials he had painted there a year and more ago still faintly legible. A lump rose in his throat.

"Good-by, Webster," he said. He lifted the suit-case and vanished. In a few minutes the campus was five miles behind him—six—ten—twenty. When he saw the first early caravan of produce headed toward the market, he slowed to a walk. The sun came over a hill and sparkled on a billion drops of dew. A bird flew singing from his path. Hugo Danner had fled beyond the gates of Webster.

X

A YEAR PASSED. In the harbour of Cristobal, at the northern end of the locks, waiting for the day to open the great steel jaws that dammed the Pacific from the Atlantic, the *Katrina* pulled at her anchor chain in the gentle swell. A few stars, liquid bright, hung in the tropical sky. A little puff of wind coming occasionally from the south carried the smell of the jungle to the ship. The crew was awakening.

A man with a bucket on a rope went to the rail and hauled up a brimming pail from the warm sea. He splashed his face and hands into it. Then he poured it back and repeated the act of dipping up water.

"Hey!" he said.

Another man joined him. "Here. Swab off your sweat. Look yonder."

The dorsal fin of a shark rippled momentarily on the surface and dipped beneath it. A third man appeared. He accepted the proffered water and washed himself. His roving eye saw the shark as it rose for

155

the second time. He dried on a towel. The off-shore breeze stirred his dark hair. There was a growth of equally dark beard on his tanned jaw and cheek. Steely muscles bulged under his shirt. His forearm, when he picked up the pail, was corded like cable. A smell of coffee issued from the galley, and the smoke of the cook's fire was wafted on deck for a pungent moment. Two bells sounded. The music went out over the water in clear, humming waves.

The man who had come first from the forecastle leaned his buttocks against the rail. One end of it had been unhooked to permit the discharge of mail. The rail ran, the man fell back, clawing, and then, thinking suddenly of the sharks, he screamed. The third man looked. He saw his fellow-seaman go overboard. He jumped from where he stood, clearing the scuppers and falling through the air before the victim of the slack rail had landed in the water. The two splashes were almost simultaneous. A boatswain, hearing the cry, hastened to the scene. He saw one man lifted clear of the water by the other, who was treading water furiously. He shouted for a rope. He saw the curve and dip of a fin. The first man seized the rope and climbed and was pulled up. The second, his rescuer, dived under water as if aware of something there that required his attention. The men above him could not know that he had felt the rake of teeth across his leg—powerful teeth, which nevertheless did not penetrate his skin. As he dived into the green depths, he saw a body lunge toward him, turn, yawn a white-fringed mouth. He snatched the lower jaw in one hand, and the upper in the other. He exerted his strength. The mouth gaped wider, a tail twelve feet behind it lashed, the thing died with fingers like steel claws tearing at its brain. It floated belly up. The man rose, took the rope, climbed aboard. Other sharks assaulted the dead one.

The dripping sailor clasped his saviour's hand. "God Almighty, man, you saved my life. Jesus!"

"That's four," Hugo Danner said abstractedly, and then he smiled. "It's all right. Forget it. I've had a lot of experience with sharks." He had never seen one before in his life. He walked aft, where the men grouped around him.

"How'd you do it?"

"It's a trick I can't explain very well," Hugo said. "You use their rush to break their jaws. It takes a good deal of muscle."

"Anyway—guy—thanks."

"Sure."

A whistle blew. The ships were lining up in the order of their arrival for admission to the Panama Canal. Gatun loomed in the feeble sun of dawn. The anchor chain rumbled. The *Katrina* edged forward at half speed.

The sea. Blue, green, restless, ghost-ridden, driven in empty quarters by devils riding the wind, secretive, mysterious, making a last gigantic, primeval stand against the conquest of man, hemming and

isolating the world, beautiful, horrible, dead god
of ten thousand voices, universal incubator, universal
grave.

The *Katrina* came to the islands in the South Pacific. Islands that issued from the water like green
wreaths and seemed to float on it. The small boats
were put out and sections of the cargo were sent
to rickety wharves where white men and brown
islanders took charge of it and carried it away into
the fringe of the lush vegetation. Hugo, looking
at those islands, was moved to smile. The place
where broken men hid from civilization, where the
derelicts of the world gathered to drown their shame
in a verdant paradise that had no particular position
in the white man's scheme of the earth.

At one of the smaller islands an accident to the
engine forced the *Katrina* to linger for two weeks.
It was during those two weeks, in a rather extraor-
dinary manner, that Hugo Danner laid the first
foundation of the fortune that he accumulated in
his later life. One day, idling away a leave on shore
in the shade of a mighty tree, he saw the outriggers
of the natives file away for the oyster beds, and,
out of pure curiosity, he followed them. For a whole
day he watched the men plunge under the surface
in search of pearls. The next day he came back and
dove with one of them.

On the bizarre floor of the ocean, among the colossal fronds of its flora, the two men swam. They
were invaders from the brilliance above the surface,

shooting like fish, horizontally, through the murk and shadow, and the denizens of that world resented their coming. Great fish shot past them with malevolent eyes, and the vises of giant clams shut swiftly in attempts to trap their moving limbs. Hugo was entranced. He watched the other man as he found the oyster bed and commenced to fill his basket with frantic haste. When his lungs stung and he could bear the agony no longer, he turned and forged toward the upper air. Then they went down again.

Hugo's blood, designed to take more oxygen from the air, and his greater density fitted him naturally for the work. The pressure did not make him suffer and the few moments granted to the divers beneath the forbidding element stretched to a longer time for him.

On the second day of diving he went alone. His amateur attempt had been surprisingly fruitful. Standing erect in the immense solitude, he searched the hills and valleys. At length, finding a promising cluster of shellfish, he began to examine them one by one, pulling them loose, feeling in their pulpy interior for the precious jewels. He occupied himself determinedly while the *Katrina* was waiting in Apia, and at the end of the stay he had collected more than sixty pearls of great value and two hundred of moderate worth.

It was, he thought, typical of himself. He had decided to make a fortune of some sort after the first bitter rage over his debacle at Webster had abated in his heart. He realized that without wealth his position in the world would be more difficult and more futile than his fates had decreed. Poverty, at least, he was not forced to bear. He could wrest fortune from nature by his might. That he had begun that task by diving for pearls fitted into his scheme. It was such a method as no other man would have considered and its achievement robbed no one while it enriched him.

When the *Katrina* turned her prow westward again, Hugo worked with his shipmates in a mood that had undergone considerable change. There was no more despair in him, little of the taciturnity that had marked his earliest days at sea, none of the hatred of mankind. He had buried that slowly and carefully in a dull year of work ashore and a month of toil on the heaving deck of the ship. For six months he had kept himself alive in a manner that he could scarcely remember. Driving a truck. Working on a farm. Digging in a road. His mind a bitter blank, his valiant dreams all dead.

One day he had saved a man's life. The reaction to that was small, but it was definite. The strength that could slay was also a strength that could succour. He had repeated the act some time later. He felt it was a kind of atonement. After that, he sought deliberately to go where he might be of assistance. In the city, again, in September, when a fire engine clanged and whooped through the streets, he followed and carried a woman from a blazing roof as if by a miracle. Then the seaman. He had counted four rescues by that time. Perhaps his self-condemnation for the boy who had fallen on the field at Webster could be stifled eventually. Human life seemed very precious to Hugo then.

He sold his pearls when the ship touched at large cities—a handful here and a dozen there, bargaining carefully and forwarding the profit to a bank in New York. He might have continued that voyage, which was a voyage commenced half in new recognition of his old wish to see and know the world and half in the quest of forgetfulness; but a slip and shifts in the history of the world put an abrupt end to it. When the *Katrina* rounded the Bec d'Aiglon and steamed into the blue and cocoa harbour of Marseilles, Hugo heard that war had been declared by Germany, Austria, France, Russia, England. . . .

XI

In a day the last veil of mist that had shrouded his feelings and thoughts, making them numb and sterile, vanished; in a day Hugo found himself—or believed that he had; in a day his life changed and flung itself on the course which, in a measure, destined its fixation. He never forgot that day.

It began in the early morning when the anchor of the freighter thundered into the harbour water. The crew was not given shore leave until noon. Then the mysterious silence of the captain and the change in the ship's course was explained. Through the third officer he sent a message to the seamen. War had been declared. The seaways were unsafe. The *Katrina* would remain indefinitely at Marseilles. The men could go ashore. They would report on the following day.

The first announcement of the word sent Hugo's blood racing. War! What war? With whom? Why? Was America in it, or interested in it? He stepped ashore and hurried into the city. The populace was in feverish excitement. Soldiers were everywhere, as if they had sprung up magically like the seed of the dragon. Hugo walked through street after street in the furious heat. He bought a paper and read the French accounts of mobilizations, of a battle impending. He looked everywhere for some one who could tell him. Twice he approached the American Consulate, but it was jammed with frantic and frightened people who were trying only to get away. Hugo's ambition, growing in him like a fire, was in the opposite direction. War! And he was Hugo Danner!

He sat at a café toward the middle of the afternoon. He was so excited by the contagion in his veins that he scarcely thrilled at the first use of his new and half-mastered tongue. The *garçon* hurried to his table.

"*De la bière,*" Hugo said.

The waiter asked a question which Hugo could not understand, so he repeated his order in the universal language of measurement of a large glass by his hands. The waiter nodded. Hugo took his beer and stared out at the people. They hurried along the sidewalk, brushing the table at which he sat. They called to each other, laughed, cried sometimes, and shook hands over and over. "*La guerre*" was on every tongue. Old men gestured the directions of battles. Young men, a little more serious perhaps, and often very drunk, were rushing into uniform as order followed order for mobilization. And there were girls, thousands of them, walking with the young men.

Hugo wanted to be in it. He was startled by the impact of that desire. All the ferocity of him, all the unleashed wish to rend and kill, was blazing in his soul. But it was a subtle conflagration, which urged him in terms of duty, in words that spoke of the war as his one perfect opportunity to put himself to a use worthy of his gift. A war. In a war what would hold him, what would be superior to him, who could resist him? He swallowed glass after glass of the brackish beer, quenching a mighty thirst and firing a mightier ambition. He saw himself charging into battle, fighting till his ammunition was gone, till his bayonet broke; and then turning like a Titan and doing monster deeds with bare hands. And teeth.

Bands played and feet marched. His blood rose to a boiling-point. A Frenchman flung himself at Hugo's table. "And you—why aren't you a soldier?"

"I will be," Hugo replied.

"Bravo! We shall revenge ourselves." The man gulped a glass of wine, slapped Hugo's shoulder, and was gone. Then a girl talked to Hugo. Then another man.

Hugo dwelt on the politics of the war and its sociology only in the most perfunctory manner. It was time the imperialistic ambitions of the Central Powers were ended. A war was inevitable for that purpose. France and England had been attacked. They were defending themselves. He would assist them. Even the problem of citizenship and the tangle of red tape his enlistment might involve did not impress him. He could see the field of battle and hear the roar of guns, a picture conjured up by his knowledge of the old wars. What a soldier he would be!

While his mind was still leaping and throbbing and his head was whirling, darkness descended. He would give away his life, do his duty and a hundred times more than his duty. Here was the thing that was intended for him, the weapon forged for his hand, the task designed for his undertaking. War. In war he could bring to a full fruition the majesty of his strength. No need to fear it there, no need to be ashamed of it. He felt himself almost the Messiah of war, the man created at the precise instant he was required. His call to serve was sounding in his ears. And the bands played.

The chaos did not diminish at night, but, rather, it increased. He went with milling crowds to a bulletin board. The Germans had commenced to move. They had entered Belgium in violation of treaties long held sacred. Belgium was resisting and Liége was shaking at the devastation of the great howitzers. A terrible crime. Hugo shook with the rage of the crowd. The first outrages and violations, highly magnified, were reported. The blond beast would have to be broken.

"God damn," a voice drawled at Hugo's side. He

turned. A tall, lean man stood there, a man who was unquestionably American. Hugo spoke in instant excitement.

"There sure is hell to pay."

The man turned his head and saw Hugo. He stared at him rather superciliously, at his slightly seedy clothes and his strong, unusual face. "American?"

"Yeah."

"Let's have a drink."

They separated themselves from the mob and went to a crowded café. The man sat down and Hugo took a chair at his side. "As you put it," the man said, "there is hell to pay. Let's drink on the payment."

Hugo felt in him a certain aloofness, a detachment that checked his desire to throw himself into flamboyant conversation. "My name's Danner," he said.

"Mine's Shayne, Thomas Mathew Shayne. I'm from New York."

"So am I, in a way. I was on a ship that was stranded here by the war. At loose ends now."

Shayne nodded. He was not particularly friendly for a person who had met a countryman in a strange city. Hugo did not realize that Shayne had been besieged all day by distant acquaintances and total strangers for assistance in leaving France, or that he expected a request for money from Hugo momentarily. And Shayne did not seem particularly wrought up by the condition of war. They lifted their glasses and drank. Hugo lost a little of his ardour.

"Nice mess."

"Time, though. Time the Germans got their answer."

Shayne's haughty eyebrows lifted. His wide, thin mouth smiled. "Perhaps. I just came from Germany. Seemed like a nice, peaceful country three weeks ago."

"Oh." Hugo wondered if there were many pro-German Americans. His companion answered the thought.

"Not that I don't believe the Germans are wrong. But war is such—such a damn fool thing."

"Well, it can't be helped."

"No, it can't. We're all going to go out and get killed, though."

"We?"

"Sure. America will get in it. That's part of the game. America is more dangerous to Germany than France—or England, for that matter."

"That's a rather cold-blooded viewpoint."

Shayne nodded. "I've been raised on it. *Garçon, l'addition, s'il vous plaît.*" He reached for his pocketbook simultaneously with Hugo. "I'm sorry you're stranded," he said, "and if a hundred francs will help, I'll be glad to let you have it. I can't do more."

Hugo's jaw dropped. He laughed a little. "Good lord, man, I said my ship was stuck. Not me. And these drinks are mine." He reached into his pocket and withdrew a huge roll of American bills and a packet of French notes.

Shayne hesitated. His calmness was not severely shaken, however. "I'm sorry, old man. You see, all day I've been fighting off starving and startled Americans and I thought you were one. I apologize for my mistake." He looked at Hugo with more interest. "As a matter of fact, I'm a little skittish about patriotism. And about war. Of course, I'm going to be in it. The first entertaining thing that has happened in a dog's age. But I'm a conscientious objector on principles. I rather thought I'd enlist in the Foreign Legion tomorrow."

He was an unfamiliar type to Hugo. He represented the American who had been educated at home and abroad, who had acquired a wide horizon for his views, who was bored with the routine of his existence. His clothes were elegant and impeccable. His face was very nearly inscrutable. Although he was only a few years older than Hugo, he made the latter feel youthful.

They had a brace of drinks, two more and two more. All about them was bedlam, as if the emotions of man had suddenly been let loose to sweep him off his feet. Grief, joy, rage, lust, fear were all obviously there in almost equal proportions.

Shayne extended his hand. "They have something to fight for, at least. Something besides money and glory. A grudge. I wonder what it is that makes me want to get in? I do."

"So do I."

Shayne shook his head. "I wouldn't if I were you. Still, you will probably be compelled to in a while." He looked at his watch. "Do you care to take dinner with me? I had an engagement with an aunt who is on the verge of apoplexy because two of the Boston Shaynes are in Munich. It scarcely seems appropriate at the moment. I detest her, anyway. What do you say?"

"I'd like to have dinner with you."

They walked down the Cannebière. At a restaurant on the east side near the foot of the thoroughfare they found a table in the corner. A pair of waiters hastened to take their order. The place was riotous with voices and the musical sounds of dining. On a special table was a great demijohn of 1870 cognac, which was fast being drained by the guests. Shayne consulted with his companion and then ordered in fluent French. The meal that was brought approached a perfection of service and a superiority of cooking that Hugo had never experienced. And always the babble, the blare of bands, the swelling and fading persistence of the stringed orchestra, the stream of purple Châteauneuf du Pape and its flinty taste, the glitter of the lights and the bright colours on the mosaics that represented the principal cities of Europe. It was a splendid meal.

"I'm afraid I'll have to ask your name again," Shayne said.

"Danner. Hugo Danner."

"Good God! Not the football player?"

"I did play football—some time ago."

"I saw you against Cornell—when was it?—two years ago. You were magnificent. How does it happen that—"

"That I'm here?" Hugo looked directly into Shayne's eyes.

"Well—I have no intention of prying into your affairs."

"Then I'll tell you. Why not?" Hugo drank his wine. "I killed a man—in the game—and quit. Beat it."

Shayne accepted the statement calmly. "That's tough. I can understand your desire to get out from under. Things like that are bad when you're young."

"What else could I have done?"

"Nothing. What are you going to do? Rather, what were you going to do?"

"I don't know," Hugo answered slowly. "What do you do? What do people generally do?" He felt the question was drunken, but Shayne accepted it at its face value.

"I'm one of those people who have too much money to be able to do anything I really care about, most of the time. The family keeps me in sight and control. But I'm going to cut away to-morrow."

"In the Foreign Legion? I'll go with you."

"Splendid!" They shook hands across the table.

Three hours later found them at another café. They had been walking part of the time in the throngs on the street. For a while they had stood outside a newspaper office watching the bulletins. They were quite drunk.

"Old man," Shayne said, "I'm mighty glad I found you."

"Me, too, old egg. Where do we go next?"

"I don't know. What's your favourite vice? We can locate it in Marseilles."

Hugo frowned. "Well, vice is so limited in its scope."

His companion chuckled. "Isn't it? I've always said vice was narrow. The next time I see Aunt Emma I'm going to say: 'Emma, vice is becoming too narrow in its scope.' She'll be furious and it will bring her to an early demise and I'll inherit a lot more money, and that will be the real tragedy. She's a useless old fool, Aunt Emma. Never did a valuable thing in her life. Goes in for charity—just like we go in for golf and what-not. Oh, well, to hell with Aunt Emma."

Hugo banged his glass on the table. *"Garçon! Encore deux whiskey à l'eau* and to hell with Aunt Emma."

"Like to play roulette?"

"Like to try."

They climbed into a taxi. Shayne gave an address and they were driven to another quarter of the town. In a room packed with people in evening clothes they played for an hour. Several people spoke to Shayne and he introduced Hugo to them. Shayne won and Hugo lost. They went out into the night. The streets were quieter in that part of town. Two girls accosted them.

"That gives me an idea," Shayne said. "Let's find a phone. Maybe we can get Marcelle and Claudine."

Marcelle and Claudine met them at the door of the old house. Their arms were laden with champagne bottles. The interior of the dwelling belied its cold, grey, ancient stones. Hugo did not remember much of what followed that evening. Short, unrelated fragments stuck in his mind—Shayne chasing the white form of Marcelle up and down the stairs; himself in a huge bath-tub washing a back in front of him, his surprise when he saw daylight through the wooden shutters of the house.

Someone was shaking him. "Come on, soldier. The leave's up."

He opened his eyes and collected his thoughts. He grinned at Shayne. "All right." But if I had to defend myself right now—I'd fail against a good strong mouse."

"We'll fix that. Hey! Marcelle! Got any Fernet-Branca?"

The girl came with two large glasses of the pick-me-up. Hugo swallowed the bitter brown fluid and shuddered. Claudine awoke. *"Chéri!"* she sighed, and kissed him.

They sat on the edge of the bed. "Boy!" Hugo said. "What a binge!"

"You like eet?" Claudine murmured.

He took her hand. "Loved it, darling. And now we're going to war."

"Ah!" she said, and, at the door: *"Bonne chance!"*

Shayne left Hugo, after agreeing on a time and place for their meeting in the afternoon. The hours passed slowly. Hugo took another drink, and then, exerting his judgment and will, he refrained from taking more. At noon he partook of a light meal. He thought, or imagined, that the ecstasy of the day before was showing some signs of decline. It occurred to him that the people might be very sober and quiet before the war was a thing to be written into the history of France.

The sun was shining. He found a place in the shade where he could avoid it. He ordered a glass of beer, tasted it, and forgot to finish it. The elation of his first hours had passed. But the thing within him that had caused it was by no means dead. As he sat there, his muscles tensed with the picturization of what was soon to be. He saw the grim shadows of the enemy. He felt the hot splash of blood. For one suspended second he was ashamed of himself, and then he stamped out that shame as being something very much akin to cowardice.

He wondered why Shayne was joining the Legion and what sort of person he was underneath his rather haughty exterior. A man of character, evidently, and one who was weary of the world to which he had been privileged. Hugo's reverie veered to his mother and father. He tried to imagine what they would think of his enlistment, of him in the war; and even what they thought of him from the scant and scattered information he had supplied. He was sure that he would justify himself. He felt purged and free and noble. His strength was a thing of wreck and ruin, given to the world at a time when wreck and ruin were needed to set it right. It was odd that such a product should emerge from the dusty brain of a college professor in a Bible-ridden town.

Hugo had not possessed a religion for a long time. Now, wondering on another tangent if the war might not bring about his end, he thought about it. He realized that he would hate himself for murmuring a prayer or asking protection. He was gamer than the Cross-obsessed weaklings who were not wise enough to look life in the face and not brave enough to draw the true conclusions from what they saw. True conclusions? He meditated. What did it matter—agnosticism, atheism, pantheism—anything but the savage and anthropomorphic twaddle that had been doled out since the Israelites singled out Jehovah from among their many gods. He would not commit himself. He would go back with his death to the place where he had been before he was born and feel no more regret than he had in that oblivious past. Meanwhile he would fight! He moved restively and waited for Shayne with growing impatience.

Until that chaotic and gorgeous hour he had lived for nothing, proved nothing, accomplished nothing.

Society was no better in any way because he had lived. He excepted the lives he had saved, the few favours he had done. That was nothing in proportion to his powers. He was his own measure, and by his own efforts would he satisfy himself. War! He flexed his arms. War. His black eyes burned with a formidable light.

Then Shayne came. Walking with long strides. A ghostly smile on his lips. A darkness in his usually pale-blue eyes. Hugo liked him. They said a few words and walked toward the recruiting-tent. A *poilu* in steely blue looked at them and saw that they were good. He proffered papers. They signed. That night they marched for the first time. A week later they were sweating and swearing over the French manual of arms. Hugo had offered his services to the commanding officer at the camp and been summarily denied an audience or a chance to exhibit his abilities. When they reached the lines—that would be time enough. Well, he could wait until those lines were reached.

XII

JUST AS the eastern horizon became light with something more steady than the flare of the guns, the command came. Hugo bit his lip till it bled darkly. He would show them—now. They might command him to wait—he could restrain himself no longer. The men had been standing there tense and calm, their needle-like bayonets pointing straight up. *"En avant!"*

His heart gave a tremendous surge. It made his hands falter as he reached for the ladder rung. "Here we go, Hugo."

"Luck, Tom."

He saw Shayne go over. He followed slowly. He looked at no man's land. They had come up in the night and he had never seen it. The scene of holocaust resembled nothing more than the municipal ash dump at Indian Creek. It startled him. The grey earth in irregular heaps, the litter of metal and equipment. He realized that he was walking forward with the other men. The ground under his feet was mushy, like ashes. Then he saw part of a human body. It changed his thoughts.

The man on Hugo's right emitted a noise like a squeak and jumped up in the air. He had been hit. Out of the corner of his eye Hugo saw him fall, get up quickly, and fall again very slowly. His foot kicked after he lay down. The rumbling in the sky grew louder and blotted out all other sound.

They walked on and on. It was like some eternal journey through the dun, vacant realms of Hades. Not much light, one single sound, and ghostly companions who faced always forward. The air in front of him was suddenly dyed orange and he felt the concussion of a shell. His ears rang. He was still walking. He walked what he thought was a number of miles.

His great strength seemed to have left him, and in its place was a complete enervation. With a deliberate effort he tested himself, kicking his foot into the earth. It sank out of sight. He squared his shoulders. A man came near him, yelling something. It was Shayne. Hugo shook his head. Then he heard the voice, a feeble shrill note. "Soon be there."

"Yeah?"

"Over that hill."

Shayne turned away and became part of the ghost escort of Hugo and his peculiarly lucid thoughts. He believed that he was more conscious of himself and things then than ever before in his life. But he did not notice one-tenth of the expression and action about himself. The top of the rise was near. He saw an officer silhouetted against it for an instant. The officer moved down the other side. He could see over the rise, then.

Across the grey ashes was a long hole. In front of it a maze of wire. In it—mushrooms. German helmets. Hugo gaped at them. All that training, all that restraint, had been expended for this. They were small and without meaning. He felt a sharp sting above his collar bone. He looked there. A row of little holes had appeared in his shirt.

"Good God," he whispered, "a machine gun."

But there was no blood. He sat down. He presumed, as a casualty, he was justified in sitting down. He opened his shirt by ripping it down. On his dark-tanned skin there were four red marks. The bullets had not penetrated him. Too tough! He stared numbly at the walking men. They had passed him. The magnitude of his realization held him fixed for a full minute. He was invulnerable! He should have known it—otherwise he would have torn himself apart by his own strength. Suddenly he roared and leaped to his feet. He snatched his rifle, cracking the stock in his fervour. He vaulted toward the helmets in the trench.

He dropped from the parapet and was confronted by a long knife on a gun. His lips parted, his eyes shut to slits, he drew back his own weapon. There was an instant's pause as they faced each other— two men, both knowing that in a few seconds one would be dead. Then Hugo, out of his scarlet fury, had one glimpse of his antagonist's face and person. The glimpse was but a flash. It was finished in quick motions. He was a little man—a foot shorter than Hugo. His eyes looked out from under his helmet with a sort of pathetic earnestness. And he was worried, horribly worried, standing there with his rifle lifted and trying to remember the precise technique of what would follow even while he fought back the realization that it was hopeless. In that split second Hugo felt a human, amazing urge to tell him that it was all right, and that he ought to hold his bayonet a little higher and come forward a bit faster. The image faded back to an enemy. Hugo acted mechanically from the rituals of drill. His own knife flashed. He saw the man's clothes part smoothly from his bowels, where the point had been inserted, up to the gray-green collar. The seam reddened, gushed blood, and a length of intestine slipped out of it. The man's eyes looked at Hugo. He shook his head twice. The look became far-away. He fell forward.

Hugo stepped over him. He was trembling and nauseated. A more formidable man approached warily. The bellow of battle returned to Hugo's ears. He pushed back the threatening rifle easily and caught the neck in one hand, crushing it to a wet, sticky handful. So he walked through the trench, a machine that killed quickly and remorselessly—a black warrior from a distant realm of the universe where the gods had bred another kind of man.

He came upon Shayne and found him engaged. Hugo stuck his opponent in the back. No thought of fair play, no object but to kill—it did not matter how. Dead Legionnaires and dead Germans mingled blood underfoot. The trench was like the floor of an *abattoir*. Someone gave him a drink. The men who remained went on across the ash dump to a second trench.

It was night. The men, almost too tired to see or move, were trying to barricade themselves against the ceaseless shell fire of the enemy. They filled bags with gory mud and lifted them on the crumbling walls. At dawn the Germans would return to do what they had done. The darkness reverberated and quivered. Hugo worked like a Trojan. His efforts had made a wide and deep hole in which machine guns were being placed. Shayne fell at his feet. Hugo lifted him up. The captain nodded. "Give him a drink."

Someone brought liquor, and Hugo poured it between Shayne's teeth. "Huh!" Shayne said.

"Come on, boy."

"How did you like it, Danner?"

Hugo did not answer. Shayne went on, "I didn't either—much. This is no gentleman's war. Jesus! I saw a thing or two this morning. A guy walking with all his—"

"Never mind. Take another drink."

"Got anything to eat?"

"No."

"Oh, well, we can fight on empty bellies. The Germans will empty them for us anyhow."

"The hell they will."

"I'm pretty nearly all in."

"So's everyone."

They put Hugo on watch because he still seemed fresh. Those men who were not compelled to stay awake fell into the dirt and slept immediately. Toward dawn Hugo heard sounds in no man's land. He leaped over the parapet. In three jumps he found himself among the enemy. They were creeping forward. Hugo leaped back. *"Ils viennent!"*

Men who slept like death were kicked conscious. They rose and fired into the night. The surprise of the attack was destroyed. The enemy came on, engaging in the darkness with the exhausted Legionnaires. Twice Hugo went among them when inundation threatened and, using his rifle barrel as a club, laid waste on every hand. He walked through them striking and shattering. And twice he saved his salient from extermination. Day came sullenly. It began to rain. The men stood silently among their dead.

Hugo lit a cigarette. His eyes moved up and down the shambles. At intervals of two yards a man, his helmet trickling rain, his clothes filthy, his face inscrutable. Shayne was there on sagging knees. Hugo could not understand why he had not been killed.

Hugo was learning about war. He thought then

that the task which he had set for himself was not altogether to his liking. There should be other and more important things for him to do. He did not like to slaughter individuals. The day passed like a cycle in hell. No change in the personnel except that made by an occasional death. No food. No water. They seemed to be exiled by their countrymen in a pool of fire and famine and destruction. At dusk Hugo spoke to the captain.

"We cannot last another night without water, food," he said.

"We shall die here, then."

"I should like, sir, to volunteer to go back and bring food."

"We need ammunition more."

"Ammunition, then."

"One man could not bring enough to assist— much."

"I can."

"You are valuable here. With your club and your charmed life, you have already saved this remnant of good soldiers."

"I will return in less than an hour."

"Good luck, then."

Where there had been a man, there was nothing. The captain blinked his eyes and stared at the place. He swore softly in French and plunged into his dugout at the sound of ripping in the sky.

A half hour passed. The steady, nerve-racking bombardment continued at an unvaried pace. Then there was a heavy thud like that of a shell landing and not exploding. The captain looked. A great bundle, tied together by ropes, had descended into the trench. A man emerged from beneath it. The captain passed his hand over his eyes. Here was ammunition for the rifles and the machine guns in plenty. Here was food. Here were four huge tins of water, one of them leaking where a shell fragment had pierced it. Here was a crate of canned meat and a sack of onions and a stack of bread loaves. Hugo broke the ropes. His chest rose and fell rapidly. He was sweating. The bundle he had carried weighed more than a ton—and he had been running very swiftly.

The captain looked again. A case of cognac. Hugo was carrying things into the dug-out. "Where?" the captain asked.

Hugo smiled and named a town thirty kilometres behind the lines. A town where citizens and soldiers together were even then in frenzied discussion over the giant who had fallen upon their stores and supplies and taken them, running off like a locomotive, in a hail of bullets that did no harm to him.

"And how?" the captain asked.

"I am strong."

The captain shrugged and turned his head away. His men were eating the food, and drinking water mixed with brandy, and stuffing their pouches with ammunition. The machine gunners were laughing. They would not be forced to spare the precious belts when the Germans came in the morning. Hugo sat among them, dining his tremendous appetite.

Three days went by. Every day, twice, five times, they were attacked. But no offence seemed capable of driving that demoniac cluster of men from their position. A demon, so the enemy whispered, came out and fought for them. On the third day the enemy retreated along four kilometres of front, and the French moved up to reclaim many, many acres of their beloved soil. The Legionnaires were relieved and another episode was added to their valiant history.

Hugo slept for twenty hours in the wooden barracks. After that he was wakened by the captain's orderly and summoned to his quarters. The captain smiled when he saluted. "My friend," he said, "I wish to thank you in behalf of my country for your labour. I have recommended you for the Croix de Guerre."

Hugo took his outstretched hand. "I am pleased that I have helped."

"And now," the captain continued, "you will tell me how you executed that so unusual coup."

Hugo hesitated. It was the opportunity he had sought, the chance that might lead to a special commission whereby he could wreak the vengeance of his muscles on the enemy. But he was careful, because he did not feel secure in trusting the captain with too much of his secret. Even in a war it was too terrible. They would mistrust him, or they would attempt to send him to their biologists. And he wanted to accomplish his mission under their permission and with their co-operation. It would be more valuable then and of greater magnitude. So he smiled and said: "Have you ever heard of Colorado?"

"No, I have not heard. It is a place?"

"A place in America. A place that has scarcely been explored. I was born there. And all the men of Colorado are born as I was born and are like me. We are very strong. We are great fighters. We cannot be wounded except by the largest shells. I took that package by force and I carried it to you on my back, running swiftly."

The captain appeared politely interested. He thumbed a dispatch. He stared at Hugo. "If that is the truth, you shall show me."

"It is the truth—and I shall show you."

Hugo looked around. Finally he walked over to the sentry at the flap of the tent and took his rifle. The man squealed in protest. Hugo lifted him off the floor by the collar, shook him, and set him down.

The man shouted in dismay and then was silent at a word from the captain. Hugo weighed the gun in his hands while they watched and then slowly bent the barrel double. Next he tore it from its stock. Then he grasped the parallel steel ends and broke them apart with a swift wrench. The captain half rose, his eyes bulged, he knocked over his inkwell. His hand tugged at his moustache and waved spasmodically.

"You see?" Hugo said.

The captain went to staff meeting that afternoon very thoughtful. He understood the difficulty of exhibiting his soldier's prowess under circumstances that would assure the proper commission. He even considered remaining silent about Hugo. With such a man in his company it would soon be illustrious along the whole broad front. But the chance came. When the meeting was finished and the officers relaxed over their wine, a colonel brought up the subject of the merits of various breeds of men as soldiers.

"I think," he said, "that the Prussians are undoubtedly our most dangerous foe. On our own side we have—"

"Begging the colonel's pardon," the captain said, "there is a species of fighter unknown, or almost unknown, in this part of the world, who excels by far all others."

"And who may they be?" the colonel asked stiffly.

"Have you ever heard of the Colorados?"

"No," the colonel said.

Another officer meditated. "They are redskins, American Indians, are they not?"

The captain shrugged. "I do not know. I know only that they are superior to all other soldiers."

"And in what way?"

The captain's eyes flickered. "I have one Colorado

in my troops. I will tell you what he did in five days near the town of Barsine." The officers listened. When the captain finished, the colonel patted his shoulder. "That is a very amusing fabrication. Very. With a thousand such men, the war would be ended in a week. Captain Crouan, I fear you have been overgenerous in pouring the wine."

The captain rose, saluted. "With your permission, I shall cause my Colorado to be brought and you shall see."

The other men laughed. "Bring him, by all means."

The captain dispatched an orderly. A few minutes later, Hugo was announced at headquarters. The captain introduced him. "Here, messieurs, is a Colorado. What will you have him do?"

The colonel, who had expected the soldier to be both embarrassed and made ridiculous, was impressed by Hugo's calm demeanour. "You are strong?" he said with a faint irony.

"Exceedingly."

"He is not humble, at least, gentlemen." Laughter. The colonel fixed Hugo with his eye. "Then, my good fellow, if you are so strong, if you can run so swiftly and carry such burdens, bring us one of our beautiful seventy-fives from the artillery."

"With your written order, if you please."

The colonel started, wrote the order laughingly, and gave it to Hugo. He left the room.

"It is a good joke," the colonel said. "But I fear it is harsh on the private."

The captain shrugged. Wine was poured. In a few minutes they heard heavy footsteps outside the tent. "He is here!" the captain cried. The officers rushed forward. Hugo stood outside the tent with the cannon they had requested lifted over his head in one hand. With that same hand clasped on the breach, he set it down. The colonel paled and gulped. "Name of the mother of God! He has brought it."

Hugo nodded. "It was as nothing, my colonel. Now I will show you what we men from Colorado can do. Watch."

They eyed him. There was a grating sound beneath his feet. Those who were quickest of vision saw his body catapult through the air high over their heads. It landed, bounced prodigiously, vanished.

Captain Crouan coughed and swallowed. He faced his superiors, trying to seem nonchalant. "That, gentlemen, is the sort of thing the Colorados do—for sport."

The colonel recovered first. "It is not human. Gentlemen, we have been in the presence of the devil himself."

"Or the Good Lord."

The captain shook his head. "He is a man, I tell you. In Colorado all the men are like that. He told me so himself. When he first enlisted, he came to me and asked for a special commission to go to

Berlin and smash the Reich—to bring back the Kaiser himself. I thought he was mad. I made him peel potatoes. He did not say any more foolish things. He was a good soldier. Then the battle came and I saw him, not believing I saw him, standing on the parapet and wielding his rifle like the lightning, killing I do not know how many men. Hundreds certainly, perhaps thousands. Ah, it is as I said, the Colorados are the finest soldiers on earth. They are more than men."

"He comes!"

Hugo burst from the sky, moving like a hawk. He came from the direction of the lines, many miles away. There was a bundle slung across his shoulder. There were holes in his uniform. He landed heavily among the officers and set down his burden. It was a German. He dropped to the ground.

"Water for him," Hugo panted. "He has fainted. I snatched him from his outpost in a trench."

XIII

AT BLAISENCOURT it was spring again. The war was nearly a year old. Blaisencourt was now a street of houses' ghosts, of rubble and dirt, populated by soldiers. A little new grass sprouted peevishly here and there; an occasional house retained enough of its original shape to harbour an industry. Captain Crouan, his arm in a sling, was looking over a heap of débris with the aid of field glasses.

"I see him," he said, pointing to a place on the boiling field where an apparent lump of soil had detached itself.

"He rises! He goes on! He takes one of his mighty leaps! Ah, God, if I only had a company of such men!"

His aide, squatted near by, muttered something under his breath. The captain spoke again. "He is very near their infernal little gun now. He has taken his rope. Ahaaaa! He spins it in the air. It falls. They are astonished. They rise up in the trench. Quick, Phèdre! Give me a rifle." The rifle barked sharply four, five times. Its bullet found a mark. Then another. "Ahaaa! Two of them! And M. Danner now has his rope on that pig's breath. It comes up. See! He has taken it under his arm! They are shooting their machine guns. He drops into a shell hole. He has been hit, but he is laughing at them. He leaps. Look out, Phèdre!"

Hugo landed behind the débris with a small German trench mortar in his arms. He set it on the floor. The captain opened his mouth, and Hugo waved to him to be silent. Deliberately, Hugo looked over the rickety parapet of loose stones. He elevated the muzzle of the gun and drew back the lanyard. The captain, grinning, watched through his glasses. The gun roared.

Its shell exploded presently on the brow of the enemy trench, tossing up a column of smoke and earth. "I should have brought some ammunition with me," Hugo said.

Captain Crouan stared at the little gun. "Pig," he said. "Son of a pig! Five of my men are in your little belly! Bah!" He kicked it.

Summer in Aix-au-Dixvaches. A tall Englishman addressing Captain Crouan. His voice was irritated by the heat. "Is it true that you French have an Indian scout here who can bash in those Minenwerfers?"

"*Pardon, mon colonel, mais je ne comprends pas l'anglais.*"

He began again in bad French. Captain Crouan smiled. "Ah? You are troubled there on your sector? You wish to borrow our astonishing soldier? It will be a pleasure, I assure you."

Hot calm night. The sky pin-pricked with stars, the air redolent with the mushy flavour of dead meat. So strong it left a taste in the mouth. So strong that food and water tasted like faintly chlorinated putrescence. Hugo, his blue uniform darker with perspiration, tramped through the blackness to a dugout. Fifteen minutes in candlelight with a man who spoke English in an odd manner.

"They've been raisin' bloody hell with us from a point about there." The tap of a pencil. "We've got little enough confidence in you, God knows—"

"Thank you."

"Don't be huffy. We're obliged to your captain for the loan of you. But we've lost too many trying to take the place ourselves not to be fed up with it. I suppose you'll want a raiding party?"

"No, thanks."

"But, cripes, you can't make it there alone."

"I can do it." Hugo smiled. "And you've lost so many of your own men—"

"Very well."

Otto Meyer pushed his helmet back on his sandy-haired head and gasped in the feverish air. A non-commissioned officer passing behind him shoved the helmet over his eyes with a muttered word of caution. Otto shrugged. Half a dozen men lounged near by. Beside and above them were the muzzles of four squat guns and the irregular silhouette of a heap of ammunition. Two of the men rolled onto their backs and panted. "I wish," one said in a soft voice, "that I was back in the Hofbrau at Munich with a tall stein of beer, with that fat *Fräulein* that kissed me in the Potsdam station last September sitting at my side and the orchestra playing—"

Otto flung a clod of dank earth at the speaker. There were chuckles from the shadows that sucked in and exhaled the rancid air. Outside the pit in which they lay, there was a gentle thud.

Otto scrambled into a sitting posture. "What is that?"

"Nothing. Even these damned English aren't low enough to fight us in this weather."

"You can never tell. At night, in the first battle of—listen!"

The thud was repeated, much closer. It was an ominous sound, like the drop of a sack of earth from a great height. Otto picked up a gun. He was a man who perspired freely, and now, in that single minute, his face trickled. He pointed the gun into the air and pulled the trigger. It kicked back and jarred his arm. In the glaring light that followed, six men peered through the spider-web of the wire. They saw nothing.

"You see?"

Their eyes smarted with the light and dark, so

swiftly exchanged. Came a thud in their midst. A great thud that spattered the dirt in all directions. "Something has fallen." "A shell!" "It's a dud!"

The men rose and tried to run. Otto had regained his vision and saw the object that had descended. A package of yellow sticks tied to a great mass of iron—wired to it. Instead of running, he grasped it. His strength was not enough to lift it. Then, for one short eternity, he saw a sizzling spark move toward the sticks. He clutched at it. "Help! The guns must be saved. A bomb!" He knew his arms surrounded death. "I cannot—"

His feeble voice was blown to the four winds at that instant. A terrible explosion burst from him, shattering the escaping men, blasting the howitzers into fragments, enlarging the pit to enormous dimensions. Both fronts clattered with machine-gun fire. Flares lit the terrain. Hugo, running as if with seven-league boots, was thrown on his face by the concussion.

Winter. Mud. A light fall of snow that was split into festers by the guns before it could anneal the ancient sores. Hugo shivered and stared into no man's land, whence a groan had issued for twenty hours, audible occasionally over the tumult of the artillery. He saw German eyes turned mutely on the same heap of rags that moved pitifully over the snow, leaving a red wake, dragging a bloody thing behind. It rose and fell, moving parallel to the two trenches. Many machine-gun bullets had either missed it or increased its crimson torment. Hugo went out and killed the heap of rags, with a revolver that cracked until the groans stopped in a low moan. Breaths on both sides were bated. The rags had been gray-green. A shout of low, rumbling praise came from the silent enemy trenches. Hugo looked over there for a moment and smiled. He looked down at the thing and vomited. The guns began again.

Another winter. Time had become stagnant. All about it was a pool of mud and suppuration, and shot through it was the sound of guns and the scent of women, the taste of wine and the touch of cold flesh. Somewhere, he could not remember distinctly where, Hugo had a clean uniform, a portfolio of papers, a jewel-case of medals. He was a great man —a man feared. The Colorado in the Foreign Legion. Men would talk about what they had seen him accomplish all through the next fifty years—at watering places in the Sahara, at the crackling fires of country-house parties in Shropshire, on the shores of the South Seas, on the moon, maybe. Old men, at the last, would clear the phlegm from their skinny throats and begin: "When I was a-fightin' with the Legion in my youngest days, there was a fellow in our company that came from some place in wild America that I disrecollect." And younger, more sanguine men would listen and shake their heads and wish that there was a war for them to fight.

Hugo was not satisfied with that. Still, he could see no decent exit and contrive no better use for himself. He clung frantically to the ideals he had taken with him and to the splendid purpose with which he had emblazoned his mad lust to enlist. Marseilles and the sentiment it had inspired seemed very far away. He thought about it as he walked toward the front, his head bent into the gale and his helmet pitched to protect his eyes from the sting of the rain.

That night he slept with Shayne, a lieutenant now, twice wounded, thrice decorated, and, like Hugo, thinner than he had been, older, with eyes grown bleak, and seldom vehement. He resembled his lean Yankee ancestors after their exhausting campaigns of the wilderness, alive and sentient only through a sheer stubbornness that brooked neither element nor disaster. Only at rare moments did the slight strain of his French blood lift him from that grim posture. Such a moment was afforded by the arrival of Hugo.

"Great God, Hugo! We haven't seen you in a dog's age." Other soldiers smiled and brought rusty cigarettes into the dug-out where they sat and smoked.

Hugo held out his hand. "Been busy. Glad to see you."

"Yes. I know how busy you've been. Up and down the lines we hear about you. *Le Colorado*. Damn

196

funny war. You'd think you weren't human, or anywhere near human, to hear these birds. Wish you'd
tell me how you get away with it. Hasn't one nicked
you yet?"

"Not yet."

"God damn. Got me here"—he tapped his
shoulder—"and here"—his thigh.

"That's tough. I guess the sort of work I do isn't
calculated to be as risky as yours," Hugo said.

"Huh! That you can tell to Sweeny." The French-
men were still sitting politely, listening to a dialogue
they could not understand. Hugo and Shayne eyed
each other in silence. A long, penetrating silence. At
length the latter said soberly: "Still as enthusiastic
as you were that night in Marseilles?"

"Are you?"

"I didn't have much conception of what war
would be then."

"Neither did I," Hugo responded. "And I'm not
very enthusiastic any more."

"Oh, well—"

"Exactly."

"Heard from your family?"

"Sure."

"Well—"

They relapsed into silence again. By and by they
ate a meal of cold food, supplemented by rank,
steaming coffee. Then they slept. Before dawn Hugo
woke feeling like a man in the mouth of a volcano
that had commenced to erupt. The universe was

shaking. The walls of the dug-out were molting chunks of earth. The scream and burst of shells were constant. He heard Shayne's voice above the din, issuing orders in French. Their batteries were to be phoned. A protective counter-fire. A *barrage* in readiness in case of attack, which seemed imminent. Larger shells drowned the voice. Hugo rose and stood beside Shayne.

"Coming over?"

"Coming over."

A shapeless face spoke in the gloom. The voice panted. "We must get out of here, my lieutenant. They are smashing in the dug-out." A methodical scramble to the orifice. Hell was rampaging in the trench. The shells fell everywhere. Shayne shook his head. It was neither light nor dark. The incessant blinding fire did not make things visible except for fragments of time and in fantastic perspectives. Things belched and boomed and smashed the earth and whistled and howled. It was impossible to see how life could exist in that caldron, and yet men stood calmly all along the line. A few of them, here and there, were obliterated.

The red sky in the southeast became redder with the rising sun. Hugo remained close to the wall. It was no novelty for him to be under shell fire. But at such times he felt the need of a caution with which he could ordinarily dispense. If one of the steel cylinders found him, even his mighty frame might not contain itself. Even he might be rent asunder.

Shayne saw him and smiled. Twenty yards away a geyser of fire sprayed the heavens. Ten feet away a fragment of shell lashed down a pile of sand-bags. Shayne's smile widened. Hugo returned it.

Then red fury enveloped the two men. Hugo was crushed ferociously against the wall and liberated in the same second. He fell forward, his ears singing and his head dizzy. He lay there, aching. Dark red stains flowed over his face from his nose and ears. Painfully he stood up. A soldier was watching him from a distance with alarmed eyes. Hugo stepped. He found that locomotion was possible. The bedlam increased. It brought a sort of madness. He remembered Shayne. He searched in the smoking, stinking muck. He found the shoulders and part of Shayne's head. He picked them up in his hands, disregarding the butchered ends of the raw gobbet. White electricity crackled in his head.

He leaped to the parapet, shaking his fists. "God damn you dirty sons of bitches. I'll make you pay for this. You got him, got him, you bastards! I'll shove your filthy hides down the devil's throat and through his guts. Oh, Jesus!" He did not feel the frantic tugging of his fellows. He ran into that bubbling, doom-ridden chaos, waving his arms and shouting maniacal profanities. A dozen times he was knocked down. He bled slowly where fragments had battered him. He crossed over and paused on the German parapet. He was like a being of steel. Bullets sprayed him. His arms dangled and lifted. Barbed wire trailed behind him.

Down before him, shoulder to shoulder, the attacking regiments waited for the last crescendo of the bombardment. They saw him come out of the fury and smiled grimly. They knew such madness. They shot. He came on. At last they could hear his voice dimly through the tumult. Someone shouted that he was mad—to beware when he fell. Hugo jumped among them. Bayonets rose. Hugo wrenched three knives from their wielders in one wild clutch. His hands went out, snatching and squeezing. That was all. No weapons, no defence. Just—hands. Whatever they caught they crushed flat, and heads fell into those dreadful fingers, sides, legs, arms, bellies. Bayonets slid from his tawny skin, taking his clothes. By and by, except for his shoes, he was naked. His fingers had made a hundred bunches of clotted pulp and then a thousand as he walked swiftly forward in that trench. Ahead of him was a file of green; behind, a clogged row of writhing men. Scarcely did the occupants of each new traverse see him before they were smitten. The wounds he inflicted were monstrous. On he walked, his voice now stilled, his breath sucking and whistling through his teeth, his hands flailing and pinching and spurting red with every contact. No more formidable engine of desolation had been seen by man, no more titanic fury, no swifter and surer death. For thirty minutes he raged through that line. The men thinned. He had crossed the attacking front.

Then the barrage lifted. But no whistles blew. No soldiers rose. A few raised their heads and then lay down again. Hugo stopped and went back into the *abattoir*. He leaped to the parapet. The French saw him, silhouetted against the sky. The second German wave, coming slowly over a far hill, saw him and hesitated. No ragged line of advancing men. No cacophony of rifle fire. Only that strange, savage figure. A man dipped in scarlet, nude, dripping, panting. Slowly in that hiatus he wheeled. His lungs thundered to the French. "Come on, you black bastards. I've killed them all. Come on. We'll send them down to hell."

The officers looked and understood that something phenomenal had happened. No Germans were coming. A man stood above their trench. "Come, quick!" Hugo shouted. He saw that they did not understand. He stood an instant, fell into the trench; and presently a shower of German corpses flung through the air in wide arcs and landed on the very edge of the French position. Then they came, and Hugo, seeing them, went on alone to meet the second line. He might have forged on through that bloody swathe to the heart of the Empire if his vitality had been endless. But, some time in the battle, he fell unconscious on the field, and his forward-leaning comrades, pushing back the startled enemy, found him lying there.

They made a little knot around him, silent, quivering. "It is the Colorado," someone said. "His friend, Shayne—it is he who was the lieutenant just killed." They shook their heads and felt a strange fear of the unconscious man. "He is breathing." They called for stretcher-bearers. They faced the enemy again, bent over on the stocks of their rifles, surged forward.

Hugo was washed and dressed in pyjamas. His wounds had healed without the necessity of a single stitch. He was grateful for that. Otherwise the surgeons might have had a surprise which would have been difficult to allay. He sat in a wheel chair, staring across a lawn. An angular woman in an angular hat and tailored clothes was trying to engage him in conversation.

"Is it very painful, my man?"

Hugo was seeing that trench again—the pulp and blood and hate of it. "Not very."

Her tongue and saliva made a noise. "Don't tell me. I know it was. I know how you all bleed and suffer."

"Madam, it happens that my wounds were quite superficial."

"Nonsense, my boy. They wouldn't have brought you to a base hospital in that case. You can't fool me."

"I was suffering only from exhaustion."

She paused. He saw a gleam in her eye. "I suppose you don't like to talk—about things. Poor boy! But I imagine your life has been so full of horror that it would be good for you to unburden yourself. Now tell me, just what does it feel like to bayonet a man?"

Hugo trembled. He controlled his voice. "Madam," he replied, "it feels exactly like sticking your finger into a warm, steaming pile of cow-dung."

"Oh!" she gasped. And he heard her repeat it again in the corridor.

XIV

"Mr. and Mrs. Ralph Jordan Shayne," Hugo
wrote. Then he paused in thought. He began again.
"I met your son in Marseilles and was with him
most of the time until his death." He hesitated. "In
fact, he died in my arms from the effect of the same
shell which sent me to this hospital. He is buried in
Carcy cemetery, on the south side. It is for that
reason I take the liberty to address you.

"I thought that you would like to know some of
the things that he did not write to you. Your son
enlisted because he felt the war involved certain
ideals that were worthy of preservation. That he
gave his life for those ideals must be a source of
pride to you. In training he was always controlled,
kindly, unquarrelsome, comprehending. In battle he
was aggressive, brilliant, and more courageous than
any other man I have ever known.

"In October, a year ago, he was decorated for
bringing in Captain Crouan, who was severely
wounded during an attack that was repulsed. Under

heavy shell fire Tom went boldly into no man's land and carried the officer from a shell pit on his back. At the time Tom himself sustained three wounds. He was mentioned a number of times in the dispatches for his leadership of attacks and patrols. He was decorated a second time for the capture of a German field officer and three of his staff, a coup which your son executed almost single-handed.

"Following his death his company made an attack to avenge him, which wiped out the entire enemy position along a sector nearly a kilometre in width and which brought a permanent advantage to the Allied lines. That is mute testimony of his popularity among the officers and men. I know of no man more worthy of the name 'American,' no American more worthy of the words 'gentleman' and 'hero.'

"I realize the slight comfort of these things, and yet I feel bound to tell you of them, because Tom was my friend, and his death is grievous to me as well as to you.

"Yours sincerely,

"(Lieutenant) Hugo Danner"

Hugo posted the letter. When the answer came, he was once again in action, the guns chugging and rumbling, the earth shaking. The reply read:

"Dear Lieutenant Danner:

"Thank you for your letter in reference to our son. We knew that he had enlisted in some foreign service. We did not know of his death. I am having your statements checked, because, if they are true, I shall be one of the happiest persons alive, and his mother will be both happy and sad. The side of young Tom which you claim to have seen is one quite unfamiliar to us. At home he was always a waster, much of a snob, and impossible to control. It may be harsh to say such things of him now that he is dead, but I cannot recall one noble deed, one unselfish act, in his life here with us.

"That I have a dead son would not sadden me. Tom had been disinherited by us, his mother and father. But that my dead son was a hero makes me feel that at last, coming into the Shayne blood and heritage, he has atoned. And so I honour him. If the records show that all you said of him is true, I shall not only honour him in this country, but I shall come to France to pay my tribute with a full heart and a knowledge that neither he nor I lived in vain.

"Gratefully yours,

"R. J. SHAYNE"

Hugo reread the letter and stood awhile with wistful eyes. He remembered Shayne's Aunt Emma, Shayne's bitter calumniation of his family. Well, they had not understood him and he had not wanted them to understand him. Perhaps Shayne had been more content than he admitted in the mud of the trenches. The war had been a real thing to him.

Hugo thought of its insufficiencies for himself. The world was not enough for Shayne, but the war had been. Both were insufficient for Hugo Danner. He listened to the thunder in the sky tiredly.

Two months later Hugo was ordered from rest billets to the major's quarters. A middle-aged man and woman accompanied by a sleek Frenchman awaited him. The man stepped forward with dignified courtesy. "I am Tom Shayne's father. This is Mrs. Shayne."

Hugo felt a great lack of interest in them. They had come too late. It was their son who had been his friend. He almost regretted the letter. He shook hands with them. Mrs. Shayne went to an automobile. Her husband invited Hugo to a café. Over the wine he became suddenly less dignified, more human, and almost pathetic. "Tell me about him, Danner. I loved that kid once, you know."

Hugo found himself unexpectedly moved. The man was so eager, so strangely happy. He stroked his white moustache and turned away moist eyes. So Hugo told him. He talked endlessly of the trenches and the dark wet nights and the fire that stabbed through them. He invented brave sorties for his friend, tripled his accomplishments, and put gaiety and wit in his mouth. The father drank every syllable as if he was committing the whole story to memory as the text of a life's solace. At last he was crying.

"That was the Tom I knew," Hugo said softly.

"And that was the Tom I dreamed and hoped and thought he would become when he was a little shaver. Well, he did, Danner."

"A thousand times he did."

Ralph Jordan Shayne blew his nose unashamedly. He thought of his patiently waiting wife. "I've got to go, I suppose. This has been more than kind of you, Mr. Danner—Lieutenant Danner. I'm glad—more glad than I can say—that you were there. I understand from the major that you're no small shakes in this army yourself." He smiled deferentially. "I wish there was something we could do for you."

"Nothing. Thank you, Mr. Shayne."

"I'm going to give you my card. In New York—my name is not without meaning."

"It is very familiar to me. Was before I met your son."

"If you ever come to the city—I mean, when you come—you must look us up. Anything we can do—in the way of jobs, positions—" He was confused.

Hugo shook his head. "That's very kind of you, sir. But I have some means of my own and, right now, I'm not even thinking of going back to New York."

Mr. Shayne stepped into the car. "I would like to do something." Hugo realized the sincerity of that desire. He reflected.

"Nothing I can think of—"

"I'm a banker. Perhaps—if I might take the liberty—I could handle your affairs?"

Hugo smiled. "My affairs consist of one bank account in the City Loan that would seem very small to you, Mr. Shayne."

"Why, that's one of my banks. I'll arrange it. You know and I know how small the matter of money is. But I'd appreciate your turning over some of your capital to me. I would consider it a blessed opportunity to return a service, a great service with a small one, I'm afraid."

"Thanks," Hugo said.

The banker scribbled a statement, asked a question, and raised his eyebrows over the amount Hugo gave him. Then he was the father again. "We've been to the cemetery, Danner. We owe that privilege to you. It says there, in French: 'The remains of a great hero who gave his life for France.' Not America, my boy; but I think that France was a worthy cause."

When they had gone, Hugo spent a disturbed afternoon. He had not been so moved in many, many months.

Now the streets of Paris were assailed by the
colour of olive drab, the twang of Yankee accents,
the music of Broadway songs. Hugo watched the
first parade with eyes somewhat proud and not a
little sombre. Each shuffling step seemed to ask a
rhythmic question. Who would not return to Paris?
Who would return once and not again? Who would
be blind? Who would be hideous? Who would be
armless, legless, who would wear silver plates and
leather props for his declining years? Hugo wondered, and, looking into those sometimes stern and
sometimes ribald faces, he saw that they had not
yet commenced to wonder.

They did not know the hammer and shock of falling shells and the jelly and putty which men became.
They chafed and bantered and stormed every café
and cocotte impartially, recklessly. Even the Legion
had been more grim and better prepared for the
iron feet of war. They fell upon Hugo with their
atrocious French—two young men who wanted a

drink and could not make the bar-tender understand.

"Hey, *fransay*," they called to him, "*comment dire que nous voulez des choses boire?*"

Hugo smiled. "What do you birds want to drink?"

"God Almighty! Here's a Frog that speaks United States. Get the gang. What's your name, bo?"

"Danner."

"Come on an' have a flock of drinks on us. You're probably dying on French pay. You order for the gang and we'll treat." Eager, grinning American faces. "Can you get whisky in this God-forsaken dump?"

"Straight or highball?"

"That's the talk. Straight, Dan. We're in the army now."

Hugo drank with them. Only for one moment did they remember they were in the army to fight: "Say, Dan, the war really isn't as tough as they claim, is it?"

"I don't know how tough they claim it is."

"Well, you seen much fightin'?"

"Three years."

"Is it true that the Heinies—?" His hands indicated his question.

"Sometimes. Accidentally, more or less. You can't help it."

"And do them machine guns really mow 'em down?"

Hugo shrugged. "There are only four men in service now who started with my company."

"Ouch! *Garçon! Encore!* An' tell him to make it double—no, triple—Dan, old man. It may be my last." To Hugo: "Well, it's about time we got here an' took the war off your shoulders. You guys sure have had a bellyful. An' I'm goin' to get me one right here and now. Bottoms up, you guys."

Hugo was transferred to an American unit. The officers belittled the recommendations that came with him. They put him in the ranks. He served behind the lines for a week. Then his regiment moved up. As soon as the guns began to rumble, a nervous second lieutenant edged toward the demoted private. "Say, Danner, you've been in this before. Do you think it's all right to keep on along this road the way we are?"

"I'm sure I couldn't say. You're taking a chance. Plane strafing and shells."

"Well, what else are we to do? These are our orders."

"Nothing," Hugo said.

When the first shells fell among them, however, Danner forgot that his transference had cost his commission and sadly bereft Captain Crouan and his command. He forgot his repressed anger at the stupidity of American headquarters and their bland assumption of knowledge superior to that gained by three years of actual fighting. He virtually took charge of his company, ignoring the bickering of a lieutenant who swore and shouted and accomplished nothing and who was presently beheaded for his lack of caution. A month later, with troops that had some feeling of respect for the enemy—a feeling gained through close and gory association—Hugo was returned his commission.

Slowly at first, and with increasing momentum, the war was pushed up out of the trenches and the Germans retreated. The summer that filled the windows of American homes with gold stars passed. Hugo worked like a slave out beyond the front trenches, scouting, spying, destroying, salvaging, bending his heart and shoulders to a task that had long since become an acid routine. September. October. November. The end of that holocaust was very near.

Then there came a day warmer than the rest and less rainy. Hugo was riding toward the lines on a *camion*. He rode as much as possible now. He had not slept for two days. His eyes were red and twitching. He felt tired—tired as if his fatigue were the beginning of death—tired so that nothing counted or mattered—tired of killing, of hating, of suffering—tired even of an ideal that had tarnished through long weathering. The *camion* was steel and it rattled and bumped as it moved over the road. Hugo lay flat in it, trying to close his eyes.

After a time, moving between the stumps of a row of poplars, they came abreast of a regiment returning from the battle. They walked slowly and dazedly. Each individual was still amazed at being alive after the things he had witnessed. Hugo raised himself and looked at them. The same expression had often been on the faces of the French. The long line of the regiment ended. Then there was an empty place on the road, and the speed of the truck increased.

Finally it stopped with a sharp jar, and the driver shouted that he could go no farther. Hugo clambered to the ground. He estimated that the battery toward which he was travelling was a mile farther. He began to walk. There was none of the former lunge and stride in his steps. He trudged, rather, his head bent forward. A little file of men approached him, and, even at a distance, he did not need a second glance to identify them. Walking wounded.

By ones and twos they began to pass him. He paid scant attention. Their field dressings were stained with the blood that their progress cost. They cursed and muttered. Someone had given them cigarettes, and a dozen wisps of smoke rose from each group. It was not until he reached the end of the straggling line that he looked up. Then he saw one man whose arms were both under bandage walking with another whose eyes were covered and whose hand, resting on his companion's shoulder, guided his stumbling feet.

Hugo viewed them as they came on and presently heard their conversation. "Christ, it hurts," one of them said.

"The devil with hurting, boy," the blinded man answered. "So do I, for that matter. I feel like there was a hot poker in my brains."

"Want another butt?"

"No, thanks. Makes me kind of sick to drag on them. Wish I had a drink, though."

"Who doesn't?"

Hugo heard his voice. "Hey, you guys," it said. "Here's some water. And a shot of cognac, too."

The first man stopped and the blind man ran into him, bumping his head. He gasped with pain, but his lips smiled. "Damn nice of you, whoever you are."

They took the canteen and swallowed. "Go on," Hugo said, and permitted himself a small lie. "I can get more in a couple of hours." He produced his flask. "And finish off on a shot of this."

He held the containers for the armless man and handed them to the other. Their clothes were ragged and stained. Their shoes were in pieces. Sweat had soaked under the blind man's armpits and stained his tunic. As Hugo watched him swallow thirstily, he started. The chin and the hair were familiar. His mind spun. He knew the voice, although its tenor was sadly changed.

"Good God," he said involuntarily, "it's Lefty!"

Lefty stiffened. "Who are you?"

"Hugo Danner."

"Hugo Danner?" The tortured brain reflected.

"Hugo! Good old Hugo! What, in the name of
Jesus, are you doing here?"

"Same thing you are."

An odd silence fell. The man with the shattered
arms broke it. "Know this fellow?"

"Do I know him! Gee! He was at college with
me. One of my buddies. Gosh!" His hand reached
out. "Put it there, Hugo."

They shook hands. "Got it bad, Lefty?"

The bound head shook. "Not so bad. I guess—I
kind of feel that I won't be able to see much any
more. Eyes all washed out. Got mustard gas in 'em.
But I'll be all right, you know. A little thing like
that's nothing. Glad to be alive. Still have my sex
appeal, anyhow. Still got the old appetite. But—
listen—what happened to you? Why in hell did you
quit? Woodman nearly went crazy looking for you."

"Oh—" Hugo's thoughts went back a distance
that seemed infinite, into another epoch and another
world—"oh, I just couldn't stick it. Say, you guys,
wait a minute." He turned. His *camion*-driver was
lingering in the distance. "Wait here." He rushed
back. The armless man whistled.

"God in heaven! Your friend there can sure cover
the ground."

"Yeah," Lefty said absently. "He always could."

In a moment Hugo returned. "I got it all fixed
up for you two to ride in. No limousine, but it'll
carry you."

Lefty's lip trembled. "Gee—Jesus Christ—" he

amended stubbornly; "that's decent. I don't feel so
dusty today. Damn it, if I had any eyes, I guess I'd
cry. Must be the cognac."

"Nothing at all, Lefty old kid. Here, I'll give you
a hand." He took Lefty's arm over his shoulder, en-
circled him with his own, and carried him rapidly
over the broken road.

"Still got the old fight," Lefty murmured as he
felt himself rushed forward.

"Still."

"Been in this mess long?"

"Since the beginning."

"I should have thought of that. I often wondered
what became of you. Iris used to wonder, too."

"How is she?"

"All right."

They reached the truck. Lefty sat down on the
metal bottom with a sigh. "Thanks, old bean. I was
just about *kaputt*. Tough going, this war. I saw my
first shell fall yesterday. Never saw a single German
at all. One of those squdgy things came across, and
before I knew it, there was onion in my eye for a
goal." The truck motor roared. The armless man
came alongside and was lifted beside Lefty. "Well,
Hugo, so long. You sure were a friend in need.
Never forget it. And look me up when the Krauts
are all dead, will you?" The gears clashed. "Thanks
again—and for the cognac, too." He waved airily.
"See you later."

Hugo stalked back on the road. Once he looked

over his shoulder. The truck was a blur of dust. "See you later. See you later. See you later." Lefty would never see him later—never see anyone ever.

That night he sat in a quiet stupor, all thought of great ideal, of fine abandon, of the fury of justice, and all flagrant phrases brought to an abrupt end by the immediate claims of his own sorrow. Tom Shayne was blasted to death. The stinging horror of mustard had fallen into Lefty's eyes. All the young men were dying. The friendships he had made, the human things that gave in memory root to the earth were ripped up and shrivelled. That seemed grossly wrong and patently ignoble. He discarded his personal travail. It was nothing. His life had been comprised of attempt and failure, of disappointment and misunderstanding; he was accustomed to witness the blunting of the edge of his hopes and the dulling of his desires when they were enacted.

Even his great sacrifice had been vain. It was always thus. His deeds frightened men or made them jealous. When he conceived a fine thing, the masses, individually or collectively, transformed it into something cheap. His fort in the forest had been branded a hoax. His effort to send himself through college and to rescue Charlotte from an unpleasant life had ended in vulgar comedy. Even that had been her triumph, her hour, and an incongruous strain of greatness had filtered through her personality rather than his. Now his years in the war were reduced to no grandeur, to a mere outlet for his savage instinct to destroy. After such a life, he reflected, he could no longer visualize himself engaged in any search for a comprehension of real values.

His mind was thorny with doubts. Seeing himself as a man made hypocritical by his gifts and the narrowness of the world, discarding his own problem as tragically solved, Hugo then looked upon the war as the same sort of colossal error. A waste. Useless, hopeless, gaining nothing but the temporal power which it so blatantly disavowed, it had exacted the price of its tawdry excitement in lives, and, now that it was almost finished, mankind was ready to emerge blank-faced and panting, no better off than before.

His heart ached as he thought of the toil, the effort, the energy and hope and courage that had been spilled over those mucky fields to satisfy the lusts and foolish hates of the demagogues. He was no longer angry. The memory of Lefty sitting smilingly on the van and calling that he would see him later was too sharp an emotion to permit brain storms and pyrotechnics.

If he could but have ended the war single-handed, it might have been different. But he was not great enough for that. He had been a thousand men, perhaps ten thousand, but he could not be millions. He could not wrap his arms around a continent and squeeze it into submission. There were too many people and they were too stupid to do more than fear him and hate him. Sitting there, he realized that his naïve faith in himself and the universe had foundered. The war was only another war that future generations would find romantic to contemplate and dull to study. He was only a species of genius who had missed his mark by a cosmic margin.

When he considered his failure, he believed that he was not thinking about himself. There he was, entrusted with special missions which he accomplished no one knew how, and no one questioned in those hectic days. Those who had seen him escape machine-gun fire, carry tons, leap a hundred yards, kill scores, still clung to their original concepts of mankind and discredited the miracle their own eyes had witnessed. Too many strange things happened in that blasting carnival of destruction for one strange sight or one strange man to leave a great mark. Personal security was at too great a premium to leave much room for interest and speculation. Even Captain Crouan believed he was only a man of freak strength and Major Ingalls in his present situation was too busy to do more than note that Hugo was capable and nod his head when Hugo reported another signal victory, ascribing it to his long experience in the war rather than to his peculiar abilities.

As he sat empty-eyed in the darkness, smoking cigarettes and breathing in his own and the world's tragic futility, his own and the world's abysmal sorrow, that stubborn ancestral courage and determination that was in him still continued to lash his reason. "Even if the war is not worth while," it whispered, "you have committed yourself to it. You are bound and pledged to see it to the bitter end. You cannot finish it on a declining note. Tonight, tomorrow, you must begin again." At the same time his lust for carnage stirred within him like a long-subdued demon. Now he recognized it and knew that it must be mastered. But it combined with his conscience to quicken his sinews anew.

It was a cold night, but Hugo perspired. Was he to go again into the holocaust to avenge a friend? Was he to live over those crimson seconds that followed the death of Shayne, all because he had helped a blind friend into a *camion?* He knew that he was not. Never again could his instinct so triumph over his reason. That was the greatest danger in being Hugo Danner. That, he commenced to see, was the explanation of all his suffering in the past. The idea warmed and encouraged him. Henceforth his emotions and sentiments would be buried even deeper than his first inbred caution had buried them. He would be a creature of intelligence, master of his caprice as well as of the power he possessed to carry out that caprice.

He lit a fresh cigarette and planned what he would do. On the next night he would prepare himself very carefully. He would eat enormously, provide himself with food and water, rest as much as he could, and then start south and east in a plane. He would drive it far into Germany. When its petrol failed, he would crash it. Stepping from the

ruins, he would hasten on in the darkness, on, on,
like Pheidippides, till he reached the centre of the
enemy government. There, crashing through the
petty human barriers, he would perform his last feat,
strangling the Emperor, slaying the generals, pulling the buildings apart with his Samsonian arms, and
disrupting the control of the war.

He had dreamed of such an enterprise even before he had enlisted. But he had known that he
lacked sufficient stamina without a great internal
cause, and no rage, no blood-madness, was great
enough to drive him to that effort. With amazement
he realized that a clenched determination depending
on the brain rather than the emotions was a greater
catalyst than any passion. He knew that he could
do such a thing. In the warmth of that knowledge
he completed his plan tranquilly and retired. For
twelve hours, by order undisturbed, Hugo slept.

In the bright morning, he girded himself. He
requisitioned the plane he needed through Major
Ingalls. He explained that requirement by saying
that he was going to bomb a battery of big guns.
The plane offered was an old one. Hugo had seen
enough of flying in his French service to understand
its navigation. He ate the huge meal he had planned.
And then, a cool and grim man, he made his way
to the hangar. In fifteen minutes his last adventure
would have commenced. But a dispatch rider, charging on to the field in a roaring motor cycle, an-

nounced the signing of the Armistice and the end of the war.

Hugo stood near his plane when he heard the news. Two men at his side began to cry, one repeating over and over: "And I'm still alive, so help me God. I wish I was dead, like Joey." Hugo was rigid. His first gesture was to lift his clenched fist and search for an object to smash with it. The fist lingered in the air. His rage passed—rage that would have required a giant vent had it occurred two days sooner. He relaxed. His arm fell. He ruffled his black hair; his blacker eyes stared and then twinkled. His lips smiled for the first time in many months. His great shoulders sagged. "I should have guessed it," he said to himself, and entered the rejoicing with a fervour that was unexpected.

XVI

THERE MUST be in heaven a certain god—a
paunchy, cynical god whose task it is to arrange for
each of the birthward-marching souls a set of circumstances so nicely adjusted to its character that
the result of its life, in triumph or defeat, will be
hinged on the finest of threads. So Hugo must have
felt coming home from war. He had celebrated the
Armistice hugely, not because it had spared his life
—most of the pomp, parade, bawdiness, and glory
had originated in such a deliverance—but because
it had rescued him from the hot blast of destructive-
ness. An instantaneous realization of that prevented
despair. He had failed in the hour of becoming
death itself; such failure was fortunate because life
to him, even at the end of the war, seemed more
the effort of creation than the business of annihila-
tion.

To know that had cost a struggle—a struggle that
took place at the hangar as the dispatch-bearer rode
up and that remained crucial only between the in-

stant when he lifted his fist and when he lowered it. Brevity made it no less intense; a second of time had resolved his soul afresh, had redistilled it and recombined it.

Not long after that he started back to America. The mass of soldiers surrounding him were undergoing a transition that Hugo felt vividly. These men would wake up sweating at night and cry out until someone whispered roughly that there were no more submarines. A door would slam and one of them would begin to weep. There were whisperings and bickerings about life at home, about what each person, disintegrated again to individuality, would do and say and think. Little fears about lost jobs and lost girls cropped out, were thrust back, came finally to remain. And no one wanted life to be what it had been; no one considered that it could be the same.

Hugo wrote to his family that the war was ended, that he was well, that he expected to see them some time in the near future. The ship that carried him reached the end of the blue sea; he was disembarked and demobilized in New York. He realized even before he was accustomed to the novelty of civilian clothes that a familiar, friendly city had changed. The retrospective spell of the eighties and nineties had vanished. New York was brand-new, blatant, rushing, prosperous. The inheritance from Europe had been assimilated; a social reality, entirely foreign and American, had been wrought and New York was ready to spread it across the parent world. Those things were pressed quickly into Hugo's mind by his hotel, the magazines, a chance novel of the precise date, the cinema, and the more general, more indefinite human pulses.

After a few days of random inspection, of casual imbibing, he called upon Tom Shayne's father. He would have preferred to escape all painful reminiscing, but he went partly as a duty and partly from necessity: he had no money whatever.

A butler opened the door of a large stone mansion and ushered Hugo to the library, where Mr. Shayne rose eagerly. "I'm so glad you came. Knew you'd be here soon. How are you?"

Hugo was slightly surprised. In his host's manner was the hardness and intensity that he had observed everywhere. "I'm very well, thanks."

"Splendid! Cocktails, Smith."

There was a pause. Mr. Shayne smiled. "Well, it's over, eh?"

"Yes."

"All over. And now we've got to beat the spears into plowshares, eh?"

"We have."

Mr. Shayne chuckled. "Some of my spears were already made into plows, and it was a great season for the harvest, young man—a great season."

Hugo was still uncertain of Mr. Shayne's deepest viewpoint. His uncertainty nettled him. "The grim

reaper has done some harvesting on his own account—" He spoke almost rudely.

Mr. Shayne frowned disapprovingly. "I made up
my mind to forget, Danner. To forget and to buckle
down. And I've done both. You'll want to know
what happened to the funds I handled for you—"

"I wasn't particularly—"

The older man shook his head with grotesque
coyness. "Not so fast, not so fast. You were particularly eager to hear. We're getting honest about
our emotions in this day and place. You're eaten with
impatience. Well—I won't hold out. Danner, I've
made you a million. A clean, cold million."

Hugo had been struggling in a rising tide of in-
comprehension; that statement engulfed him. "Me?
A million?"

"In the bank in your name waiting for a blonde
girl."

"I'm afraid I don't exactly understand, Mr.
Shayne."

The banker readjusted his glasses and swallowed
a cocktail by tipping back his head. Then he rose,
paced across the broad carpet, and faced Hugo.
"Of course you don't understand. Well, I'll tell
you about it. Once you did a favour for me which
has no place in this conversation." He hesitated;
his face seemed to flinch and then to be jerked back
to its former expression. "In return I've done a
little for you. And I want to add a word to the gift
of your bank book. You have, if you're careful,

leisure to enjoy life, freedom, the world at your feet. No more strife for you, no worry, and no care. Take it. Be a hedonist. There is nothing else. I've lain in bed nights enjoying the life that lies ahead of you, my boy. Vicariously voluptuous. Catchy phrase, isn't it? My own. I want to see you do it up brown."

Hugo rubbed his hand across his forehead. It was not long ago that this same man had sat at an *estaminet* and wept over snatches of a childhood which death had made sacred. Here he stood now, asking that a life be done up brown, and meaning cheap, obvious things. He wished that he had never called on Tom's father.

"That wasn't my idea of living—" he said slowly.

"It will be. Forget the war. It was a dream. I realized it suddenly. If I had not, I would still be—just a banker. Not a great banker. The great banker. I saw, suddenly, that it was a dream. The world was mad. So I took my profit from it, beginning on the day I saw."

"How, exactly?"

"Eh?"

"I mean—how did you profit by the war?"

Mr. Shayne smiled expansively. "What was in demand then, my boy? What were the stupid, traduced, misguided people raising billions to get? What? Why, shells, guns, foodstuffs. For six months I had a corner on four chemicals vitally necessary to the government. And the government got them—

at my price. I owned a lot of steel. I mixed food and
diplomacy in equal parts—and when the pie was
opened, it was full of solid gold."

Hugo's voice was strange. "And that is the way
—my money was made?"

"It is." Mr. Shayne perceived that Hugo was
angry. "Now, don't get sentimental. Keep your eye
on the ball. I—" He did not finish, because Mrs.
Shayne came into the room. Hugo stared at him
fixedly, his face livid, for several seconds before he
was conscious of her. Even then it was only a partial
consciousness.

She was stuffed into a tight, bright dress. She was
holding out her hand, holding his hand, holding his
hand too long. There was mascara around her eyes
and they dilated and blinked in a foolish and flirtatious way; her voice was syrup. She was taking a
cocktail with the other hand—maybe if he gave her
hand a real squeeze, she would let go. A tall, sallow
young man had come in behind her; he was Mr.
Jerome Leonardo Bateau, a perfect dear. Mrs.
Shayne was still holding his hand and murmuring;
Mr. Shayne was patting his shoulder; Mr. Bateau
was staring with haughty and jealous eyes. Hugo
excused himself.

In the hall he asked for Mr. Shayne's secretary.
He collected himself in a few frigid sentences.
"Please tell Mr. Shayne I am very grateful. I wish
to transfer my entire fortune to my parents in

Indian Creek, Colorado. The name is Abednego Danner. Make all arrangements."

A faint "But—" followed him futilely through the door. In the space of a block he had cut a pace that set other pedestrians gaping to a fast walk.

XVII

HUGO SAT in Madison Square Park giving his attention in a circuit to the Flatiron Building, the clock on the Metropolitan Tower, and the creeping barrage of traffic that sent people scampering, stopped, moved forward again. He had sat on the identical bench at the identical time of day during his obscure undergraduate period. To repeat that contemplative stasis after so much living had intervened ought to have produced an emotion. He had gone to the park with that idea. But the febrile fires of feeling were banked under the weight of many things and he could suffer nothing, enjoy nothing and think but one fragmentary routine.

He had tried much and made no progress. He would be forced presently to depart on a different course from a new threshold. That idea went round and round in his head like a single fly in a big room. It lost poignancy and eventually it lost meaning. Still he sat in feeble sunshine trying to move beyond stagnancy. He remembered the small man with the huge roll of bills who had moved beside him and asked for a cup of coffee. He remembered the woman who had robbed him; silk ankles crossed his line of vision, and a gusty appetite vaporized even as it steamed into the coldness of his indecision.

He was without money now, as he had been then, so long ago. He budged on the bench and challenged himself to think.

What would you do if you were the strongest man in the world, the strongest thing in the world, mightier than the machine? He made himself guess answers for that rhetorical query. "I would—I would have won the war. But I did not. I would run the universe single-handed. Literally single-handed. I would scorn the universe and turn it to my own ends. I would be a criminal. I would rip open banks and gut them. I would kill and destroy. I would be a secret, invisible blight. I would set out to stamp crime off the earth; I would be a super-detective, following and summarily punishing every criminal until no one dared to commit a felony. What would I do? What will I do?"

Then he realized that he was hungry. He had not eaten enough in the last few days. Enough for him. With some intention of finding work he had left Mr. Shayne's house. A call on the telephone from Mr. Shayne himself volunteering a position had crystallized that intention. In three days he had discovered the vast abundance of young men, the embarrassment of young men, who were walking along the streets looking for work. He who had always worked with his arms and shoulders had determined to try to earn his living with his head. But the white-collar ranks were teeming, overflowing, supersaturated. He went down in the scale of clerkships and inexperienced clerkships. There was no work.

Thence he had gone to the park, and presently he rose. He had seen the clusters of men on Sixth Avenue standing outside the employment agencies. He could go there. Any employment was better than hunger—and he had learned that hunger could come swiftly and formidably to him. Business was slack, hands were being laid off; where an apprentice was required, three trained men waited avidly for work. It was appalling and Hugo saw it as appalling. He was not frightened, but, as he walked, he knew that it was a mistake to sit in the park with the myriad other men. Walking made him feel better. It was action, it bred the thought that any work was better than none. Work would not hinder his dreams, meantime.

When he reached Forty-second Street he could see the sullen, watchful groups of men. He joined one of them. A loose-jointed, dark-faced person came down a flight of stairs, wrote on a blackboard in chalk, and went up again. Several of the group detached themselves and followed him—to compete for a chance to wash windows.

A man at his side spoke to him. "Tough, ain't it, buddy?"

"Yeah, it's tough," Hugo said.

"I got three bones left. Wanna join me in a feed an' get a job afterward?"

Hugo looked into his eyes. They were troubled and desirous of companionship. "No, thanks," he replied.

They waited for the man to scribble again in chalk.

"They was goin' to fix up everybody slick after the war. Oh, hell, yes."

"You in it?" Hugo asked.

"Up to my God-damned neck, buddy."

"Me, too. Guess I'll go up the line."

"I'll go witcha."

"Well—"

They waited a moment longer, for the man with the chalk had reappeared. Hugo's comrade grunted. "Wash windows an' work in the steel mills. Break your neck or burn your ear off. Wha' do they care?" Hugo had taken a step toward the door, but the youth with the troubled eyes caught his sleeve. "Don't go up for that, son. They burn you in them steel mills. I seen guys afterward. Two years an' you're all done. This is tough, but that's tougher. Sweet Jesus, I'll say it is."

Hugo loosened himself. "Gotta eat, buddy. I don't happen to have even three bones available at the moment."

The man looked after him. "Gosh," he murmured. "Even guys like that."

He was in a dingy room standing before a grilled

window. A voice from behind it asked his name, age, address, war record. Hugo was handed a piece of paper to sign and then a second piece that bore the scrawled words: "Amalgamated Crucible Steel Corp., Harrison, N. J."

Hugo's emotional life was reawakened when he walked into the mills. His last nickel was gone. He had left the train at the wrong station and walked more than a mile. He was hungry and cold. He came, as if naked, to the monster and he did it homage.

Its predominant colour scheme was black and red. It had a loud, pagan voice. It breathed fire. It melted steel and rock and drank human sweat, with human blood for an occasional stimulant. On every side of him were enormous buildings and woven between them a plaid of girders, cables, and tracks across which masses of machinery moved. Inside, Thor was hammering. Inside, a crane sped overhead like a tarantula, trailing its viscera to the floor, dangling a gigantic iron rib. A white speck in its wounded abdomen was a human face.

The bright metal gushed from another hole. It was livid and partially alive; it was hot and had a smell; it swept away the thought of the dark descending night. It made a pool in a great ladle; it made a cupful dipped from a river in hell. A furnace exhaled sulphurously, darting a snake's tongue into the sky. The mills roared and the earth shook. It was bestial, reptilian—labour, and the labour of creation, and the engine that turned the earth could be no more terrible.

Hugo, standing sublimely small in its midst, measured his strength against it, soaked up its warmth, shook his fist at it, and shouted in a voice that could not be heard for a foot: "Christ Almighty! This—is something!"

"Name?"

"Hugo Danner."

"Address?"

"None at present."

"Experience?"

"None."

"Married?"

"No."

"Union?"

"What?"

"Lemme see your union card."

"I don't belong."

"Well, you gotta join."

He went to the headquarters of the union. Men were there of all sorts. The mills were taking on hands. There was reconstruction to be done abroad and steel was needed. They came from Europe, for the most part. Thickset, square-headed, small-eyed men. Men with expressionless faces and bulging muscles that held more meaning than most countenances. They gave him room and no more. They answered the same questions that he answered. He stood in a third queue with them, belly to back, mouths closed. He was sent to a lodging-house, advanced five dollars, and told that he would be boarded and given a bed and no more until the employment agency had taken its commission, and the union its dues. He signed a paper. He went on the night shift without supper.

He ran a wheelbarrow filled with heavy, warm slag for a hundred feet over a walk of loose bricks. The job was simple. Load, carry, dump, return, load. On some later night he would count the number of loads. But on this first night he walked with excited eyes, watching the tremendous things that happened all around him. Men ran the machinery that dumped the ladle. Men guided liquid iron from the furnaces into a maze of channels and cloughs, clearing the way through the sand, cutting off the stream, making new openings. Men wheeled the slag and steered the trains and trams and cranes. Men operated the hammers. And almost all of the men were nude to the waist, sleek and shining with sweat; almost all of them drank whisky.

One of the men in the wheelbarrow line even offered a drink to Hugo. He held out the flask and bellowed in Czech. Hugo took it. The drink was raw and foul. Pouring into his empty stomach, it had a powerful effect, making him exalted, making him work like a demon. After a long, noisy time that did not seem long a steam whistle screamed faintly and the shift was ended.

The Czech accompanied Hugo through the door.

The new shift was already at work. They went out. A nightmare of brilliant orange and black fled from Hugo's vision and he looked into the pale, remote chiaroscuro of dawn.

"Me tired," the Czech said in a small, aimless tone.

They flung themselves on dirty beds in a big room. But Hugo did not sleep for a time—not until the sun rose and day was evident in the grimy interior of the bunk house.

That he could think while he worked had been Hugo's thesis when he walked up Sixth Avenue. Now, working steadily, working at a thing that was hard for other men and easy for him, he nevertheless fell into the stolid vacuum of the manual labourer. The mills became familiar, less fantastic. He remembered that oftentimes the war had given a more dramatic passage of man's imagination forged into fire and steel.

His task was changed numerous times. For a while he puddled pig iron with the long-handled, hoe-like tool.

"Don't slip in," they said. It was succinct, graphic.

Then they put him on the hand cars that fed the furnaces. It was picturesque, daring, and for most men too hard. Few could manage the weight or keep up with the pace. Those who did were honoured by their fellows. The trucks were moved forward by human strength and dumped by hand-windlasses. Occasionally, they said, you became tired and fell

into the furnace. Or jumped. If you got feeling
woozy, they said, quit. The high rails and red mouths
were hypnotic, like burning Baal and the Juggernaut.

Hugo's problems had been abandoned. He worked
as hard as he dared. The presence of grandeur and
din made him content. How long it would have lasted
is uncertain; not forever. On the day when he had
pushed up two hundred and three loads during his
shift, the boss stopped him in the yard.

A tall, lean, acid man. He caught Hugo's sleeve
and turned him round. "You're one of the bastards
on the furnace line."

"Yes."

"How many cars did you push up today?"

"Two hundred and three."

"What the hell do you think this is, anyway?"

"I don't get you."

"Oh, you don't, huh? Well, listen here, you God-
damned athlete, what are you trying to do? You got
the men all sore—wearing themselves out. I had to
lay off three—why? Because they couldn't keep up
with you, that's why. Because they got their guts in a
snarl trying to bust your record. What do you think
you're in? A race? Somebody's got to show you your
place around here and I think I'll just kick a lung out
right now."

The boss had worked himself into a fury. He
became conscious of an audience of workers. Hugo

smiled. "I wouldn't advise you to try that—even if you are a big guy."

"What was that?" The words were roared. He gathered himself, but when Hugo did not flinch, did not prepare himself, he was suddenly startled. He remembered, perhaps, the two hundred and three cars. He opened his fist. "All right. I ain't even goin' to bother myself tryin' to break you in to this game. Get out."

"What?"

"Get out. Beat it. I'm firing you."

"Firing me? For working too hard?" Hugo laughed. He bent double with laughter. His laughter sounded above the thunder of the mill. "Oh, God, that's funny. Fire me!" He moved toward the boss menacingly. "I've a notion to twist your liver around your neck myself."

The workers realized that an event of some magnitude was taking place. They drew nearer. Hugo's laughter came again and changed into a smile—an emotion that cooled visibly. Then swiftly he peeled up the sleeve of his shirt. His fist clenched; his arm bent; under the nose of his boss he caused his mighty biceps to swell. His whole body trembled. With his other hand he took the tall man's fingers and laid them on that muscle.

"Squeeze," he shouted.

The boss squeezed. His face grew pallid and he let go suddenly. He tried to speak through his dry mouth, but Hugo had turned his back. At the brick gate post he paused and drew a breath.

His words resounded like the crack of doom. "So long!"

XVIII

IN THE next four weeks Hugo knew the pangs of hunger frequently. He found odd jobs, but none of them lasted. Once he helped to remove a late snowstorm from the streets. He worked for five days on a subway excavation. His clothes became shabby, he began to carry his razor in his overcoat pocket and to sleep in hotels that demanded only twenty-five cents for a night's lodging. When he considered the tens of thousands of men in his predicament, he was not surprised at or ashamed of himself. When, however, he dwelt on his own peculiar capacities, he was both astonished and ashamed to meander along the dreary pavements.

Hunger did curious things to him. He had moments of fury, of imagined violence, and other moments of fantasy when he dreamed of a rich and noble life. Sometimes he meditated the wisdom of devouring one prodigious meal and fleeing through the dead of night to the warm south. Occasionally he considered going back to his family in Colorado.

His most bitter hours were spent in thinking of Mr. Shayne and of accepting a position in one of Mr. Shayne's banks.

In his maculate, threadbare clothes, with his dark, aquiline face matured by the war he was a sharp contrast of facts and possibilities. It never occurred to him that he was young, that his dissatisfaction, his idealism, his *Weltschmerz* were integral to the life-cycle of every man.

At the end of four weeks, with hunger gnawing so avidly at his core that he could not pass a restaurant without twitching muscles and quivering nerves, he turned abruptly from the street into a cigar store and telephoned to Mr. Shayne. The banker was full of sound counsel and ready charity. Hugo regretted the call as soon as he heard Mr. Shayne's voice; he regretted it when he was ravishing a luxurious dinner at Mr. Shayne's expense. It was the weakest thing he had done in his life.

Nevertheless he accepted the position offered by Mr. Shayne. That same evening he rented a small apartment, and, lying on his bed, a clean bed, he wondered if he really cared about anything or about anyone. In the morning he took a shower and stood for a long time in front of the mirror on the bath-room door, staring at his nude body as if it were a rune he might learn to read, an engima he might solve by concentration. Then he went to work. His affiliation with the Down Town Savings Bank lasted into the spring and was terminated by one of the oddest incidents of his career.

Until the day of that incident his incumbency was in no way unusual. He was one of the bank's young men, receiving fifty dollars weekly to learn the banking business. They moved him from department to department, giving him mentally menial tasks which afforded him in each case a glimpse of a new facet of financial technique. It was fairly interesting. He made no friends and he worked diligently.

One day in April when he had returned from lunch and a stroll in the environs of the Battery— returned to a list of securities and a strip from an adding machine, which he checked item by item— he was conscious of a stirring in his vicinity. A woman employee on the opposite side of a wire wicket was talking shrilly. A vice-president rose from his desk and hastened down the corridor, his usually composed face suddenly white and disconcerted. The tension was cumulative. Work stopped and clusters of people began to chatter. Hugo joined one of them.

"Yeah," a boy was saying, "it's happened before. A couple o' times."

"How do they know he's there?"

"They got a telephone goin' inside and they're talkin' to him."

"I'll be damned."

The boy nodded rapidly. "Yeah—some talk! Tellin' him what to try next."

"Poor devil!"

"What's the matter?" Hugo asked.

The boy was glad of a new and uninformed listener. "Aw, some dumb vault clerk got himself locked in, an' the locks jammed an' they can't get him out."

"Which vault? The big one?"

"Naw. The big one's got pipes for that kinda trouble. The little one they moved from the old building."

"It's not so darn little at that," someone said.

Another person, a man, chuckled. "Not so darn. But there isn't air in there to last three hours. Caughlin said so."

"Honest to God?"

"Honest. An' he's been there more than an hour already."

"Jeest!" There was a pregnant, pictorial silence. Someone looked at Hugo.

"What's eatin' you, Danner? Scared?"

His face was tense and his hands were opening and closing convulsively. "No," he answered. "Guess I'll go down and have a look."

He rang for an elevator in the corridor and was carried to the basement. In the small room on which the vault opened were five or six people, among them a woman who seemed to command the situation. The men were all smoking; their attitudes were relaxed, their voices hushed.

One repeated nervously: "Jesus Christ, Jesus Christ, Jesus Christ."

"That won't help, Mr. Quail. I've sent for the expert and he will probably have the safe open in a short time."

"Blowtorches?" the swearing man asked abruptly.

"Absurd. He would cook before he was out. And three feet of steel and then two feet more."

"Nitroglycerin?"

"And make jelly out of him?" The woman tapped her finger-nails with her glasses.

Another arrival, who carried a small satchel, talked with her in an undertone and then took off his coat. He went first to a telephone on the wall and said: "Gi' me the inside of the vault. Hello. . . . Hello? You there? Are you all right? . . . Try that combination again." The safe-expert held the wire and waited. Not even the faintest sounds of the attempt were audible in the front room. "Hello? You tried it? . . . Well, see if those numbers are in this order." He repeated a series of complicated directions. Finally he hung up. "Says it's getting pretty stuffy in there. Says he's lying down on the floor."

People came and went. The president himself walked in calmly and occupied a chair. He lit a cigar, puffed on it, and stared with ruminative eyes at the shiny mechanism on the front of the safe.

"We are doing everything possible," the woman said to him crisply.

"Of course," he nodded. "I called up the insurance company. We're amply covered." A pause.

"Mrs. Robinson, post one of the guards to keep people from running in and out of here. There are enough around already."

No one had given Hugo any attention. He stood quietly in the background. The expert worked and all eyes were on him. Occasionally he muttered to himself. The hands of an electric clock moved along in audible jerks. Nearly an hour passed and the room had become hazy with tobacco smoke. The man working on the safe was moist with perspiration. His blue shirt was a darker blue around the armpits. He lit a cigarette, set it down, whirled the dials again, lit another cigarette while the first one burned a chair arm, and threw a crumpled, empty package on the floor.

At last he went to the phone again. He waited for some time before it was answered, and he was compelled to make the man inside repeat frequently. The new series of stratagems was without result. Before he went again to his labours, he addressed the group. "Air getting pretty bad, I guess."

"Is it dark?" one of them asked tremulously.

"No."

Fifteen minutes more. The expert glanced at the bank's president, hesitated, struggled frenziedly for a while, and then sighed. "I'm afraid I can't get him out, sir. The combination is jammed and the time-lock is all off."

The president considered. "Do you know of anyone else who could do this?"

The man shook his head. "No. I'm supposed to be the best. I've been called out for this—maybe six times. I never missed before. You see, we make this safe—or we used to make it. And I'm a specialist. It looks serious."

The president took his cigar from his mouth. "Well, go ahead anyway—until it's too late."

Hugo stepped away from the wall. "I think I can get him out."

They turned toward him. The president looked at him coldly. "And who are you?"

Mrs. Robinson answered. "He's the new man Mr. Shayne recommended so highly."

"Ah. And how do you propose to get him out, young man?"

Hugo stood pensively for a moment. "By methods known only to me. I am certain I can do it—but I will undertake it only if you will all leave the room."

"Ridiculous!" Mrs. Robinson said.

The president's mouth worked. He looked more sharply at Hugo. Then he rose. "Come on, everybody." He spoke quietly to Hugo. "You have a nerve. How much time do you want?"

"Five minutes."

"Only five minutes," the president murmured as he walked from the chamber.

Hugo did not move until they had all gone. Then he locked the door behind them. He walked to the safe and rapped on it tentatively with his knuckles. He removed his coat and vest. He planted his feet

against the steel sill under the door. He caught
hold of the two handles, fidgeted with his elbows,
drew a deep breath, and pulled. There was a reso-
nant, metallic sound. Something gave. The edge of
the seven-foot door moved outward and a miasma
steamed through the aperture. Hugo changed his
stance and took the door itself in his hands. His back
bent. He pulled again. With a reverberating clang
and a falling of broken steel it swung out. Hugo
dragged the man who lay on the floor to a window
that gave on a grated pit. He broke the glass with
his fist. The clerk's chest heaved violently; he panted,
opened his eyes, and closed them tremblingly.

Hugo put on his coat and vest and unlocked the
door. The people outside all moved toward him.

"It's all right," Hugo said. "He's out."

Mrs. Robinson glanced at the clerk and walked
to the safe. "He's ruined it!" she said in a shrill
voice.

The president was behind her. He looked at the
handles of the vault, which had been bent like hair-
pins, and he stooped to examine the shattered bolts.
Then his eyes travelled to Hugo. There was a pro-
foundly startled expression in them.

The clerk was sobbing. Presently he stopped.
"Who got me out?"

They indicated Hugo and he crossed the floor on
tottering feet. "Thanks, mister," he said piteously.
"Oh, my God, what a wonderful thing to do! I—I

just passed out when I saw your fingers reaching around—"

"Never mind," Hugo interrupted. "It's all right, buddy."

The president touched his shoulder. "Come up to my office." A doctor arrived. Several people left. Others stood around the demolished door.

The president was alone when Hugo entered and sat down. He was cold and he eyed Hugo coldly. "How did you do that?"

Hugo shrugged. "That's my secret, Mr. Mills."

"Pretty clever, I'd say."

"Not when you know how." Hugo was puzzled. His ancient reticence about himself was acting together with a natural modesty.

"Some new explosive?"

"Not exactly."

"Electricity? Magnetism? Thought-waves?"

Hugo chuckled. "No. All wrong."

"Could you do it on a modern safe?"

"I don't know."

President Mills rubbed his fingers on the mahogany desk. "I presume you were planning that for other purposes?"

"What!" Hugo said.

"Very well done. Very well acted. I will play up to you, Mr. —"

"Danner."

"Danner. I'll play up to this assumption of innocence. You have saved a man's life. You are, of course, blushingly modest. But you have shown your hand rather clearly. Hmmm." He smiled sardonically. "I read a book about a safe-cracker who opened a safe to get a child out—at the expense of his liberty and position—or at the hazard of them, anyhow. Maybe you have read the same book."

"Maybe," Hugo answered icily.

"Safe-crackers—blasters, light fingers educated to the dials, and ears attuned to the tumblers—we can cope with those things, Mr. —"

"Danner."

"But this new stunt of yours. Well, until we find out what it is, we can't let you go. This is business, Mr. Danner. It involves money, millions, the security of American finance, of the very nation. You will understand. Society cannot afford to permit a man like you to go at large until it has a thoroughly effective defence against you. Society must disregard your momentary sacrifice, momentary nobleness. Your process, unknown by us, constitutes a great social danger. I do not dare overlook it. I cannot disregard it even after the service you have done— even if I thought you never intended to put it to malicious use."

Hugo's thoughts were far away—to the fort he had built when he was a child in Colorado, to the wagon he had lifted up, to the long, discouraging gauntlet of hard hearts and frightened eyes that his miracles had met with. His voice was wistful when, at last, he addressed the banker.

"What do you propose to do?"

"I shan't bandy words, Danner. I propose to hang on to you until I get that secret. And I shall be absolutely without mercy. That is frank, is it not?"

"Quite."

"You comprehend the significance of the third degree?"

"Not clearly."

"You will learn about it—unless you are reasonable."

Hugo bowed sadly. The president pressed a button. Two policemen came into the room. "McClaren has my instructions," he said.

"Come on." Hugo rose and stood between them. He realized that the whole pantomime of his arrest was in earnest. For one brief instant the president was given a glimpse of a smile, a smile that worried him for a long time. He was so worried that he called McClaren on the telephone and added to his already abundant instructions.

A handful of bystanders collected to watch Hugo cross from the bank to the steel patrol wagon. It moved forward and its bell sounded. The policemen had searched Hugo and now they sat dumbly beside him. He was handcuffed to both of them. Once he looked down at the nickel bonds and up at the dull faces. His eyebrows lifted a fraction of an inch.

Captain McClaren received Hugo in a bare room shadowed by bars. He was a thick-shouldered, red-haired man with a flabby mouth from which protruded a moist and chewed toothpick. His eyes were blue and bland. He made Hugo strip nude and gave him a suit of soiled clothes. Hugo remained alone in that room for thirty hours without food or water. The strain of that ordeal was greater than his jailers could have conceived, but he bore it with absolute stoicism.

Early in the evening of the second day the lights in the room were put out, a glaring automobile lamp was set up on a table, he was seated in front of it, and men behind the table began to question him in voices that strove to be terrible. They asked several questions and ultimately boiled them down to one: "How did you get that safe open?" which was bawled at him and whispered hoarsely at him from the darkness behind the light until his mind rang with the words, until he was waiting frantically for each new issue of the words, until sweat glistened on his brow and he grew weak and nauseated. His head ached splittingly and his heart pounded. They desisted at dawn, gave him a glass of water, which he gulped, and a dose of castor oil, which he allowed them to force into his mouth. A few hours later they began again. It was night before they gave up.

The remnant of Hugo's clenched sanity was dumbfounded at what followed after that. They beat his face with fists that shot from the blackness. They threw him to the floor and kicked him. When his skin did not burst and he did not bleed, they beat and kicked more viciously. They lashed him with

253

rubber hoses. They twisted his arms as far as they could—until the bones of an ordinary man would have become dislocated.

Except for thirst and hunger and the discomfort caused by the castor oil, Hugo did not suffer. They refined their torture slowly. They tried to drive a splinter under his nails; they turned on the lights and drank water copiously in his presence; they finally brought a blowtorch and prepared to brand him. Hugo perceived that his invulnerability was to stand him in stead no longer. His tongue was swollen, but he could still talk. Sitting placidly in his bonds, he watched the soldering iron grow white in the softly roaring flame. When, in the full light that shone on the bare and hideous room, they took up the iron and approached him, Hugo spoke.

"Wait. I'll tell you."

McClaren put the iron back. "You will, eh?"

"No."

"Oh, you won't."

"I shan't tell you, McClaren; I'll show you. And may God have mercy on your filthy soul."

There were six men in the room. Hugo looked from one to another. He could tolerate nothing more; he had followed the course of President Mills's social theory far enough to be surfeited with it. There was decision in his attitude, and not one of the six men who had worked his torment in relays could have failed to feel the chill of that decision.

They stood still. McClaren's voice rang out: "Cover him, boys."

Hugo stretched. His bonds burst; the chair on which he sat splintered to kindling. Six revolvers spat simultaneously. Hugo felt the sting of the bullets. Six chambers were emptied. The room eddied smoke. There was a harsh silence.

"Now," Hugo said gently, "I will demonstrate how I opened that safe."

"Christ save us," one of the men whispered, crossing himself.

McClaren was frozen still. Hugo walked to the wall of the jail and stabbed his fist through it. Brick and mortar burst out on the other side and fell into the cinder yard. Hugo kicked and lashed with his fists. A large hole opened. Then he turned to the men. They broke toward the door, but he caught them one by one—and one by one he knocked them unconscious. That much was for his own soul. Only McClaren was left. He carried McClaren to the hole and dropped him into the yard. He wrenched open the iron gate and walked out on the street, holding the policeman by the arm. McClaren fainted twice and Hugo had to keep him upright by clinging to his collar. It was dark. He hailed a cab and lifted the man in.

"Just drive out of town," Hugo said.

McClaren came to. They bumped along for miles and he did not dare to speak. The apartment buildings thinned. Street lights disappeared. They traversed a stretch of woodland and then rumbled through a small town.

"Who are you?" McClaren said.

"I'm just a man, McClaren—a man who is going to teach you a lesson."

The taxi was on a smooth turnpike. It made swift time. Twice Hugo satisfied the driver that the direction was all right. At last, on a deserted stretch, Hugo called to the driver to stop. McClaren thought that he was going to die. He did not plead. Hugo still held him by the arm and helped him from the cab.

"Got any money on you?" Hugo asked.

"About twenty dollars."

"Give me five."

With trembling fingers McClaren produced the bill. He put the remainder of his money back in his pocket automatically. The taxi-driver was watching, but Hugo ignored him.

"McClaren," he said soberly, "here's your lesson. I just happen to be the strongest man in the world. Never tell anybody that. And don't tell anyone where I took you tonight—wherever it is. I shan't be here anyway. If you tell either of those two things, I'll eat you. Actually. There was a poor devil smothering in that safe and I yanked it open and dragged him out. As a reward you and your dirty scavengers were put to work on me. If I weren't as merciful as God Himself, you'd all be dead. Now, that's your lesson. Keep your mouth shut. Here is the final parable."

Still holding the policeman's arm, he walked to the taxi and, to the astonishment of the driver, gripped the axle in one hand, lifted up the front end like a derrick, and turned the entire car around. He put McClaren in the back seat.

"Don't forget, McClaren." To the driver: "Back to where you picked us up. The bird in the back seat will be glad to pay."

The red lamp of the cab vanished. Hugo turned in the other direction and began to run in great leaps. He slowed when he came to a town. A light was burning in an all-night restaurant. Hugo produced the five-dollar bill.

"Give me a bucket of water—and put on about five steaks. Five."

XIX

IT WAS bright morning when Hugo awoke. Through the window-pane in the room where he had slept, he could see a straggling back yard; damp clothes moved in the breeze, and beyond was a depression green with young shoots. He descended to the restaurant and ate his breakfast. Automobiles were swishing along the road outside and he could hear a clatter of dishes in the kitchen. Afterwards he went out doors and walked through the busy centre of the village and on into the country.

Sun streamed upon him; the sky was blue; birds twittered in the budding bushes. He had almost forgotten the beauty and peacefulness of springtime; now it came over him with a rush—pastel colours and fecund warmth, smells of earth and rain, melodious, haphazard wind. He knew intuitively that McClaren would never send for him; he wondered what Mr. Mills would say to Mr. Shayne about him. Both thoughts passed like white clouds

over his mind and he forgot them for an indolent
vegetative tranquillity.

The road curved over hills and descended into
tinted valleys. Farmers were ploughing and plant-
ing. The men at the restaurant had told him that
he was in Connecticut. That did not matter, for
any other place would have been the same on this
May morning. A truck-driver offered him a ride,
which Hugo refused, and then, watching the cubic
van surge away in the distance, he wished fugitively
that he had accepted.

Two half dollars and a quarter jingled in his
pocket. His suit was seedy and his beard unshaven.
A picture of New York ran through his mind: he
stood far off from it gazing at the splendour of its
towers in the morning light; he came closer and
the noise of it smote his ears; suddenly he plunged
into the city, his perspective vanished, and there rose
about him the ugly, unrelated, inchoate masses of
tawdriness that had been glorious from a distance,
while people—dour, malicious, selfish people who
scuttled like ants—supplanted the vista of stone and
steel. The trite truth of the ratio between approach
and enchantment amused him. It was so obvious,
yet so few mortals had the fine sense to withdraw
themselves. He was very happy walking tirelessly
along that road.

After his luncheon he allowed a truck to carry him
farther from the city, deeper into the magic of
spring. The driver bubbled with it—he wore a

purple tulip in his greasy cap and he slowed down on the hilltops with an unassuming reverence and a naïve slang that fitted well with Hugo's mood. When he reached his destination, Hugo walked on with reluctance. Shadows of the higher places moved into the lowlands. He crossed a brook and leaned over its middle on the bridge rail, fascinated by an underwater landscape, complete, full of colour, less than a foot high. From every side came the strident music of frogs. Spring, spring, spring, they sang, rolling their liquid gutturals and stopping abruptly when he came too near.

In the evening, far from the city, he turned from the pavement on a muddy country road, walking on until he reached the skeleton of an old house. There he lay down, taking his supper from his pocket and eating it slowly. The floor of the second story had fallen down and he could see the stars through a hole in the roof. In such houses, he thought, the first chapters of American history had been lived. When it was entirely dark, a whippoorwill began to make its sweet and mournful music. Warmth and chilliness came together from the ground. He slept.

In the morning he followed the road into the hills. Long stretches of woodland were interrupted by fields. He passed farmhouses and the paved drive of an estate. More than a mile from the deserted farm, more than two miles from the main road, half hidden in a skirt of venerable trees, he saw an old, green house behind which was a row of barns. It was a big house; tile medallions had been set in its foundations by an architect whose tombstone must now be aslant and illegible. It was built on a variety of planes and angles; gables cropped at random from its mossy roof. Grass grew in the broad yard under the trees, and in the grass were crocuses, yellow and red and blue, like wind-strewn confetti.

Hugo paused to contemplate this peaceful edifice. A man walked briskly from one of the barn doors. He perceived Hugo and stopped, holding a spade in his hand. Then, after starting across to the house, he changed his mind and, dropping the spade, approached Hugo.

"Looking for work, my man?"

Hugo smiled. "Why—yes."

"Know anything about cattle?"

"I was reared in a farming country."

"Good." He scrutinized Hugo minutely. "I'll try you at eight dollars a week, room, and board." He opened the gate.

Hugo paused. The notion of finding employment somewhere in the country had been fixed in his mind and he wondered why he waited, even as he did, when the charm of the old manor had offered itself to him as if by a miracle. The man swung open the gate; he was lithe, sober, direct.

"My name is Cane—Ralph Cane. We raise blooded Guernsey stock here. At the moment we haven't a man."

"I see," Hugo said.

261

"I could make the eight ten—in a week—if you were satisfactory."

"I wasn't considering the money—"

"How?"

"I wasn't considering the money."

"Oh! Come in. Try it." An eagerness was apparent in his tone. While Hugo still halted on a knoll of indecision, a woman opened the French windows which lined one façade of the house and stepped down from the porch. She was very tall and very slender. Her eyes were slaty blue and there was a delicate suggestion—almost an apparition—of grey in her hair.

"What is it, Ralph?" Her voice was cool and pitched low.

"This is my wife," Cane said.

"My name is Danner."

Cane explained. "I saw this man standing by the gate, and now I'm hiring him."

"I see," she said. She looked at Hugo. The crystalline substance of her eyes glinted transiently with some inwardness—surprise, a vanishing gladness, it might have been. "You are looking for work?"

"Yes," Hugo answered.

Cane spoke hastily. "I offered him eight a week and board, Roseanne."

She glanced at her husband and returned her attention inquisitively to Hugo. "Are you interested?"

"I'll try it."

Cane frowned nervously, walked to his wife, and nodded with averted face. Then he addressed Hugo: "You can sleep in the barn. We have quarters there. I don't think we'll be in for any more cold weather. If you'll come with me now, I'll start you right in."

Until noon Hugo cleaned stables. There were two dozen cows—animals that would have seemed beautiful to a rustic connoisseur—and one lordly bull with malignant horns and bloodshot eyes. He shoveled the pungent and not offensive débris into a wheelbarrow and transferred it to a dung-heap that sweated with internal humidity. At noon Cane came into the barn.

"Pretty good," he said, viewing floors fairly shaved by Hugo's diligence. "Lunch is ready. You'll eat in the kitchen."

Hugo saw the woman again. She was toiling over a stove, her hair in disarray, a spotted apron covering her long body. He realized that they had no servants, that the three of them constituted the human inhabitants of the estate—but there were shades, innumerable shades, of a long past, and some of those ghosts had crept into Roseanne's slaty eyes. She carried lunch for herself and her husband into a front room and left him to eat in the soft silence.

After lunch Cane spoke to him again. "Can you plough?"

"It's been a long time—but I think so."

"Good. I have a team. We'll drive to the north

field. I've got to start getting the corn in pretty soon."

The room in the barn was bare: four board walls, a board ceiling and floor, an iron cot, blankets, the sound and smell of the cows beneath. Hugo slept dreamlessly, and when he woke, he was ravenous.

His week passed. Cane drove him like a slave-master, but to drive Hugo was an unhazardous thing. He did not think much, and when he did, it was to read the innuendo of living that was written parallel to the existence of his employer and Rose-anne. They were troubled with each other. Part of that trouble sprang from an evident source: Cane was a miser. He resented the amount of food that Hugo consumed, despite the unequal ratio of Hugo's labours. When Hugo asked for a few dollars in advance, he was curtly refused. That had happened at lunch one day. After lunch, however, and evidently after Cane had debated with his wife, he inquired of Hugo what he wanted. A razor and some shaving things and new trousers, Hugo had said.

Cane drove the station wagon to town and returned with the desired articles. He gave them to Hugo.

"Thank you," Hugo said.

Cane chuckled, opening his thin lips wide. "All right, Danner. As a matter of fact, it's money in my bank."

"Money in your bank?"

"Sure. I've lived here for years and I get a ten-per-cent discount at the general store. But I'm charging you full price—naturally."

"Naturally," Hugo agreed.

That was one thing that would make the tribulation in her eyes. Hugo wished that he could have met these two people on a different basis, so that he could have learned the truth about them. It was plain that they were educated, cultured, refined. Cane had said something once about raising cattle in England, and Roseanne had cooked peas as she had learned to cook them in France. *"Petits pois au beurre,"* she had murmured—with an unimpeachable accent.

Then the week had passed and there had been no mention of the advance in wages. For himself, Hugo did not care. But it was easy to see why no one had been working on the place when Hugo arrived, why they were eager to hire a transient stranger.

He learned part of what he had already guessed from a clerk in the general store. One of the cows was ailing. Mr. Cane could not drive to town (Mrs. Cane, it seemed, never left the house and its environs) and they had sent Hugo.

"You working for the Canes?" the clerk had asked.

"Yes."

"Funny people."

Hugo replied indirectly. "Have they lived here long?"

265

"Long? Roseanne Cane was a Bishop. The Bishops built that house and the house before it—back in the seventeen hundreds. They had a lot of money. Have it still, I guess, but Cane's too tight to spend it." There was nothing furtive in the youth's manner; he was evidently touching on common village gossip. "Yes, sir, too tight. Won't give her a maid. But before her folks died, it was Europe every year and a maid for every one of 'em, and 'Why, deary, don't tell me that's the second time you've put on that dress! Take it right off and never wear it again.'" The joke was part of the formula for telling about the Canes, and the clerk snickered appreciatively. "Yes, sir. You come down here some day when I ain't got the Friday orders to fill an' I'll tell you some things about old man Cane that'll turn your stummick."

Hugo accepted his bundle, set it in the seat beside himself, and drove back to the big, green house.

Later in the day he said to Cane: "If you will want me to drive the station wagon very often, I ought to have a license."

"Go ahead. Get one."

"I couldn't afford it at the moment, and since it would be entirely for you, I thought—"

"I see," Cane answered calmly. "Trying to get a license out of me. Well, you're out of luck. You probably won't be needed as a chauffeur again for the next year. If you are, you'll drive without a license, and drive damn carefully, too, because any fines or any accidents would come out of your wages."

Hugo received the insult unmoved. He wondered what Cane would say if he smashed the car and made an escape. He knew he would not do it; the whole universe appeared so constructed that men like Cane inevitably avoided their desserts.

June came, and July. The sea-shore was not distant and occasionally at night Hugo slipped away from the woods and lay on the sand, sometimes drinking in the firmament, sometimes closing his eyes. When it was very hot he undressed behind a pile of barnacle-covered boulders and swam far out in the water. He swam naked, unmolested, stirring up tiny whirlpools of phosphorescence, and afterwards, damp and cool, he would dress and steal back to the barn through the forest and the hay-sweet fields.

One day a man in Middletown asked Mr. Cane to call on him regarding the possible purchase of three cows. Cane's cows were raised with the maximum of human care, the minimum of extraneous expense. His profit on them was great and he sold them, ordinarily, one at a time. He was so excited at the prospect of a triple sale that for a day he was almost gay, very nearly generous. He drove off blithely—not in the sedan, but in the station wagon, because its gasoline mileage was greater.

It was a day filled with wonder for Hugo. When Cane drove from the house, Roseanne was standing beside the drive. She walked over to the barn and said to Hugo in an oddly agitated voice: "Mr. Danner, could you spare an hour or two this morning to help me get some flowers from the woods?"

"Certainly."

She glanced in the direction her husband had taken and hurried to the kitchen, returning presently with two baskets and a trowel. He followed her up the road. They turned off on an overgrown path, pushed through underbrush, and arrived in a few minutes at the side of a pond. The edges were grown thick with bushes and water weeds, dead trees lifted awkward arms at the upper end, and dragon flies skimmed over the warm brown water.

"I used to come here to play when I was a little girl," she said. "It's still just the same." She wore a blue dress; branches had dishevelled her hair; she seemed more alive than he had ever seen her.

"It's charming," Hugo answered.

"There used to be a path all the way around— with stones crossing the brook at the inlet. And over there, underneath those pine trees, there are some orchids. I've always wanted to bring them down to the house. I think I could make them grow. Of course, this is a bad time to transplant anything— but I so seldom get a chance. I can't remember when —when—"

He realized with a shock that she was going to cry. She turned her head away and peered into the green wall. "I think it's here," she said tremulously.

They followed a dimly discernible trail; there were deer tracks in it and signs of other animals whose feet had kept it passable. It was hot and damp and they were forced to bend low beneath the tangle to make progress. Almost suddenly they emerged in a grove of white pines. They stood upright and looked: wind stirred sibilantly in the high tops, and the ground underfoot was a soft carpet; the lake reflected the blue of the sky instead of the brown of its soft bottom.

"Let's rest a minute," she said. And then: "I always think a pine grove is like a cathedral. I read somewhere that pines inspired Gothic architecture. Do you suppose it's true?"

"There was the lotos and the Corinthian column," Hugo answered.

They sat down. This was a new emotion—a paradoxical emotion for him. He had come to an inharmonious sanctuary and he could expect both tragedy and enchantment. There was Roseanne herself, a hidden beautiful thing in whom were prisoned many beauties. She was growing old in the frosty seclusion of her husband's company. She was feeding on the toothless food of dreams when her hunger was still strong. That much anyone might see; the reason alone remained invisible. He was acutely conscious of an hour at hand, an imminent moment of vision.

"You're a strange man," she said finally.

That was to be the password. "Yes?"

"I've watched you every day from the kitchen

269

window." Her depression had gone now and she was talking with a vague excitement.

"Have you?"

"Do you mind if we pretend for a minute?"

"I'd like it."

"Then let's pretend this is a magic carpet and we've flown away from the world and there's nothing to do but play. Play," she repeated musingly. "I'll be Roseanne and you'll be Hugo. You see, I found out your name from the letters. I found out a lot about you. Not facts like born, occupation, father's first name; just—things."

He dared a little then. "What sort of things, Roseanne?"

She laughed. "I knew you could do it! That's one of them. I found out you had a soul. Souls show even in barn-yards. You looked at the peonies one day and you played with the puppies the next. In one way—Hugo—you're a failure as a farm hand."

"Failure?"

"A flop. You never make a grammatical mistake." She saw his surprise and laughed again. "And your manners—and, then, you understood French. See— the carpet is taking us higher and farther away. Isn't it fun! You're the hired man and I'm the farmer's wife and all of a sudden—we're—"

"A prince and princess?"

"That's exactly right. I won't pretend I'm not curious—morbidly curious. But I won't ask questions, either, because that isn't what the carpet is for."

"What is it for, Roseanne?"

"To get away from the world, silly. And now— there's a look about you. When I was a little girl, my father was a great man, and many great men used to come to our house. I know what the frown of power is and the attitude of greatness. You have them—much more than any pompous old magnate I ever laid eyes on. The way you touch things and handle them, the way you square your shoulders. Sometimes I think you're not real at all and just an imaginary knight come to storm my castle. And sometimes I think you're a very famous man whose afternoon walk just has been extended for a few months. The first thought frightens me, and the second makes me wonder why I haven't seen your picture in the Sunday rotogravures."

Hugo's shoulders shook. "Poor Princess Roseanne. And what do I think about you, then—"

She held up her hand. "Don't tell me, Hugo. I should be sad. After all, my life—"

"May be what it does not appear to be."

She took a brittle pine twig and dug in the mould of the needles until it broke. "Ralph—was different once. He was a chemist. Then—the war came. And he was there and a shell—"

"Ah," Hugo said. "And you loved him before?"

"I had promised him before. But it changed him so. And it's hard."

"The carpet," he answered gently. "The carpet—"

"I almost dropped off, and then I'd have been hurt, wouldn't I?"

"A favour for a favour. I'm not a great man, but I hope to be one. I have something that I think is a talent. Let it go at that. The letters come from my father and mother—in Colorado."

"I've never seen Colorado."

"It's big—"

"Like the nursery of the Titans, I think," she said softly, and Hugo shuddered. The instinct had been too true.

Her eyes were suddenly stormy. "I feel old enough to mother you, Hugo. And yet, since you came, I've been a little bit in love with you. It doesn't matter, does it?"

"I think—I know—"

"Sit closer to me then, Hugo."

The sun had passed the zenith before they spoke connectedly again. "Time for the magic carpet to come to earth," she said gaily.

"Is it?"

"Don't be masculine any longer—and don't be rudely possessive. Of course it is. Aren't you hungry?"

"I was hungry—" he began moodily.

"All off at earth. Come on. Button me. Am I a sight?"

"I disregard the bait."

"You're being funny. Come. No—wait. We've forgotten the orchids. I wonder if I really came for orchids. Should you be terribly offended if I said I thought I did?"

"Extravagantly offended."

Cane returned late in the day. The cows had been sold—"I even made five hundred clear and above the feeding and labour on the one with the off leg. She'll breed good cattle." The barns were as clean as a park, and Roseanne was singing as she prepared dinner.

Nothing happened until a hot night in August. The leaves were still and limp, the moon had set. Hugo lay awake and he heard her coming quietly up the stairs.

"Ralph had a headache and he took two triple bromides. Of course, I could always have said that I heard one of the cows in distress and came to wake you. But he's jealous, poor dear. And then—but who could resist a couple of simultaneous alibis?"

"Nobody," he whispered. She sat down on his bed. He put his arm around her and felt that she was in a nightdress. "I wish I could see you now."

"Then take this flashlight—just for an instant. Wait." He heard the rustle of her clothing. "Now."

She heard him draw in his breath. Then the light went out.

With the approach of autumn weather Roseanne caught a cold. She continued her myriad tasks, but he could see that she was miserable. Even Cane sympathized with her gruffly. When the week of the cattle show in New York arrived, the cold was worse and she begged off the long trip on the trucks with the animals. He departed alone with his two most precious cows, scarcely thinking of her, muttering about judges and prizes.

Again she came out to the barn. "You've made me a dreadful hypocrite."

"I know it."

"You were waiting for me! Men are so disgustingly sure of everything!"

"But——"

"I've made myself cough and sniffle until I can't stop."

Hugo smiled broadly. "All aboard the carpet. . . ."

They lay in a field that was surrounded by trees. The high weeds hid them. Goldenrod hung over them. "Life can't go on——"

"Like this," he finished for her.

"Well—can it?"

"It's up to you, Roseanne. I never knew there were women——"

"Like me? You should have said 'was a woman.'"

"Would you run away with me?"

"Never."

"Aren't we just hunting for an emotion?"

"Perhaps. Because there was a day—one day—in the pines——"

He nodded. "Different from these other two. That's because of the tragic formation of life. There is only one first, only one commencement, only one virginity. Then—"

"Character sets in."

"Then it becomes living. It may remain beautiful, but it cannot remain original."

"You'd be hard to live with."

"Why, Roseanne?"

"Because you're so determined not to have an illusion."

"And you—"

"Go on. Say it. I'm so determined to have one."

"Are we quarreling? I can fix that. Come closer, Roseanne." Her face changed through delicate shades of feeling to tenderness and to intensity. Abruptly Hugo leaped to his feet.

The rhythmic thunder rode down upon them like the wind. A few yards away, head down, tail straight, the big bull charged over the ground like an avalanche. Roseanne lifted herself in time to see Hugo take two quick steps, draw back his fist, and hit the bull between the horns. It was a diabolical thing. The bull was thrown back upon itself. Its neck snapped loudly. Its feet crumpled; it dropped dead. Twenty feet to one side was a stone wall. Hugo picked up a hoof and dragged the carcass to the base of the wall. With his hand he made an indenture in the rocks, and over the face of the hollow he splashed the bull's blood. Then he approached Roseanne. The whole episode had occupied less than a minute.

She had hunched her shoulders together, and her face was pale. She articulated with difficulty. "The bull"—her hands twitched—"broke in here—and you hit him."

"Just in time, Roseanne."

"You killed him. Then—why did you drag him over there?"

"Because," Hugo answered slowly, "I thought it would be better to make it seem as if he charged the wall and broke his neck that way."

Her frigidity was worse than any hysteria. "It isn't natural to be able to do things like that. It isn't human."

He swallowed; those words in that stifled intonation were very familiar. "I know it. I'm very strong."

Roseanne looked down at the grass. "Wipe your hand, will you?"

He rubbed it in the earth. "You mustn't be frightened."

"No?" She laughed a little. "What must I be, then? I'm alive, I'm crawling with terror. Don't touch me!" She screamed and drew back.

"I can explain it."

"You can explain everything! But not that."

"It was an idiotic, wild, unfair thing to have happen at this time," he said. "My life's like that." He looked beyond her. "I began wanting to do tremendous things. The more I tried, the more dis-

couraged I became. You see, I was strong. There
have been other things figuratively like the bull.
But the things themselves get littler and more preposterous, because my ambition and my nerve grows
smaller." He lowered his head. "Some day—I
shan't want to do anything at all any more. Con-
tinuous and unwonted defeat might infuriate some
men to a great effort. It's tiring me." He raised
his eyes sadly to hers. "Roseanne—!"

She gathered her legs under herself and ran.
Hugo made no attempt to follow her. He merely
watched. Twice she tripped and once she fell. At
the stone wall she looked back at him. It was not
necessary to be able to see her expression. She went
on across the fields—a skinny, flapping thing—at
last a mere spot of moving colour.

Hugo turned and stared at the brown mound of
the bull. After a moment he walked over and stood
above it. Its tongue hung out and its mouth grinned.
It lay there dead, and yet to Hugo it still had life:
the indestructibility of a ghost and the immortality
of a symbol. He sat beside it until sundown.

At twilight he entered the barn and tended the
cows. The doors of the house were closed. He
went without supper. Cane returned jubilantly later
in the evening. He called Hugo from the back porch.

"Telegram for you."

Hugo read the wire. His father was sick and
failing rapidly. "I want my wages," he said. Then
he went back to the barn. His trifling belongings

were already wrapped in a bundle. Cane reluctantly counted out the money. Hugo felt nauseated and feverish. He put the money in his pocket, the bundle under his arm; he opened the gate, and his feet found the soft earth of the road in the darkness.

XX

Hugo had three hours to wait for a Chicago train. His wages purchased his ticket and left him in possession of twenty dollars. His clothing was nondescript; he had no baggage. He did not go outside the Grand Central Terminal, but sat patiently in the smoking-room, waiting for the time to pass. A guard came up to him and asked to see his ticket. Hugo did not remonstrate and produced it mechanically; he would undoubtedly be mistaken for a tramp amid the sleek travellers and commuters.

When the train started, his fit of perplexed lethargy had not abated. His hands and feet were cold and his heart beat slowly. Life had accustomed him to frustration and to disappointment, yet it was agonizing to assimilate this new cudgeling at the hands of fate. The old green house in the Connecticut hills had been a refuge; Roseanne had been a refuge. They were, both of them, peaceful and whimsical and they had seemed innocent of the capacity for great anguish. Every man dreams of the season-changed countryside as an escape; every man dreams of a woman on whose broad breast he may rest, beneath whose tumbling hair and moth-like hands he may discover forgetfulness and freedom. Some men are successful in a quest for those anodynes. Hugo could understand the sharp contours of one fact: because he was himself, such a quest would always end in failure. No woman lived who could assuage him; his fires would not yield to any temporal powers.

He was barren of desire to investigate deeper into the philosophy of himself. All people turned aside by fate fall into the same morass. Except in his strength, Hugo was pitifully like all people: wounds could easily be opened in his sensitiveness; his moral courage could be taxed to the fringe of dilemma; he looked upon his fellow men sometimes with awe at the variety of high places they attained in spite of the heavy handicap of being human—he looked upon them again with repugnance—and very rarely, as he grew older, did such inspections of his kind include a study of the difference between them and him made by his singular gift. When that thought entered his mind, it gave rise to peculiar speculations.

He approached thirty, he thought, and still the world had not re-echoed with his name; the trumps, banners, and cavalcade of his glory had been only shadows in the sky, dust at sunset that made evanescent and intangible colours. Again, he thought, the very perfection of his prowess was responsible for its inapplicability; if he but had an Achilles' heel so that his might could taste the occasional tonic of inadequacy, then he could meet the challenge of possible failure with successful effort. More frequently he condemned his mind and spirit for not being great enough to conceive a mission for his thews. Then he would fall into a reverie, trying to invent a creation that would be as magnificent as the destructions he could so easily envision.

In such a painful and painstaking mood he was carried over the Alleghenies and out on the Western plains. He changed trains at Chicago without having slept, and all he could remember of the journey was a protracted sorrow, a stabbing consciousness of Roseanne, dulled by his last picture of her, and a hopeless guessing of what she thought about him now.

Hugo's mother met him at the station. She was unaltered, everything was unaltered. The last few instants in the vestibule of the train had been a series of quick remembrances; the whole countryside was like a long-deserted house to which he had returned. The mountains took on a familiar aspect, then the houses, then the dingy red station. Lastly his mother, upright and uncompromisingly grim, dressed in her perpetual mourning of black silk. Her recognition of Hugo produced only the slightest flurry and immediately she became mundane.

"Whatever made you come in those clothes?"

"I was working outdoors, mother. I got right on a train. How is father?"

"Sinking slowly."

"I'm glad I'm in time."

"It's God's will." She gazed at him. "You've changed a little, son."

"I'm older." He felt diffident. A vast gulf had risen between this vigorous, religious woman and himself.

She opened a new topic. "Whatever in the world made you send us all that money?"

Hugo smiled. "Why—I didn't need it, mother. And I thought it would make you and father happy."

"Perhaps. Perhaps. It has done some good. I've sent four missionaries out in the field and I am thinking of sending two more. I had a new addition put on the church, for the drunkards and the fallen. And we put a bathroom in the house. Your father wanted two, but I wouldn't hear of it."

"Have you got a car?"

"Car? I couldn't use one of those inventions of Satan. Your father made me hire this one to meet you. There's Anna Blake's house. She married that fellow she was flirting with when you went away. And there's our house. It was painted last month."

Now all the years had dropped away and Hugo was a child again, an adolescent again. The car stopped.

"You can go right up. He's in the front room. I'll get lunch."

Hugo's father was lying on the bed watching the door. A little wizened old man with a big head and thin yellow hands. Illness had made his eyes rheumy, but they lighted up when his son entered, and he half raised himself.

"Hello, father."

"Hugo! You've come back."

"Yes, father."

"I've waited for you. Sit down here on the bed. Move me over a little. Now close the door. Is it cold out? I was afraid you might not get here. I was afraid you might get sick on the train. Old people are like that, Hugo." He shaded his eyes. "You aren't a very big man, son. Somehow I always remembered you as big. But—I suppose"—his voice thinned—"I suppose you don't want to talk about yourself."

"Anything you want to hear, father."

"I can't believe you came back." He ruminated. "There were a thousand things I wanted to ask you, son—but they've all gone from my mind. I'm not so easy in your presence as I was when you were a little shaver."

Hugo knew what those questions would be. Here, on his death-bed, his father was still a scientist. His soul flinched from giving its account. He saw suddenly that he could never tell his father the truth; pity, kindredship, kindness, moved him. "I know what you wanted to ask, father. Am I still strong?" It took courage to suggest that. But he was rewarded.

The old man sighed ecstatically. "That's it, Hugo, my son."

"Then—father, I am. I grew constantly stronger when I left you. In college I was strong. At sea I was strong. In the war. First I wanted to be mighty in games and I was. Then I wanted to do services. And I did, because I could."

The head nodded on its feeble neck. "You found things to do? I—I hoped you would. But I always worried about you. Every day, son, every day for all these years, I picked up the papers and looked at them with misgivings. 'Suppose,' I said to myself, 'suppose my boy lost his temper last night. Suppose someone wronged him and he undertook to avenge himself.' I trusted you, Hugo. I could not quite trust—the other thing. I've even blamed myself and hated myself." He smiled. "But it's all right—all right. So I am glad. Then, tell me—what—what—"

"What have I done?"

"Do you mind? It's been so long and you were so far away."

"Well—" Hugo swept his memory back over his career—"so many things, father. It's hard to recite one's own—"

"I know. But I'm your father, and my ears ache to hear."

"I saved a man pinned under a wagon. I saved a man from a shark. I pulled open a safe in which a man was smothering. Many things like that. Then—there was the war."

"I know. I know. When you wrote that you had gone to war, I was frightened—and happy. Try as I might, I could not think of a great constructive cause for you to enter. I had to satisfy myself by thinking that you could find such a cause. Then the war came. And you wrote that you were in it. I was happy. I am old, Hugo, and perhaps my nationalism and my patriotism are dead. Sides in a war did not seem to matter. But peace mattered to me, and I thought—I hoped that you could hasten peace. Four years, Hugo. Your letters said nothing. Four years. And then it stopped. And I understood. War is property fighting property, not David fighting Goliath. The greatest David would be unavailing now. Even you could do little enough."

"Perhaps not so little, father."

"There were things, then?"

Hugo could not disappoint his father with the whole formidable truth. "Yes." He lied with a steady gaze. "I stopped the war."

"You!"

"After four years I perceived the truth of what you have just said. War is a mistake. It is not sides that matter. The object of war is to make peace. On a dark night, father, I went alone into the enemy lines. For one hundred miles that night I upset every gun, I wrecked every ammunition train, I blew up every dump—every arsenal, that is. Alone I did it. The next day they asked for peace. Remember the false armistice? Somehow it leaked out that there would be victory and surrender the next night—because of me. Only the truth about me was never known. And a day later—it came."

The weak old man was transported. He raised himself up on his elbows. "You did that! Then all my work was not in vain. My dream and my prayer were justified! Oh, Hugo, you can never know how glad I am you came and told me this. How glad."

He repeated his expression of joy until his tongue was weary; then he fell back. Hugo sat with shining eyes during the silence that followed. His father at length groped for a glass of water. Strength returned to him. "I could ask for no more, son. And yet we are petulant, insatiable creatures. What is doing now? The world is wicked. Yet it tries halfheartedly to rebuild itself. One great deed is not enough—or are you tired?"

Hugo smiled. "Am I ever tired, father? Am I vulnerable?"

"I had forgotten. It is so hard for the finite mind to think beyond itself. Not tired. Not vulnerable. No. There was Samson—the cat." He was embarrassed. "I hurt you?"

"No, father." He repeated it. Every gentle fall of the word "father" from his lips and every mention of "son" by his father was rare privilege, unfamiliar elixir to the old man. His new lie took its cue from Abednego Danner's expressions. "My work goes on. Now it is with America. I expect to go to Washington soon to right the wrongs of politics and government. Vicious and selfish men I shall force from their high places. I shall secure the idealistic and the courageous." It was a theory he had never considered, a possible practice born of necessity. "The pressure I shall bring against them will be physical and mental. Here a man will be driven from his house mysteriously. There a man will slip into the limbo. Yonder an inconspicuous person will suddenly be braced by a new courage; his enemies will be gone and his work will progress unhampered. I shall be an invisible agent of right—right as best I can see it. You understand, father?"

Abednego smiled like a happy child. "I do, son. To be you must be splendid."

"The most splendid thing on earth! And I have you to thank, you and your genius to tender gratitude to. I am merely the agent. It is you that created and the whole world that benefits."

Abednego's face was serene—not smug, but transfigured. "I yearned as you now perform. It is strange that one cloistered mortal can become inspired with the toil and lament of the universe. Yet there is a danger of false pride in that, too. I am apt to fall into the pit because my cup is so full here at the last. And the greatest problem of all is not settled."

"What problem?" Hugo asked in surprise.

"Why, the problem that up until now has been with me day and night. Shall there be made more men like you—and women like you?"

The idea staggered Hugo. It paralyzed him and

he heard his father's voice come from a great distance. "Up in the attic in the black trunk are six notebooks wrapped in oilpaper. They were written in pencil, but I went over them carefully in ink. That is my life-work, Hugo. It is the secret—of you. Given those books, a good laboratory worker could go through all my experiments and repeat each with the same success. I tried a little myself. I found out things—for example, the effect of the process is not inherited by the future generations. It must be done over each time. It has seemed to me that those six little books—you could slip them all into your coat pocket—are a terrible explosive. They can rip the world apart and wipe humanity from it. In malicious hands they would end life. Sometimes, when I became nervous waiting for the newspapers, waiting for a letter from you, I have been sorely tempted to destroy them. But now—"

"Now?" Hugo echoed huskily.

"Now I understand. There is no better keeping for them than your own. I give them to you."

"Me!"

"You, son. You must take them, and the burden must be yours. You have grown to manhood now and I am proud of you. More than proud. If I were not, I myself would destroy the books here on this bed. Matilda would bring them and I would watch them burn so that the danger would go with—" he cleared his throat—"my dream."

"But—"

"You cannot deny me. It is my wish. You can see what it means. A world grown suddenly—as you are."

"I, father—"

"You have not avoided responsibility. You will not avoid this, the greatest of your responsibilities. Since the days when I made those notes—what days! —biology has made great strides. For a time I was anxious. For a time I thought that my research might be rediscovered. But it cannot be. Theory has swung in a different direction." He smiled with inner amusement. "The opticians have decided that the microscope I made is impossible. The biochemists, moving through the secretions of such things as hippuric acid in the epithelial cells, to enzymes, to hormones, to chromosomes, have put a false construction on everything. It will take hundreds, thousands of years to see the light. The darkness is so intense and the error so plausible that they may never see again exactly as I saw. The fact of you, at best, may remain always no more than a theory. This is not vanity. My findings were a combination of accidents almost outside the bounds of mathematical probability. It is you who must bear the light."

Hugo felt that now, indeed, circumstance had closed around him and left him without succour or recourse. He bowed his head. "I will do it, father."

"Now I can die in peace—in joy."

With an almost visible wrench Hugo brought himself back to his surroundings. "Nonsense, father. You'll probably get well."

"No, son. I've studied the progress of this disease in the lower orders—when I saw it imminent. I shall die—not in pain, but in sleep. But I shall not be dead —because of you." He held out his hand for Hugo.

Some time later the old professor fell asleep and Hugo tiptoed from the room. Food was sizzling downstairs in the kitchen, but he ignored it, going out into the sharp air by the front door. He hastened along the streets and soon came to the road that led up the mountain. He climbed rapidly, and when he dared, he discarded the tedious little steps of all mankind. He reached the side of the quarry where he had built the stone fort, and seated himself on a ledge that hung over it. Trees, creepers, and underbrush had grown over the place, but through the October-stripped barricade of their branches he could see a heap of stones that was his dolmen, on which the hieroglyph of him was inscribed.

Two tears scalded his cheeks; he trembled with the welter of his emotions. He had failed his father, failed his trust, failed the world; and in the abyss of that grief he could catch no sight of promise or hope. Having done his best, he had still done nothing, and it was necessary for him to lie to put the thoughts of a dying man to rest. The pity of that lie! The folly of the picture he had painted of himself— Hugo Danner the scourge of God, Hugo Danner the destroying angel, Hugo Danner the hero of a quick love-affair that turned brown and dead like a plucked flower, the sentimental soldier, the involuntary misanthrope.

"I must do it!" he whispered fiercely. The ruined stones echoed the sound of his voice with a remote demoniac jeer. Do what? What, strong man? What?

XXI

Now THE winds keened from the mountains, and snow fell. Abednego Danner, the magnificent Abednego Danner, was carried to his last resting-place, the laboratory of nature herself. His wife and his son followed the bier; the dirge was intoned, the meaningless cadence of ritual was spoken to the cold ground; a ghostly obelisk was lifted up over his meagre remains. Hugo had a wish to go to the hills and roll down some gigantic chunk of living rock to mark that place until the coming of a glacier, but he forbore and followed all the dark conventions of disintegration.

The will was read and the bulk of Hugo's sorry gains was thrust back into his keeping. He went into the attic and opened the black trunk where the six small notebooks lay in oilpaper. He took them out and unwrapped them. The first two books were a maze of numbered experiments. In the third a more vigorous calligraphy, a quivering tracery of excitement, marked the repressed beginning of a new earth.

He bought a bag and some clothes and packed; the false contralto of his mother's hymns as she went about the house filled him with such despair that he left after the minimum interval allowed by filial decency. She was a grim old woman still, one to whom the coming of the kingdom to Africa was a passion, the polishing of the coal stove a duty, and the presence of her unfamiliar son a burden.

When he said good-by, he kissed her, which left her standing on the station platform looking at the train with a flat, uncomprehending expression. Hugo knew where he was going and why: he was on his way to Washington. The great crusade was to begin. He had no plans, only ideals, which are plans of a sort. He had told his father he was making the world a better place, and the idea had taken hold of him. He would grapple the world, his world, at its source; he would no longer attempt to rise from a lowly place; he would exert his power in the highest places; government, politics, law, were malleable to the force of one man.

Most of his illusion was gone. As he had said so glibly to his father, there were good men and corrupt in the important situations in the world; to the good he would lend his strength, to the corrupt he would exhibit his embattled antipathy. He would be not one impotent person seeking to dominate, but the agent of uplift. He would be what he perceived life had meant him to be: an instrument. He could not be a leader, but he could create a leader.

Such was his intention; he had seen a new way to reform the world, and if his inspiration was clouded occasionally with doubt, he disavowed the doubts as a Christian disavows temptation. This was to be his magnificent gesture; he closed his eyes to the inferences made by his past.

He never thought of himself as pathetic or quixotic; his ability to measure up to external requirements was infinite; his disappointment lay always (he thought) in his spirit and his intelligence. He went to Washington: the world was pivoting there.

His first few weeks were dull. He installed himself in a pleasant house and hired two servants. The use to which he was putting his funds compensated for their origin. It was men like Shayne who would suffer from his mission. And such a man came into view before very long.

Hugo interested himself in politics and the appearance of politics. He read the *Congressional Record,* he talked with everyone he met, he went daily to the Capitol and listened to the amazing pattern of harangue from the lips of innumerable statesmen. In looking for a cause his eye fell naturally on the problem of disarmament. Hugo saw at once that it was a great cause and that it was bogged in the greed of individuals. It is not difficult to become politically partisan in the Capitol of any nation. It was patent to Hugo that disarmament meant a removal of the chance for war; Hugo hated war. He moved hither and thither, making friends, learning, entertaining, never exposing his plan— which his new friends thought to be lobbying for some impending legislation.

He picked out an individual readily enough. Some of the men he had come to know were in the Senate, others in the House of Representatives, others were diplomats, newspaper reporters, attachés. Each alliance had been cemented with care and purpose. His knowledge of an enemy came by whisperings, by hints, by plain statements.

Congressman Hatten, who argued so eloquently for laying down arms and picking up the cause of humanity, was a guest of Hugo's.

"Danner," he said, after a third highball, "you're a sensible chap. But you don't quite get us. I'm fighting for disarmament—"

"And making a grand fight—"

The Congressman waved his hand. "Sure. That's what I mean. You really want this thing for itself. But, between you and me, I don't give a rap about ships and guns. My district is a farm district. We aren't interested in paying millions in taxes to the bosses and owners in a coal and iron community. So I'm against it. Dead against it—with my constituency behind me. Nobody really wants to spend the money except the shipbuilders and steel men. Maybe they don't, theoretically. But the money in it is too big. That's why I fight."

"And your speeches?"

"Pap, Danner, pure pap. Even the yokels in my home towns realize that."

"It doesn't seem like pap to me."

"That's politics. In a way it isn't. Two boys I was fond of are lying over there in France. I don't want to make any more shells. But I have to think of something else first. If I came from some other district, the case would be reversed. I'd like to change the tariff. But the industrials oppose me in that. So we compromise. Or we don't. I think I could put across a decent arms-limitation bill right now, for example, if I could get Willard Melcher out of town for a month."

"Melcher?"

"You know him, of course—at least, who he is. He spends the steel money here in Washington—to keep the building program going on. Simple thing to do. The Navy helps him. Tell the public about the Japanese menace, the English menace, all the other menaces, and the public coughs up for bigger guns and better ships. Run 'em till they rust and nobody ever really knows what good they could do."

"And Melcher does that?"

The Congressman chuckled. "His pay-roll would make your eyes bulge. But you can't touch him."

Hugo nodded thoughtfully. "Don't you think any-one around here works purely for an idea?"

"How's that? Oh—I understand. Sure. The cranks!" And his laughter ended the discussion.

Hugo began. He walked up the brick steps of Melcher's residence and pulled the glittering brass knob. A servant came to the door.

"Mr. Danner to see Mr. Melcher. Just a moment."

A wait in the hall. The servant returned. "Sorry, but he's not in."

Hugo's mouth was firm. "Please tell him that I saw him come in."

"I'm sorry, sir, but he is going right out."

"Tell him—that he will see me."

The servant raised his voice. "Harry!" A heavy person with a flattened nose and cauliflower ears stepped into the hall. "This gentleman wishes to see Mr. Melcher, and Mr. Melcher is not in—to him. Take care of him, Harry." The servant withdrew.

"Run along, fellow."

Hugo smiled. "Mr. Melcher keeps a bouncer?"

An evil light flickered in the other's eyes. "Yeah, fellow. And I came up from the Pennsy mines. I'm a tough guy, so beat it."

"Not so tough your ears and nose aren't a sight," Hugo said lightly.

The man advanced. His voice was throaty. "Git!"

"You go to the devil. I came here to see Melcher and I'm going to see him."

"Yeah?"

The tough one drew back his fist, but he never

understood afterwards what had taken place. He came to in the kitchen an hour later. Mr. Melcher heard him rumble to the floor and emerged from the library. He was a huge man, bigger than his bouncer; his face was hard and sinister and it lighted with an unpleasant smile when he saw the unconscious thug and measured the size of Hugo. "Pulled a fast one on Harry, eh?"

"I came to see you, Melcher."

"Well, might as well come in now. I worked up from the mines myself, and I'm a hard egg. If you got funny with me, you'd get killed. Wha' daya want?"

Hugo sat down in a leather chair and lit a cigarette. He was comparatively without emotion. This was his appointed task and he would make short shrift of it. "I came here, Melcher," he began, "to talk about your part in the arms conferences. It happens that I disagree with you and your propaganda. It happens that I have a method of enforcing my opinion. Disarmament is a great thing for the world, and putting the idea across is the first step toward even bigger things. I know the relative truths of what you say about America's peril and what you get from saying it. Am I clear?"

Melcher had reddened. He nodded. "Perfectly."

"I have nothing to add. Get out of town."

Melcher's eyes narrowed. "Do you really believe that sending me out of town would do any good? Do you have the conceit to think that one nutty shrimp like you can buck the will and ideas of millions of people?"

Hugo did not permit his convictions to be shaken. "There happen to be extenuating circumstances, Melcher."

"Really? You surprise me." The broad sarcasm was shaken like a weapon. "And do you honestly think you could chase me—me—out of here?"

"I am sure of it."

"How?"

Hugo extinguished his cigarette. "I happen to be more than a man. I am—" he hesitated, seeking words—"let us say, a devil, or an angel, or a scourge. I detest you and what you stand for. If you do not leave—I can ruin your house and destroy you. And I will." He finished his words almost gently.

Melcher appeared to hesitate. "All right. I'll go. Immediately. This afternoon."

Hugo was astonished. "You will go?"

"I promise. Good afternoon, Mr. Danner."

Hugo rose and walked toward the door. He was seething with surprise and suspicion. Had he actually intimidated Melcher so easily? His hand touched the knob. At that instant Melcher hit him on the head with a chair. It broke in pieces. Hugo turned around slowly.

"I understand. You mistook me for a dangerous lunatic. I was puzzled for a moment. Now—"

Melcher's jaw sagged in amazement when Hugo

did not fall. An instant later he threw himself forward, arms out, head drawn between his shoulders. With one hand Hugo imprisoned his wrists. He lifted Melcher from the floor and shook him. "I meant it, Melcher. And I will give you a sign. Rotten politics, graft, bad government, are doomed." Melcher watched with staring eyes while Hugo, with his free hand, rapidly demolished the room. He picked up the great desk and smashed it, he tore the stone mantelpiece from its roots; he kicked the fireplace apart; he burst a hole in the brick wall— dragging the bulk of a man behind him as he moved. "Remember that, Melcher. No one else on earth is like me—and I will get you if you fail to stop. I'll come for you if you squeal about this—and I leave it to you to imagine what will happen."

Hugo walked into the hall. "You're all done for —you cheap swindlers. And I am doom." The door banged.

Melcher swayed on his feet, swallowed hard, and ran upstairs. "Pack," he said to his valet.

He had gone; Hugo had removed the first of the public enemies. Yet Hugo was not satisfied. His approach to Melcher had been dramatic, terrifying, effective. There were rumours of that violent morning. The rumours said that Melcher had been attacked, that he had been bought out for bigger money, that something peculiar was occurring in Washington. If ten, twenty men left and those rumours multiplied by geometrical progression, sheer intimidation would work a vast good.

But other facts disconcerted Hugo. In the first place, his mind kept reverting to Melcher's words: "Do you have the conceit to think that one person can buck the will of millions?" No matter how powerful that person, his logic added. Millions of dollars or people? the same logic questioned. After all, did it matter? People could be perjured by subtler influences than gold. Secondly, the parley over arms continued to be an impasse despite the absence of Melcher. Perhaps, he argued, he had not removed Melcher soon enough. A more carefully focused consideration showed that, in spite of what Hatten had said. It was not individuals against whom the struggle was made, but mass stupidity, gigantic bulwarks of human incertitude. And a new man came in Melcher's place—a man who employed different tactics. Hugo could not exorcise the world.

A few days later Hugo learned that two radicals had been thrown into jail on a charge of murder. The event had taken place in Newark, New Jersey. A federal officer had attempted to break up a meeting. He had been shot. The men arrested were blamed, although it was evident that they were chance seizures, that their proved guilt could be at most only a social resentfulness. At first no one gave the story much attention. The slow wheels of Jersey justice—printed always in quotation marks by the dailies—began to turn. The men were summarily tried and convicted of murder in the first degree. A mob assaulted the jail where they were confined —without success. Two of the mob were wounded by riot guns.

A meeting was held in Berlin, one in London, another in Paris. Moscow was silent, but Moscow was reported to be in an uproar. The trial assumed international proportions overnight. Embassies were stormed; legations from America were forced to board cruisers. Strikes were ordered; long queues of sullen men and women formed at camp kitchens. The President delivered a message to Congress on the subject. Prominent personages debated it in public halls, only to be acclaimed and booed concomitantly. The sentence imposed on two Russian immigrants rocked the world. In some cities it was not safe for American tourists to go abroad in the streets. And all the time the two men drew nearer to the electric chair.

It was then that Hugo met Skorvsky. Many people knew him; he was a radical, a writer; he lived in Washington, he styled himself an unofficial ambassador of the world. A small, dark man with a black moustache who attended one of Hugo's informal afternoon discussions on a vicarious invitation. "Come over and see Hugo Danner. He's something new in Washington."

"Something new in Washington? I shall omit the obvious sarcasm. I shall go." Skorvsky went.

Hugo listened to him talk about the two prisoners.

He was lucid; he made allowances for the American democracy, which in themselves were burning criticism. Hugo asked him to dinner. They dined at Hugo's house.

"You have the French taste in wines," Skorvsky said, "but, as it is to my mind the finest taste in the world, I can say only that."

Hugo tried to lead him back to the topic that interested both of them so acutely. Skorvsky shrugged. "You are polite—or else you are curious. I know you—an American business man in Washington with a purpose. Not an apparent purpose—just now. No, no. Just now you are a host, cultivated and genial, and retiring. But at the proper time—ah! A dam somewhere in Arizona. A forest that you covet in Alaska. Is it not so?"

"What if it is not?"

Skorvsky stared at the ceiling. "What then? A secret? Yes, I thought that about you while we were talking to the others today. There is something deep about you, my new friend. You are a power. Possibly you are not even really an American."

"That is wrong."

"You assure me that I am right. But I will agree with you. You are, let us say, the very epitome of the man Mr. Mencken and Mr. Lewis tell us about so charmingly. I am Russian and I cannot know all of America. You might divulge your errand, perhaps?"

"Suppose I said it was to set the world aright?"

Skorvsky laughed lightly. "Then I should throw myself at your feet."

Both men were in deadly earnest, Hugo not quite willing to adopt the Russian's almost effeminate delicacy, yet eager to talk to him, or to someone like him—someone who was more than a great self-centred wheel in the progress of the nation. Hugo yielded a little further. "Yet that is my purpose. And I am not altogether impotent. There are things I can do—" He got up from the table and stretched himself with a feline grace.

"Such as?"

"I was thinking of your two compatriots who were recently given such wretched justice. Suppose they were liberated by force. What then?"

"Ah! You are an independent communist?"

"Not even that. Just a friend of progress."

"So. A dreamer. One of the few who have wealth. And you have a plan to free these men?"

Hugo shrugged. "I merely speculated on the possible outcome of such a thing; assume that they were snatched from prison and hidden beyond the law."

Skorvsky meditated. "It would be a great victory for the cause, of course. A splendid lift to its morale."

"The cause of Bolshevism?"

"A higher and a different cause. I cannot explain it briefly. Perhaps I cannot explain it at all. But the old world of empires is crumbled. Democracy is at its farcical height. The new world is not yet manifest. I shall be direct. What is your plan, Mr. Danner?"

"I couldn't tell you. Anyway, you would not believe it. But I could guarantee to deliver those two men anywhere in the country within a few days without leaving a trace of how it was done. What do you think of that, Skorvsky?"

"I think you are a dangerous and a valuable man."

"Not many people do." Hugo's eyes were moody. "I have been thinking about it for a long time. Nothing that I can remember has happened during my life that gives me a greater feeling of understanding than the imprisonment and sentencing of those men. I know poignantly the glances that are given them, the stupidity of the police and the courts, the horror-stricken attitude of those who condemn them without knowledge of the truth or a desire for such knowledge." He buried his face in his hands and then looked up quickly. "I know all that passionately and intensely. I know the blind fury to which it all gives birth. I hate it. I detest it. Selfishness, stupidity, malice. I know the fear it engenders —a dreadful and a justified fear. I've felt it. Very little in this world avails against it. You'll forgive so much sentiment, Skorvsky?"

"It makes us brothers." The Russian spoke with force and simplicity. "You, too—"

Hugo crossed the room restlessly. "I don't know.

I am always losing my grip. I came to Washington with a purpose and I cannot screw myself to it unremittingly. These men seem——"

Skorvsky was thinking. "Your plan for them. What assistance would you need?"

"None."

"None!"

"Why should I need help? I——never mind. I need none."

"You have your own organization?"

"There is no one but me."

Skorvsky shook his head. "I cannot——and yet——looking at you——I believe you can. I shall tell you. You will come with me tonight and meet my friends——those who are working earnestly for a new America, an America ruled by intelligence alone. Few outsiders enter our councils. We are all——nearly all——foreigners. Yet we are more American than the Maine fisherman, the Minnesota farmer. Behind us is a party that grows apace. This incident in New Jersey has added to it, as does every dense mumble of Congress, every scandalous metropolitan investigation. I shall telephone."

Hugo allowed himself to be conducted half-dubiously. But what he found was superficially, at least, what he had dreamed for himself. The house to which he was taken was pretentious; the people in its salon were amiable and educated; there was no sign of the red flag, the ragged reformer, the anarchist. The women were gracious; the men witty. As he talked to them, one by one, he began to believe that here was the nucleus around which he could construct his imaginary empire. He became interested; he expanded.

It was late in the night when Skorvsky raised his voice slightly, so that everyone would listen, and made an announcement: "Friends, I have had the honour to introduce Mr. Danner to you. Now I have the greater honour of telling you his purpose and pledge. Tomorrow night he will go to New Jersey"—the silence became absolute—"and two nights later he will bring to us in person from their cells Davidoff and Pletzky."

A quick, pregnant pause was followed by excitement. They took Hugo by the hand, some of them applauded, one or two cheered, they shouldered near him, they asked questions and expressed doubts. It was broad daylight before they dispersed. Hugo walked to his house, listening to a long rhapsody from Skorvsky.

"We will make you a great man if you succeed," Skorvsky said. "Good-night, comrade."

"Good-night." Hugo went into the hall and up to his bedroom. He sat on his bed. A dullness overcame him. He had never been patronized quite in the same way as he had that night; it exerted at once a corrosive and a lethargic influence. He undressed slowly, dropping his shoes on the floor. Splendid people they were, he thought. A smaller voice suggested to him that he did not really care to go to New Jersey for the prisoners. They would be hard to locate. There would be a sensation and a mystery again. Still, he had found a purpose.

His telephone rang. He reached automatically from the bed. The room was bright with sunshine, which meant that it was late in the day. His brain took reluctant hold on consciousness. "Hello?"

"Hello? Danner, my friend—"

"Oh, hello, Skorvsky—"

"May I come up? It is important."

"Sure. I'm still in bed. But come on."

Hugo was under the shower bath when his visitor arrived. He invited Skorvsky to share his breakfast, but was impatiently refused. "Things have happened since last night, Comrade Danner. For one, I saw the chief."

"Chief?"

"You have not met him as yet. We conferred about your scheme. He—I regret to say—opposed it."

Hugo nodded. "I'm not surprised. I'll tell you what to do. You take me to him—and I'll prove conclusively that it will be successful. Then, perhaps, he will agree to sanction it. Every time I think of those two poor devils—snatched from a mob— waiting there in the dark for the electric chair—it makes my blood boil."

"Quite," Skorvsky agreed. "But you do not understand. It is not that he doubts your ability—if you failed it would not be important. He fears you might accomplish it. I assured him you would. I have faith in you."

"He's afraid I would do it? That doesn't make sense, Skorvsky."

"It does, I regret to say." His expressive face stirred with discomfort. "We were too hasty, too precipitate. I see his reason now. We cannot afford as a group to be branded as jail-breakers."

"That's—weak," Hugo said.

Skorvsky cleared his throat. "There are other matters. Since Davidoff and Pletzky were jailed, the party has grown by leaps and bounds. Money has poured in—"

"Ah," Hugo said softly, "money."

Skorvsky raged. "Go ahead. Be sarcastic. To free those men would cost us a million dollars, perhaps."

"Too bad."

"With a million—the million their electrocution will bring from the outraged—we can accomplish more than saving two paltry lives. We must be hard, we must think ahead."

"In thinking ahead, Skorvsky, do you not think of the closing of a switch and the burning of human flesh?"

"For every cause there must be martyrs. Their names will live eternally."

"And they themselves—?"

"Bah! You are impractical."

"Perhaps." Hugo ate a slice of toast with outward calm. "I was hoping for a government that—did not weigh people against dollars—"

"Nor do we!"

"No?"

Skorvsky leaped to his feet. "Fool! Dreamer! Preposterous idealist! I must be going."

Hugo sighed. "Suppose I went ahead?"

"One thing!" The Russian turned with a livid face. "One thing the chief bade me tell you. If those men escape—you die."

"Oh," Hugo said. He stared through the window. "And supposing I were to offer your chief a million—or nearly a million—for the privilege of freeing them?"

Skorvsky's face returned to its look of transfiguration, the look that had accompanied his noblest words of the night before. "You would do that, comrade?" he whispered. "You would give us—give the cause—a million? Never since the days of our Saviour has a man like you walked on this—"

Hugo stood up suddenly. "Get out of here!" His voice was a cosmic menace. "Get out of here, you dirty swine. Get out of here before I break you to matchwood, before I rip out your guts and stuff them back through your filthy, lying throat. Get out, oh, God, get out!"

XXII

HUGO REALIZED at last that there was no place in his world for him. Tides and tempest, volcanoes and lightning, all other majestic vehemences of the universe had a purpose, but he had none. Either because he was all those forces unnaturally locked in the body of a man, or because he was a giant compelled to stoop and pander to live at all among his feeble fellows, his anachronism was complete.

That much he perceived calmly. His tragedy lay in the lie he had told to his father: great deeds were always imminent and none of them could be accomplished because they involved humanity, humanity protecting its diseases, its pettiness, its miserable convictions and conventions, with the essence of itself—life. Life not misty and fecund for the future, but life clawing at the dollar in the hour, the security of platitudes, the relief of visible facts, the hope in rationalization, the needs of skin, belly, and womb.

Beyond that, he could see destiny by interpreting his limited career. Through a sort of ontogenetic recapitulation he had survived his savage childhood, his barbaric youth, and the Greeces, Romes, Egypts, and Babylons of his early manhood, emerging into a present that was endowed with as much aspiration and engaged with the same futility as was his contemporary microcosm. No life span could observe anything but material progress, for so mean and inalterable is the gauge of man that his races topple before his soul expands, and the eventualities of his growth in space and time must remain a problem for thousands and tens of thousands of years.

Searching still further, he appreciated that no single man could force a change upon his unwilling fellows. At most he might inculcate an idea in a few and live to see its gradual spreading. Even then he could have no assurance of its contortions to the desire for wealth and power or of the consequences of those contortions.

Finally, to build, one must first destroy, and he questioned his right to select unaided the objects for destruction. He looked at the Capitol in Washington and pondered the effect of issuing an ultimatum and thereafter bringing down the great dome like Samson. He thought of the churches and their bewildering, stupefying effect on masses who were mulcted by their own fellows, equally bewildered, equally stupefied. Suppose through a thousand nights he ravaged the churches, wrecking every structure in the land, laying waste property, making the loud, unattended volume of worship an impossibility, taking away the purple-robed gods of his forbears? Suppose he sank the navy, annihilated the army, set up a despotism? No matter how efficiently and well he ruled, the millions would hate him, plot against him, attempt his life; and every essential agent would be a hypocritical sycophant seeking selfish ends.

He reached the last of his conclusions sitting beside a river whither he had walked to think. An immense loathing for the world rose up in him. At its apex a locomotive whistled in the distance, thundered inarticulately, and rounded a bend. It came very near the place where Hugo reclined, black, smoking, and noisy, drivers churning along the rails, a train of passenger cars behind. Hugo could see the dots that were people's heads. People! Human beings! How he hated them! The train was very near. Suddenly all his muscles were unsprung. He threw himself to his feet and rushed toward the train, with a passionate desire to get his fingers around the sliding piston, to up-end the locomotive and to throw the ordered machinery into a blackened, blazing, bloody tangle of ruin.

His lips uttered a wild cry; he jumped across the river and ran two prodigious steps. Then he stopped. The train went on unharmed. Hugo shuddered.

If the world did not want him, he would leave the world. Perhaps he was a menace to it. Perhaps he should kill himself. But his burning, sickened heart refused once more to give up. Frenzy departed, then numbness. In its place came a fresh hope, new determination. Hugo Danner would do his utmost until the end. Meanwhile, he would remove himself some distance from the civilization that had tortured him. He would go away and find a new dream.

The sound of the locomotive was dead in the distance. He crossed the river on a bridge and went back to his house. He felt strong again and glad— glad because he had won an obscure victory, glad because the farce of his quest in political government had ended with no tragic dénouement.

They were electrocuting Davidoff and Pletzky that day. The news scarcely interested Hugo. The part he had very nearly played in the affair seemed like the folly of a dimly remembered acquaintance. The relief of resigning that impossible purpose overwhelmed him. He dismissed his servants, closed his house, and boarded a train. When the locomotive pounded through the station, he suffered a momentary pang. He sat in a seat with people all around him. He was tranquil and almost content.

XXIII

HUGO HAD no friends. One single individual whom he loved, whom he could have taken fully into his confidence, might, in a measure, have resolved his whole life. Yet so intense was the pressure that had conditioned him that he invariably retreated before the rare opportunities for such confidences. He had known many persons well: his father and mother, Anna Blake, Lefty Foresman, Charlotte, Iris, Tom Shayne, Roseanne, even Skorvsky—but none of them had known him. His friendlessness was responsible for a melancholy yearning to remain with his kind. Having already determined to go away, he sought for a kind of compromise.

He did not want to be in New York, or Washington, or any other city; the landscape of America was haunted for him. He would leave it, but he would not open himself to the cruel longing for his own language, the sight of familiar customs and manners. From his hotel in New York he made excursions to various steamship agencies and travel bureaus. He had seen many lands, and his *Wanderlust* demanded novelty. For days he was undecided.

It was a chance group of photographs in a Sunday newspaper that excited his first real interest. One of the pictures was of a man—erect, white-haired, tanned, clear-eyed—Professor Daniel Hardin—a procession of letters—head of the new expedition to Yucatan. The other pictures were of ruined temples, unpiled stone causeways, jungle. He thought instantly that he would like to attach himself to the party.

Many factors combined to make the withdrawal offered by an expedition ideal. The more Hugo thought about it, the more excited he became. The very nascency of a fresh objective was accompanied by and crowded with new hints for himself and his problems. The expedition would take him away from his tribulations, and it would not entirely cut him off from his kind: Professor Hardin had both the face and the fame of a distinguished man.

A thought that had been in the archives of his mind for many months came sharply into relief: of all human beings alive, the scientists were the only ones who retained imagination, ideals, and a sincere interest in the larger world. It was to them he should give his allegiance, not to the statesmen, not to industry or commerce or war. Hugo felt that in one quick glimpse he had made a long step forward.

Another concept, far more fantastic and in a way even more intriguing, dawned in his mind as he read

316

accounts of the Maya ruins which were to be excavated. The world was cluttered with these great lumps of incredible architecture. Walls had been builded by primitive man, temples, hanging gardens, obelisks, pyramids, palaces, bridges, terraces, roads —all of them gigantic and all of them defying the penetration of archæology to find the manner of their creation. Was it not possible—Hugo's heart skipped a beat when it occurred to him—that in their strange combination of ignorance and brilliance the ancients had stumbled upon the secret of human strength—his secret! Had not those antique and migratory peoples carried with them the formula which could be poured into the veins of slaves, making them stronger than engines? And was it not conceivable that, as their civilizations crumbled, the secret was lost, together with so many other formulæ of knowledge?

He could imagine plumed and painted priests with prayer and sacrifice cutting open the veins of prehistoric mothers and pouring in the magic potion. When the babies grew, they could raise up the pyramids, walls, and temples; they could do it rapidly and easily. A great enigma was thus resolved. He set out immediately to locate Professor Hardin and with difficulty arranged an interview with him.

Preparations for the expedition were being carried on in an ordinary New York business office. A secretary announced Hugo and he was conducted before the professor. Daniel Hardin was no dusty pedagogue. His knowledge was profound and academic, his books were authoritative, but in himself he belonged to the type of man certain to succeed, whatever his choice of occupation. Much of his life had been spent in field work—arduous toil in bizarre lands where life depended sometimes on tact and sometimes on military strategy. He appraised Hugo shrewdly before he spoke.

"What can I do for you, Mr. Danner?"

Hugo came directly to the point. "I should like to join your Yucatan expedition."

Professor Hardin smiled. "I'm sorry. We're full up."

"I'd be glad to go in any capacity—"

"Have you special qualifications? Knowledge of the language? Of archæology?"

"No."

The professor picked up a tray of letters. "These letters—more than three hundred—are all from young men—and women—who would like to join my expedition."

"I think I should be useful," Hugo said, and then he played his trump, "and I should be willing to contribute, for the favour of being included, a sum of fifty thousand dollars."

Professor Hardin whistled. Then his eyes narrowed. "What's your object, young man? Treasure?"

"No. A life—let us say—with ample means at my disposal and no definite purpose."

"Boredom, then." He smiled. "A lot of these other young men are independently wealthy, and bored. I must say, I feel sorry for your generation. But—no—I can't accept. We are already adequately financed."

Hugo smiled in response. "Then—perhaps—I could organize my own party and camp near you."

"That would hamper me."

"Then—a hundred thousand dollars."

"Good Lord. You are determined."

"I have decided. I am familiar with the jungle. I am an athlete. I speak a little Spanish—enough to boss a labour gang. I propose to assist you in that way, as well as financially. I will make any contract with you that you desire—and attach no strings whatever to my money."

Professor Hardin pondered for a long time. His eyes twinkled when he replied. "You won't believe it, but I don't give a damn for your money. Not that it wouldn't assist us. But—the fact is—I could use a man like you. Anybody could. I'll take you—and you can keep your money."

"There will be a check in the mail tomorrow," Hugo answered.

The professor stood. "We're hoping to get away in three weeks. You'll leave your address with my secretary and I'll send a list of the things you'll want for your kit." He held out his hand and Hugo shook it. When he had gone, the professor looked over the roof-tops and swore gleefully to himself.

Hugo discovered, after the ship sailed, that every-one called Professor Hardin "Dan" and they used Hugo's first name from the second day out. Dan Hardin was too busy to be very friendly with any of the members of his party during the voyage, but they themselves fraternized continually. There were deck games and card games; there were long and erudite arguments about the people whom they were going to study. What was the Mayan time cycle and did it correspond to the Egyptian Sothic cycle or the Greek Metonic cycle. Where did the Mayans get their jade? Did they come from Asia over Bering Strait or were they a colony of Atlantis? When they knew so much about engineering, why did they not use the keystone arch and the wheel? Why was their civilization decadent, finished when the *conquistadores* discovered it? How old were they—four thousand years or twelve thousand years? There were innumerable other debates to which Hugo listened like a man new-born.

The cold Atlantic winds were transformed over-night to the balm of the Gulf stream. Presently they passed the West Indies, which lay on the water like marine jewels. Ages turned back through the days of buccaneering to the more remote times. In the port of Xantl a rickety wharf, a single white man, a zinc bar, and a storehouse filled with chicle blocks marked off the realm of the twentieth century. The ship anchored. During the next year it would make two voyages back to the homeland for supplies. But the explorers would not emerge from the jungle in that time.

An antiquated, wood-burning locomotive, which rocked along over treacherous rails, carried them inland. The scientists became silent and pensive. In another car the Maya Indians who were to do the manual labour chattered incessantly in their explosive tongue. At the last sun-baked stop they disembarked, slept through an insect-droning night, and entered the jungle. For three weeks they hacked and hewed their way forward; the vegetation closed behind them, cutting off the universe as completely as the submerging waves of the sea. It was hot, difficult work, to which Hugo lent himself with an energy that astounded even Hardin, who had judged him valuable.

One day, when the high mountains loomed into view, Hugo caught his first glimpse of Uctotol, the Sacred City. A creeper on the hillside fell before his machete, then another—a hole in the green wall— and there it stood, shining white, huge, desolate, still as the grave. His arm hung in mid-air. Over him passed the mystic feeling of familiarity, that fugitive sense of recognition which springs so readily into a belief in immortality. It seemed to him during that staggering instant that he knew every contour of those great structures, that he had run in the streets, lived, loved, died there—that he could almost remember the names and faces of its inhabitants, dead for thousands of years—that he could

nearly recall the language and the music—that destiny itself had arranged a home-coming. The vision
died. He gave a great shout. The others rushed to
his side and found him trembling and pointing.

Tons of verdure were cut down and pushed aside.
A hacienda was constructed and a camp for the
labourers. Then the shovels and picks were broken
from their boxes; the scientists arranged their para-
phernalia, and the work began, interrupted frequently by the exultant shouts that marked a new
finding. No one regretted Hugo. He made his men
work magically; his example was a challenge. He
could do more than any of them, and his hair and
eyes, black as their own, his granite face, stern and
indefatigable, gave him a natural dominion over
them.

All this—the dark, starlit, plushy nights with their
hypnotic silences, the vivid days of toil, the patient
and single-minded men—was respite to Hugo. It
salved his tribulations. It brought him to a gradual
assurance that any work with such men would be
sufficient for him. He was going backward into the
world instead of forward; that did not matter. He
stood on the frontier of human knowledge. He was
a factor in its preparation, and if what they carried
back with them was no more than history, if it cast
no new light on existing wants and perplexities, it
still served a splendid purpose. Months rolled by
unheeded; Hugo gathered friends among these men

—and the greatest of those friends was Daniel Hardin.

In their isolation and occasional loneliness each of them little by little stripped his past for the others. Only Hugo remained silent about himself until his reticence was conspicuous. He might never have spoken, except for the accident.

It was, in itself, a little thing, which happened apart from the main field of activity. Hugo and two Indians were at work on a small temple at the city's fringe. Hardin came down to see. The great stone in the roof, crumbled by ages, slipped and teetered. Underneath the professor stood, unheeding. But Hugo saw. He caught the mass of rock in his arms and lifted it to one side. And Dan Hardin turned in time to perceive the full miracle.

When Hugo lifted his head, he knew. Yet, to his astonishment, there was no look of fear in Hardin's blue eyes. Instead, they were moderately surprised, vastly interested. He did not speak for some time. Then he said: "Thanks, Danner. I believe you saved my life. Should you mind picking up that rock again?"

Hugo dismissed the Indians with a few words. He glanced again at Hardin to make sure of his composure. Then he lifted the square stone back to its position.

Hardin was thinking aloud. "That stone must weigh four tons. No man alive can handle four tons like that. How do you do it, Hugo?"

Hot, streaming sun. Tumbled débris. This profound question asked again, asked mildly for the first time. "My father—was a biologist. A great biologist. I was—an experiment."

"Good Lord! And—and that's why you've kept your past dark, Hugo?"

"Of course. Not many people—"

"Survive the shock? You forget that we—here—are all scientists. I won't press you."

"Perhaps," Hugo heard himself saying, "I'd like to tell you."

"In that case—in my room—tonight. I should like to hear."

That night, after a day of indecision, Hugo sat in a dim light and poured out the story of his life. Hardin never interrupted, never commented, until the end. Then he said softly: "You poor devil. Oh, you poor bastard." And Hugo saw that he was weeping. He tried to laugh.

"It isn't as bad as that—Dan."

"Son"—his voice choked with emotion—"this thing—this is my life-work. This is why you came to my office last winter. This is—the most important thing on earth. What a story! What a man you are!"

"On the contrary—"

"Don't be modest. I know. I feel. I understand."

Hugo's head shook sadly. "Perhaps not. You can see—I have tried everything. In itself, it is great. I can see that. It is, objectively, the most important thing on earth. But the other way— What can I do?

Tell me that. You cannot tell me. I can destroy. As nothing that ever came before or will come again, I can destroy. But destruction—as I believe, as you believe—is at best only a step toward re-creation. And what can I make afterwards? Think. Think, man! Rack your brains! What?" His hands clenched and unclenched. "I can build great halls and palaces. Futile! I can make bridges. I can rip open mountains and take out the gold. I am that strong. It is as if my metabolism was atomic instead of molecular. But what of it? Stretch your imagination to its uttermost limits—and what can I do that is more than an affair of petty profit to myself? Mankind has already extended its senses and its muscles to their tenth powers. He can already command engines to do what I can do. It is not necessary that he become an engine himself. It is preposterous that he should think of it—even to transcend his engines. I defy you, I defy you with all my strength, to think of what I can do to justify myself!"

The words had been wrung from Hugo. Perspiration trickled down his face. He bit his lips to check himself. The older man was grave. "All your emotions, your reflections, your yearnings and passions, come—to that. And yet—"

"Look at me in another light," Hugo went on. "I've tried to give you an inkling of it. You were the first who saw what I could do—glimpsed a fraction of it, rather—and into whose face did not come fear, loathing, even hate. Try to live with a sense

325

of that. I can remember almost back to the cradle
that same thing. First it was envy and jealousy.
Then, as I grew stronger, it was fear, alarm, and
the thing that comes from fear—hatred. That is
another and perhaps a greater obstacle. If I found
something to do, the whole universe would be against
me. These little people! Can you imagine what it is
to be me and to look at people? A crowd at a ball
game? A parade? Can you?"

"Great God," the scientist breathed.

"When I see them for what they are, and when
they exert the tremendous bulk of their united detes-
tation and denial against me, when I feel rage rising
inside myself—can you conceive—?"

"That's enough. I don't want to try to think. Not
of that. I—"

"Shall I walk to my grave afraid that I shall let
go of myself, searching everywhere for something
to absorb my energy? Shall I?"

"No."

The professor spoke with a firm concentration.
Hugo arrested himself. "Then what?"

"Did it ever dawn on you that you had missed
your purpose entirely?"

The words were like cold water to Hugo. He
pulled himself together with a physical effort and
replied: "You mean—that I have not guessed it so
far?"

"Precisely."

"It never occurred to me. Not that I had missed it entirely."

"You have."

"Then, for the love of God, what is it?"

Hardin smiled a gentle, wise smile. "Easy there. I'll tell you. And listen well, Hugo, because tonight I feel inspired. The reason you have missed it is simple. You've tried to do everything single-handed—"

"On the contrary. Every kind of assistance I have enlisted has failed me utterly."

"Except one kind."

"Science?"

"No. Your own kind, Hugo."

The words did not convey their meaning for several seconds. Then Hugo gasped. "You mean—other men like me?"

"Exactly. Other men like you. Not one or two. Scores, hundreds. And women. All picked with the utmost care. Eugenic offspring. Cultivated and reared in secret by a society for the purpose. Not necessarily your children, but the children of the best parents. Perfect bodies, intellectual minds, your strength. Don't you see it, Hugo? You are not the reformer of the old world. You are the beginning of the new. We begin with a thousand of you. Living by yourselves and multiplying, you produce your own arts and industries and ideals. The new Titans! Then—slowly—you dominate the world. Conquer and stamp out all these things to which you and I and all men of intelligence object. In the end—you are alone and supreme."

Hugo groaned. "To make a thousand men live my life—"

"But they will not. Suppose you had been proud of your strength. Suppose you had not been compelled to keep it a secret. Suppose you could have found glorious uses for it from childhood—"

"In the mountains," Hugo whispered, his eyes bemused, "where the sun is warm and the days long—these children growing. Even here, in this place—"

"So I thought. Don't you see, Hugo?"

"Yes, I see. At last, thank God, I do see!"

For a long time their thoughts ran wild. When they cooled, it was to formulate plans. A child taken here. Another there. A city in the jungle—the jungle had harboured races before: not only these Mayas, but the Incas, Khmers, and others. A modern city for dwellings, and these tremendous ruins would be the blocks for the nursery. They would teach them art and architecture—and science. Engineering, medicine—their own, undiscovered medicine—the new Titans, the sons of dawn—so ran their inspired imaginations.

When the night was far advanced and the camp was wrapped in slumber, they made a truce with this divine fire. They shook each other's hands.

"Good-night, Hugo. And tomorrow we'll go over the notes."

"I'll bring them."

"Till evening, then."

Hugo lay on his bed, more ecstatic than he had ever been in his life. By and by he slept. Then, as if the ghosts of Uctotol had risen, his mind was troubled by a host, a pageant of dreams. He turned in his sleep, rending his blankets. He moaned and mumbled. When he woke, he understood that his soul had undergone another of its diametric inversions. The mad fancies of the night before had died and memory could not rekindle them. Little dreads had goaded away their brightness. Conscience was bickering inside him. Humanity was content; it would hate his new race. And the new race, being itself human, might grow top-heavy with power. If his theory about the great builders of the past was true, then perhaps this incubus would explain why the past was no more. If his Titans disagreed and made war on each other—surely that would end the earth. He quailed.

Overcome by a desire to think more about this giants' scheme, he avoided Hardin. In the siesta hour he went back to his tent and procured the books wherein his father had written the second secret of life. He crammed them into his pocket and broke through the jungle. When he was beyond sight and sound, he dropped his machete and made his way as none but he could do. With his body he cut a swath toward the mountains and emerged from the green veil on to the bare rocks, panting and hot.

Upward he climbed until he had gained the summit. To the west were strewn the frozen billows of the range. To the east a limitless sea of verdure. At his feet the ruins in neat miniature, like a model. Above, scalding sun and blue sky. Around him a wind, strangely chill. And silence.

He sat with his head on his hands until his thoughts were disturbed. A humid breath had risen sluggishly from the jungle floor. The sun was dull. Looking toward the horizon, he could see a black cloud. For an instant he was frightened, the transformation had been so gigantic and so soundless. He knew a sudden, urgent impulse to go back to the valley. He disobeyed it and watched the coming of the storm. The first rapier of lightning through the bowels of the approaching cloud warned him again. Staunchly he stood. He had come there to think.

"I must go back and begin this work," he told himself. "I have found a friend!" The cloud was descending. Thunder ruminated in heaven's garret. "It is folly," he repeated, "folly, folly, folly in the face of God." Now the sun went out like an extinguished lamp, and the horizon crept closer. A curtain of torrential rain was lowered in the north. "They will make the earth beautiful," he said, and ever and again: "This thing is not beautiful. It is wrong." His agitation increased rapidly. The cloud was closing on the mountain like a huge hand. The muscles in his legs quivered.

"If there were only a God," he whispered, "what

a prayer I would make!" Then the wind came like a visible thing, pushing its fingers over the vegetation below, and whirling up the mountain, laden with dust. After the wind, the rain—heavy, roaring rain that fell, not in separate drops, but in thick streams. The lightning was incessant. It illuminated remote, white-topped peaks, which, in the fury of the storm, appeared to be swaying. It split clouds apart, and the hurricane healed the rents. All light went out. The world was wrapped in darkness.

Hugo clutched his precious books in the remnants of his clothing and braced himself on the bare rock. His voice roared back into the storm the sounds it gave. He flung one hand upward.

"Now—God—oh, God—if there be a God—tell me! Can I defy You? Can I defy Your world? Is this Your will? Or are You, like all mankind, impotent? Oh, God!" He put his hand to his mouth and called God like a name into the tumult above. Madness was upon him and the bitter irony with which his blood ran black was within him.

A bolt of lightning stabbed earthward. It struck Hugo, outlining him in fire. His hand slipped away from his mouth. His voice was quenched. He fell to the ground.

After three days of frantic searching, Daniel Hardin came upon the incredible passage through the jungle and followed it to the mountain top. There he found the blackened body of Hugo Danner, lying face down. His clothing was burned to ashes, and an

331

accumulation of cinders was all that remained of the notebooks. After discovering that, Professor Hardin could not forbear to glance aloft at the sun and sky. His face was saddened and perplexed.

"We will carry him yonder to Uctotol and bury him," he said at last; "then—the work will go on."

In the Bison Frontiers of Imagination series

Gullivar of Mars
By Edwin L. Arnold
Introduced by Richard A. Lupoff
Afterword by Gary Hoppenstand

A Journey in Other Worlds: A
Romance of the Future
By John Jacob Astor
Introduced by S. M. Stirling

The Wonder
By J. D. Beresford
Introduced by Jack L. Chalker

At the Earth's Core
By Edgar Rice Burroughs
Introduced by Gregory A. Benford
Afterword by Phillip R. Burger

Beyond Thirty
By Edgar Rice Burroughs
Introduced by David Brin
Essays by Phillip R. Burger and
Richard A. Lupoff

The Eternal Savage: Nu of the
Niocene
By Edgar Rice Burroughs
Introduced by Tom Deitz

The Land That Time Forgot
By Edgar Rice Burroughs
Introduced by Mike Resnick

Lost on Venus
By Edgar Rice Burroughs
Introduced by Kevin J. Anderson

The Moon Maid: Complete and
Restored
By Edgar Rice Burroughs
Introduced by Terry Bisson

Pellucidar
By Edgar Rice Burroughs
Introduced by Jack McDevitt
Afterword by Phillip R. Burger

Pirates of Venus
By Edgar Rice Burroughs
Introduced by F. Paul Wilson
Afterword by Phillip R. Burger

Under the Moons of Mars
By Edgar Rice Burroughs
Introduced by James P. Hogan

The Poison Belt: Being an
Account of Another Amazing
Adventure of Professor Challenger
By Sir Arthur Conan Doyle
Introduced by Katya Reimann

The Circus of Dr. Lao
By Charles G. Finney
Introduced by John Marco

Omega: The Last Days of the
World
By Camille Flammarion
Introduced by Robert Silverberg

Ralph 124C 41+
By Hugo Gernsback
Introduced by Jack Williamson

The Lost Continent: The Story of Atlantis
By C. J. Cutcliffe Hyne
Introduced by Harry Turtledove
Afterword by Gary Hoppenstand

Mizora: A World of Women
By Mary E. Bradley Lane
Introduced by Joan Saberhagen

A Voyage to Arcturus
By David Lindsay
Introduced by John Clute

Before Adam
By Jack London
Introduced by Dennis L. McKiernan

Fantastic Tales
By Jack London
Edited by Dale L. Walker

The Moon Pool
By A. Merritt
Introduced by Robert Silverberg

The Purple Cloud
By M. P. Shiel
Introduced by John Clute

The Skylark of Space
By E. E. "Doc" Smith
Introduced by Vernor Vinge

Skylark Three
By E. E. "Doc" Smith
Introduced by Jack Williamson

Tales of Wonder
By Mark Twain
Edited, introduced, and with notes by David Ketterer

The Chase of the Golden Meteor
By Jules Verne
Introduced by Gregory A. Benford

In the Days of the Comet
By H. G. Wells
Introduced by Ben Bova

The Last War: A World Set Free
By H. G. Wells
Introduced by Greg Bear

The Sleeper Awakes
By H. G. Wells
Introduced by J. Gregory Keyes
Afterword by Gareth Davies-Morris

The War in the Air
By H. G. Wells
Introduced by Dave Duncan

Gladiator
By Philip Wylie
Introduced by Janny Wurts

When Worlds Collide
By Philip Wylie and Edwin Balmer
Introduced by John Varley